HEROTICA

ADVENTURES
IN LOVE AND TIME

KERRY GREENWOOD

CLAN
DESTINE
PRESS

First published in paperback in Australia 2017
by Clan Destine Press

PO Box 121 Bittern
Victoria 3918 Australia

Copyright © Kerry Greenwood 2016

National Library of Australia CIP entry
    Greenwood, Kerry.
    Herotica
    ISBN: 978-0-9954394-4-3
    Series: Adventures in Love and Time

Cover Design © Ran Valerhon
    www.valerhon.com

Design & Typesetting: Clan Destine Press
Printed & Bound: Lightning Source

www.clandestinepress.com.au

CONTENTS

THE LAMENT OF ACHILLES	5
THE EVACUATION OF ATLANTIS	9
SAPPHO OF LESBOS	15
BABYLON	21
THE LIBRARY ANGEL	27
THE GUARDIANS OF MAIDEN CASTLE	35
ESCAPE FROM HERCULANEUM	42
AELFWINE & THE SUCCUBUS	48
HAERN DARA	54
SKARA BRAE	59
SKALDIC SAGA	67
THREE WISHES	74
SNOW WHITE	82
THE CRUSADER'S HEART	91
A GESTE OF ROBYN HODE	97
THE SAMURAI	107
MERLIN	114
THE HIGHWAY MAN	122
RED RIDING HOOD	128
THE DRYSDALE SETTLERS	134
THE PIPES OF LUCKNOW	143
THE LAST OF THE NAVAJO	150
STEAMPUNK'D	161
THE ARTIFICER OF BEAUME	170
THE NAUTILUS	178
KHEPHEREN & PTAH-HOTEP	186
THE TILEDAN BAND	196
THE SECRET DIARY OF JOHN WATSON	203
THE EVOLUTION OF THE VAMPYRE	214
ALL ALONG THE WATCHTOWER	220
IT'S SO VERY LONELY	228
I NEVER GOT THE HANG OF THURSDAYS	233

THE LAMENT OF ACHILLES

He tasted my blood when I was only eleven years old and now I shall burn a city and slaughter a people in revenge for his murder.

He wasn't a lamia, of course, a creature that drinks blood for sustenance. He was Ariston Patroclus, who found me sitting and bleeding from the knees, having fallen while training. I was stung with defeat - I hate losing - and also with the grazes, which were full of gravel which I could not remove.

'Prince,' said Patroclus, who was fourteen to my eleven years and even then calm, grave and serene in presence, 'let me tend you.'

'Sir,' I responded, wiping my face, 'why would you do so?'

'Because you are hurt,' he said, and took my hand.

He sat me down on the river bank, brought water in his helmet, and washed my injuries. They were minor. I should have ignored them except that it was so pleasant to be cared for. Patroclus was strong, fast, a good fighter. I respected him. He didn't appear to want anything from me but for me to sit still while he tended me.

So I, Achilles, Grey-eyed, Swift Runner, Sacker of Cities to be, pre-destined greatest hero in the world, sat still, as requested.

He washed all the small injuries and then examined the sad state of my knees.

'I can't prise every speck out without injuring you more, and I will not have such a perfect body develop scarred knees,' he told me. 'So I will do as the animals do.'

He knelt down and started to lick and suck the grazes.

It felt very good, like being licked by a large, friendly dog. His hair was long and curly and moved tickling across my thighs. His two hands held me in place. Lick, suck, spit: he was drawing the gravel out. The injuries felt warm. Soon he moved to the other knee, comforting it with his mouth. He sat back on his heels, pleased by his work. No gravel remained.

'You have drunk my blood,' I observed. 'You are mine, now. We are brothers.'

He looked up with a flash of bright eyes. Then he took his little knife and just nicked the heel of his hand. A bead of blood appeared. He held the hand up to my face. I sucked the wound. Then he kissed his own blood off my lips.

'Brother,' he affirmed.

It was an oath. He never broke it.

My foster father knew that I was fated to be a great hero and to die young. Therefore he taught me - mercilessly, relentlessly - to fight for my life. With sword and shield. Without a shield, without a sword, with a spear, with a knife, with a noose, with a rock, with my bare hands and teeth. My master would not have me die, lest I die untimely and miss my destiny.

And Patroclus, who was a prince, no lowly slave, stayed by my side, as close as I would allow him. Sometimes a battle madness took me, and I would not recognise my friends. I feared I might slay him in error, so he watched from a safe distance as I hacked my way through bushes and briars. When the rage was spent, he would take me by the hand and lead me back to our tent, where he would tend me and kiss me and kneel at my feet.

'My prince, the brambles have defended themselves well today,' he would observe, again extracting thorns with his mouth from the long scratches striping my sides and back.

'A fierce enemy indeed,' I would answer. I looked down at his bent head and loved him with all my stony heart.

For I loved no one else. When Agamemnon proposed the adventure of Troy, I joined the League. My fate was drawing in upon me: I could sense it. But I had no idea it would take ten years to manifest.

My myrmidons accompanied me, of course, as was right and in accordance with their oaths. But Patroclus came because he loved me.

He was always there when we slept rough. His chest was ever a pillow for my head. We made love, now, as soldiers do, as lovers do. Not in the Godless Achaean exchange of master and slave. We kissed fiercely, made love gently or passionately as I desired, and lay together in the holy incense of our seed.

Once, when battle madness seized me untimely, when Patroclus saw the God-given glaze come over my grey eyes, at a moment when, if I had gone raging, I would have lost us the battle, he fell to his knees, bared his body, and offered himself to me.

I fell upon him and ravished him like a conquered city. I thrust into his willing, loving body as though he was my worst enemy. I bruised him wherever I grasped. Shoulders bloomed purple under my handling. He braced himself to receive me and he held his position against my full strength, against my rage. I heard him cry out in pain with every stroke, but I could not stop and the madness did not abate until I screamed like a hawk in his stooping and collapsed on him. He lay bleeding beneath me, my battle rage expended.

But then he gently disengaged us, held me in his arms as I ruefully wept, comforted me and kissed away my tears. I slept.

When I woke I kissed every bite and fingermark and tenderly sucked him to spill his seed in my mouth. I was horrified at how I had hurt him, Achilles' only love. But he told me there was nothing to forgive.

'If one consorts with heroes, there will be pain,' he told me, and limped off to see the Asclepid.

When I dreamed bad dreams in the darkness, he was always there. He always woke and embraced me. He would tell me long tales of our ancestors or silly stories such as goat herds tell, to while away the long hours with the flocks. His voice went softly in the night, banishing the monsters. I hardly remember any of his stories and now bitterly wish that I did. For he is dead. Now my dreams are uncomforted, and the night contains nothing but revenge.

He was a fierce fighter, but in his own, grave way. He would confront an enemy and consider him, deflect every stroke, watch, circle, and then strike. Once. That was usually enough. I used to tease him about this. Was his sword so precious, I asked, that he did not like to clash it against another, lest it be damaged? He liked to point out that if one stroke was enough, then it would remain unscathed. It was a fine blade, war booty from Achaea. I had given it to him, to replace his old sword, which had broken when he deflected an attacker who was trying to stab me in the back. For Patroclus came from an old but poor family and his gear was not anything like as splendid as he deserved.

When we were between battles he delighted to tend me. H would uncoil and wash my hair, rinsing it with herbs, and then comb it like a mother would. Gently but relentlessly, until every strand was perfect and the comb ran freely from scalp to tip. Then he would knot it again above my forehead, a pad to support my helmet, or leave it loose, a curtain to hide a lover in.

I have shorn it now, and burned it in Patroclus' funeral pyre, along with a hundred Trojan prisoners.

How shall I live without you, my love, my spirit, my soul? I killed Hector for you, but you did not return to comfort me with the honey-sweet kisses of your mouth.

Troy will fall. I will slaughter them all. I will be a Divine Hero. Then I will die in battle, and across the sea I will see you standing there, arms outstretched, as I have often seen you before, and I shall feel your embrace again, feel your arms fold around me, taste your lips.

And we will live forever in the Island of heroes, in Elysium.

A very little time, now, my love. Be patient. I am coming. I just have to die.

THE EVACUATION OF ATLANTIS

He joined Gnathos in the grav-sled storage niche at the harbour of Atlantis. Above him, the city circled its heights like a series of wheels, each set of walls laminated a different colour. Smoke was rising from their mountain. Daringly, Andros brushed the light, fluffy ash, which had been falling like snow for days, from his friend's long curly red hair. Affection was frowned on in Atlantis. He longed for Gnathos with all his soul, but had never lain down with him, for fear that they would both be discovered and expunged.

'Gnathos, why are we here, and what is that lump wriggling in your bag?' he asked.

'It is I,' said a clear, scornful voice, stinging a little in his head.

'Basht?' he asked, staggered at the magnitude of his friend's crime. 'You stole one of the experimental felines?'

'No, of course not,' soothed Gnathos, stroking his cheek. 'That would mean instant death.' Andros relaxed until Gnathos continued. 'I stole both.'

'I am here,' said a deeper voice, also stinging. Bashtet, mate of Basht.

'But they're telepathic and empathic and they said... the Ephors said they were to be euthanised, the experiment was over and we're leaving, we can't take them to Home Dimension! Gnathos, what have you done?'

'Made a mistake about you, that is plain,' said Gnathos. He clutched the cat closer. 'Can I at least ask you to give us time to escape, before you call the Hounds on us?'

'No, wait, Gnathos, my honey, you took me by surprise,' protested Andros, catching at his friend's shoulder. Basht rose from her bag and bit him on the wrist.

'He is afraid,' said the cat. 'He is a fool. We must hurry. Already I feel the sea and land cry out. This mountain is going to explode soon.'

'I won't leave you,' said Andros. 'Where are you going?'

'Away,' said Gnathos. 'The Ephors are already gone, into the tunnel, en route to Shambala in the Mother Mountains. The others are packing up and climbing to the Highest so that the portal can open. When it does, this part of the city will be destroyed. So I came down here to take a grav-sled. The cats and I can ride out the wave. I know a cave we can stay in until we can find refuge. And I had always thought you would come too, my Andros,' he said sadly. 'I thought you would come with me, to escape, to enjoy music, to be able to love each other apart from three stolen kisses. To be able to dance. To have a future where eyes don't watch our every move, where science doesn't rule. We might even be able to laugh, even though an Atlantean never laughs, once we get away.'

'I would!' cried Andros. 'I will!'

'Basht doesn't believe you,' said Gnathos. Andros dropped to his knees, resting his head on his friend's belt. Gnathos' free hand came down to touch his hair.

'She's a cat. They're suspicious. Let me come too! I...' The long censored words would not come to his lips. He could not speak. But Basht pricked up her ears.

'He loves you!' she said, surprised. 'If that is settled, can we go now?'

The grav-sled had been a good choice. It carried a lot of goods – Gnathos had evidently sacked and looted the deserted parts of the city – and it moved fast and very close to the waves. It was easy to see the high-prowed Antlantean ships, sailing under power towards Hellas.

'We're not going that way?' asked Andros. Still afraid, he

had snuggled up almost against his friend before the liquid screen, watching the Atlanteans sail at right angles.

'We're going north,' said Gnathos. Andros felt that he still did not trust him. Curled up with her mate on Gnathos' best bed-cover, Basht yawned, and he felt the yawn in his mind and yawned in reflex.

'I told him you loved him,' she said. 'He knows. Kiss him. You are disturbing my rest, and my kittens are due soon. I need my sleep.'

Instantly, a strong cramp made Andros bend double, clutching his belly. The conditioning against this behaviour had been very strong. He fought down a wave of nausea. Instead of replying, Andros kissed the side of Gnathos' throat, very gently, little butterfly kisses, which tickled. The heavens did not fall. The Ephors did not appear. No robot hands dragged him out of the embrace of his only friend. The sickness receded, the cramp faded. It appeared that, once broken, the terror reactions would not return.

Gnathos turned his head and took Andros' mouth with his own and kissed him fiercely, deeply, biting into his bottom lip. Then he disengaged and looked into the liquid screen. Andros saw his beautiful green eyes widen.

'We're away!' he announced. 'Look back at the mountain!'

All his life Andros had known the shape of that mountain, the city of Atlantis, and now it was covered in a bright silver mist, as though a cloud had come down. The portal had opened. The populace were leaving.

'Goodbye, Ephors,' he breathed. 'Goodbye, Practicality Lessons and beatings. Farewell, Atlantean Deportment and Philosophy and Calm and Stillness. And Forced Learning and Behaviour Modification. They never managed to make me want anyone else, you know, Gnathos.'

'Or me, you,' breathed Gnathos.

They kissed until they were afire. Neither had been allotted a partner, so they had not participated in the State Sanctioned Joining once a month of the married Atlanteans. The coupling of men with men was punishable by death, as pollutants in the carefully balanced gene pool. They had no guide but desire. They fumbled, stroked, grabbed, and sighed, and at one point Gnathos could feel the amusement of both cats, colouring the roaring red fog in his head that made him try to get closer, closer!

Later they lay in a puddle of garments, sticky and exhausted, and Andros stretched out a hand to see if he was, actually, glowing. Both he and his lover were.

They reached the cave high in the Ebruz Mountains a day before the Great Wave. It was comfortable. Gnathos had visited it before. It was more of a cache than a home, but the cats appreciated the sanitary facilities and the small planetary motion generator kept the cave toasty warm. The grav-sled slid into its prepared place and dropped into re-charge.

They spent the whole day eating, sleeping, and learning how to make love. Gnathos had bought a small pipe from a fisherman, and they both tried to compose tunes.

In the middle of the second night, Andros saw a strange light, and woke the others. Together, men and cats sat and watched the red flame scorching the clouds, the bombs of pumice exploding in the air, all so far away as to make the destruction of the city no taller than a candle flame.

Then they went back to sleep. Because the water would be coming soon. They heard it first as a rumble in the ground, which disturbed the cats. Basht and her mate washed furiously, trying to block out the subsonics, until each cat came to a human and compelled them to put their hands over their sensitive ears.

Then there was a crash which shook the mountains end to end and sounded like the end of the planet.

'The Nile must be at full,' commented Gnathos, stroking Andros and Basht at the same time. 'Outgoing tide crashing into incoming Great Wave. The water's already moving up. By morning we'll be in the midst of an ocean.'

'It will go down again?' asked Andros.

'Yes, of course, in most places. This is all our fault, you know. The stadia covered in salt water that will not bear next year. The drowned people and animals. We were careless of their lives.'

'You aren't,' said Andros, kissing him on the hand. 'You rescued the cats.'

'Yes, there's that. The Ephors would have killed them,' admitted Gnathos.

'All right then. We no longer belong to those people, but to the humans,' said Andros. 'And what will become of us? Humans are short lived, prone to disease and wars.'

We will live long lives, together my, my love; as will the cats. And we will just have to find a kingdom that doesn't engage in unsafe behaviour,' replied Gnathos. 'I have just the place in mind, Stable government, polytheic, civilised. Also they are very musical.'

'And you will stay with me?' asked Andros.

'Of course. Always. And with the cats.'

They kissed again until Basht interrupted.

'You not only rescued us from death, but you said you would take us to a land where our kittens would be worshipped as gods,' Basht reminded Gnathos.

'That's true, we will go there just as soon as the water goes down. I have a lovely place in mind for the City of Cats.'

'Come and lie down with me,' suggested Andros, embracing his lover and drawing him down on the second best bed cover. 'Now we are humans, and we can love, and dance and sing, and maybe we will laugh, as well.'

Gnathos subsided into his arms with great joy. His lips curved, his mouth opened. He laughed. Andros laughed. And both cats purred.

ARCHAEOLOGICAL NOTE:

The city of Bubastis, centre of the worship of the Cat Goddess, Basht, has many mummified cats. Such as have been examined have been DNA tested to belong to a strain of *felis sylvestris* and *felis lybica*, a striped cat such as one sees in Egypt even today. No one has ever found the neat, elegant black cats, who were the model for the innumerable statues of the Goddess herself.

Striped cats can undergo chinchillisation, or melanisation, which fades their stripes, but the avatars of the Goddess are all black, unrelieved by any marks. Further investigation at Bubastis may elucidate this puzzle.

SAPPHO OF LESBOS

I desire
And I crave
You.

Phaon had just reached the highest step of the white marble villa when he stopped abruptly. As a fisherman from the bay, he had no errand high on this hill, where the legendary poet Sappho dwelt with her coterie. But it was not social embarrassment which had caused him to stay his footsteps.

It was the long and above all, *sharp* spear which was levelled in a workmanlike manner at his breastbone by Demetrius of Lesbos, the guard. Demetrius was long limbed, sloe eyed, and very attractive, with a half-moon smile. At this moment, however, he was regarding Phaon with disapproval.

'You can't come in,' he told the fisherman. 'You're Phaon, aren't you? Seen you leering at the Lady Sappho down at the beach, where we go bathing.'

'No,' said Phaon. 'I just–'

'You're wasting your time, pretty man,' said Demetrius, sympathetically. 'She just doesn't do men. Not ever. There must be some girl who'd have you, look at you, broad shoulders, hair in ringlets...'

'You don't–' Phaon tried.

'But never mind. I stay out here to make sure that no one disrupts her songs. They're having a poetic duel tonight. If you want to sit here, with me, on the top step, you can see into the hall and hear what they're saying. Would that suit you?'

'Yes,' said Phaon.

'And you promise not to rush inside and try to embrace her? Because I have this spear, and I'd hate to ruin that beautiful back by sticking holes in it. Not to mention that the Lady of the House can't abide mess.'

'I'll be good,' promised Phaon. 'I'll sit here with you and I won't move.'

'Excellent,' said Demetrius. They sat down together on the highest step. 'It'll be nice to have some company,' added the guard.

'Demetrius–' Phaon began, and the guard hushed him.

'Duel's starting,' he said, and Phaon looked into Sappho's symposium. To his surprise, there were men there. Phaon raised an eyebrow at Demetrius.

'That's Alcaeus and his young men. He lives next door. They don't do girls. Perfect match, in my view. Only male company she can stand. Pity he's such a bad poet. But she, ah Sappho, she's a genius. Aphrodite inspires her, breathing poetry into her mouth in a kiss.'

'He's good looking,' observed Phaon. Alcaeus was slim and epicene, dressed, as were all his followers, in expensive tunics dyed blue with woad.

As the season was early spring, Sappho and all of her women were wearing a delicate green; from Sappho's tunic, Rhodopis' chlamys, revealing her bare thighs and hips, to the wisp of cloth which almost concealed the pubis of the lovely Cleis, Sappho's lover. Unlike Alcaeus' boys, who all tended to the willowy, Sappho's maidens were diverse: Cleis was plump, Sappho herself stocky and small, Rhodopis tall and thin. The only thing that united them, thought Phaon, was the fierce light of intelligence in their eyes.

They were drinking wine from golden cups and eating black grapes.

'Those Aeolians,' commented Demetrius, 'drink like fish. Someone'll come out soon with my supper. You're welcome to share it.'

'Thank you,' said Phaon absently, eyes on the golden light inside. It came from olive oil lamps, but Phaon was prepared to swear that it actually came from poetry. He heard Demetrius chuckle.

'They are divine, aren't they?' he asked. 'And you and me out here in the cold darkness, spying on the Gods. They sleep in all morning, you know, rise for a little meal, then go walking. They stay in the temple of Aphrodite for a while, dedicating the songs of the night before, and you've seen them, at dusk, strolling down to the sea-foam, slipping naked as the newborn Aphrodite into the waves.'

'I've seen them,' murmured Phaon.

'Beautiful,' agreed Demetrius.

'I always watch them,' replied Phaon.

'I'm so sorry,' said Demetrius. 'The boats rock as the sailors pleasure themselves, and that's all the pleasure they'll get out of Divine Sappho. Then the ladies come back here, laze around in the fresh water baths, and dine and dance and make more songs. Once every ten days, they have this sort of party. Alcaeus usually visits.'

'Demetrius—' Phaon began again.

A well dressed slave girl brought a supper basket and a large jug of diluted wine. She saw Phaon, blushed, and scurried away.

'Oh,' said Demetrius. 'Sorry. They're a bit wary around strange men. We'll just have to drink out of the same cup.' He filled it. 'Rejoice,' he said, and raised the cup in salute.

'*Chiarete*!' answered Phaon, taking it from Demetrius's warm hand and sipping. It was good wine, rich and sweet and dark. Demetrius nudged Phaon with an elbow.

'It's starting,' he said. In order to see, he shifted closer to Phaon on the marble step, They were sitting shoulder to shoulder and thigh to thigh when the verse duel began.

Alcaeus began in a fine, strong voice:

> *'Lord Apollo, good shepherd,*
> *Your sheep beg for release.'*

In return, Sappho her voice like Hymettus honey, sang:

> *'Queen Aphrodite,*
> *Don't let him shear my fleece!'*

There was a laugh, and Alcaeus continued:

> *'Lord Archer, fire arrows of love into her bed.'*

Sappho, pulling one of Alcaeus' boys in front of her, squeaked:

> *'Lady Aphrodite, be my strong shield instead!'*

The young *pais* stumbled and laughed, so Alcaeus embraced his young man, drew him away from Sappho and sang:

> *'No stronger force, lord, in Aeolis than her love.'*

Sappho, glancing up, as though her Goddess was indeed looking down on her, sang:

> *'Lift me, then, Lady, to Divine realms above.'*

'Change?' suggested Alcaeus. 'To a theme of your choosing.'

'I will,' replied Sappho with a smile, 'but only because you're losing.'

The company laughed and drank more wine. Sappho sang:

> *'To my Cleis, my honeyed maiden,*
> *'Fairer than the morning, swift as the light.'*

Alcaeus capped this with:

> *'To my Larichos, my dancer,*
> *'No one more beautiful in my sight.'*

When Phaon winced, Demetrius nodded. 'I told you he was a terrible poet.'

Sappho sang:

> *'I tell you, they will remember us in centuries to come*
> *'For the beauty of my Cleis will enchant even time.'*

Alcaeus capped:

> *'A flame through my loins as I see him move*
> *'My Larichos, of all men the most prime.'*

'His loins are afire?' Phaon said. 'Shat sounds dangerous.'

'Have some more wine,' Demetrius soothed.

Sappho sang:

> *'I drape myself with many garlands of flowers*
> *'But Cleis' skin smells sweeter than roses.'*

Cleis blushed. Alcaeus made the gesture that said he was beaten, but Sappho continued:

> *'So gentle her love, as the breeze from the mountains*
> *'Carrying the scent of bee-grazed blossoms*
> *'Strong magical herbs, that will transform*
> *'Hatred into Love, Death into Life. And I*
> *'Would live thus with you forever, Cleis.'*

The audience broke into applause. Cleis kissed Sappho's hands. The lyre was passed from person to person as they began improvising bawdy songs.

Demetrius stood up. 'Well, that's all there is to see. Sorry about your disappointed hopes.'

'Demetrius,' Phaon said, putting both hands on the guard's shoulders. 'You have few faults, most adorable of men, but you never *will* let anyone finish a sentence. I tried to tell you I didn't come up to this villa in pursuit of Sappho.'

'You didn't?' Demetrius was puzzled. 'Shall I pick up my spear?'

'No,' said Phaon, taking the guard's hand and placing it under his tunic. 'You will find here the only spear we need.'

'You came up here to seduce *me*?' asked Demetrius, incredulity in every word.

'I did,' replied Phaon, 'though I am glad to have seen the divine Sappho. You do not have to sit out here all night, surely.'

'No, here comes my relief now,' said Demetrius. 'So when you said you were watching Sappho's maidens–'

'Always escorted by an extremely attentive and delightful guard.'

Demetrius began to lead Phaon away, toward his own sleeping place.

'*With precious and royal perfume,*' he said. '*I will anoint you. There will be no holy rite—*'

'*From which we will be absent,*' Phaon completed the poem, and they clasped and kissed fervently, leaning against the white pillars of Sappho's villa, while the company inside the house sang of legendary lovers of astounding potency.

'*Some say an army of horsemen,*' said Phaon.
'*Some say soldiers, some say ships,*' said Demetrius.
'*Is the fairest thing on the black earth,*' recited Phaon.
'*But I say, it is what one loves,*' replied Demetrius.

The guard slept in an alcove, screened by a curtain. Phaon descended into Demetrius' embrace, slotting in beside him in the narrow space: foot, shin, knee, thigh, hip, torso, shoulder.

They wrapped their arms around each other, still half-bespelled by desire and now by Sappho's voice, heard clearly through the curtain. They lay unmoving while she sang.

'Glorious Aphrodite, hear our prayer.
'Breathe on us your perfumes
'Cypress, rose and sea-foam
'The blessings of your ocean birth.

'Lie down with us, Lady, here
'In our earthly and tumbled beds
'Smile on our loves, anoint us here
'Where mouth meets hungry mouth.'

When Phaon at last fully embraced Demetrius, he found that they were both crying.

BABYLON

We hanged our harps upon the willows in the midst thereof.
For they that carried us away captive required of us a song;
And they that wasted us required of us mirth, saying
Sing us one of the songs of Zion.
How shall we sing the Lord's song in a strange land?

ASSYRIAN EMPIRE, 720 BC

The deep green shadow blinded him as effectively as a bright light, and he halted and blinked. It was cool and scented under the trees.

Trees? This was Ninevah, great city of the Assyrians, brick and stone and dust. He had been shoved and lashed if he looked up, dragging a heavy cart full of little trees in barrels. Now he was ordered to drop the hauling ropes and he slumped down onto damp grass.

Grass? The overseer, the Assyrian Kul, gave Nahum a final flick of the whip and stomped away to torture another child of Naphtali. How many of us can be left? thought Nahum, dragging in deep breaths. Surely not many now. Babylon wanted to steal our lives, our daughters, our songs. Assyria just wants to kill us all if we do not follow their ways.

And we cannot abandon God, though he has abandoned us for our sins. If we abandon God, we will no longer be Israel. Someone put a rough palm on his shoulder, and when he flinched away from the contact, said in Hebrew 'Shalom, brother, peace. Can you stand?'

'In a moment. Shalom, brother, is this paradise? If so the road was long and hard.'

Nahum could see, now, in the leafy gloom under the dense fruit trees. The man who was patting his shoulder was no older than he. He wore the simple cloth of a labouring slave, and over it the gown of an employee of the court. His voice was warm and amused.

'No, Eden happened already. This is the Hanging Gardens, and we are its keepers. The Great King Sennacharib comes here every now and again. Only he, and his wives. There must always be fruit, and not a fallen leaf may be seen.

'Therefore, he set us here. There are twelve of us, all Israelites, because we are so good with gardens.'

'That bastard Kul made me drag this cart all the way from the market. Are the trees for you? I can't thank you for the task, brother.'

'My name is Aaron of the tribe of Dan,' said the other man gravely.

'I am Nahum of the tribe of Naphtali.'

They exchanged the kiss of peace, as between brethren. Aaron smelt fragrant, of jasmine and roses. Nahum knew that he stank of sweat, blood, and fear.

'Soon we shall talk, and eat, and I shall introduce you to the others. You are the only one of your tribe here,' he said, forestalling the question. 'We all are. Our captors chose us, one from each tribe. And hatred must not devour us,' he added, hauling Nahum to his feet. 'Now, my little trees. They need a drink. So do you!'

'What sort are they?' asked Nahum, taking the cup Aaron held out and drinking gratefully. Cool, earthy water. He had never tasted anything so delicious.

'The Babylonians call them citron,' replied Aaron. 'Come, with both of us hauling, it will not be too long before we can get their roots into good rich earth. Then you can wash and eat. I will tend your welts, and you can lie down in peace.'

'I would love to believe you, my Aaron,' replied Nahum. 'But I can't.'

But it seemed to be true, at least, for the moment. They were lodged in pairs, in little houses on each level of the structure. One man from, as Aaron had said, each of the twelve tribes: Dan, Asher, Naphtali, Reuben, Simeon, Levi, Zebulun, Gad Judah, Issachur, Levi, and Benjamin.

The news of all of them was uniformly dire. All the Northern Kingdoms had been conquered and swept away. Only the tribe of Judah in the land of Judah held out against the Assyrian siege.

'And soon, surely, Jerusalem, the Holy City, will fall again,' commented Isaac, gulping down the sour wine they had managed to make, covertly, of the Great King's surplus grapes.

'Even if it does,' said Aaron, 'Israel shall not break.'

'Look around you,' scoffed Asher. 'We *are* broken! What is left of our tribes, but the bare remnant which is us?'

'Even so,' Aaron said. 'Put some honey in your wine, Nahum, the bees have been feeding on the roses. We are not yet dead. While we live, while only one of us lives, Israel lives. So drink up and don't be so gloomy!

'And look at this palace of trees,' he said, waving a work-worn hand around at the orchard in which they were sitting.

'It's made by coating many reed mats in tar, building two courses of mortared brick on that, then a coating of melted lead to make it waterproof. The walls are 22 cubits thick, the causeways five cubits wide, and water is supplied by the aqueduct and lifted by Archimedes screws. So that it is always wet, always growing? And in 20 years the trees have grown so high that the Gardens are a mass of green, a relief to sore eyes in this city of enamel and clashing colours and dust and stone. Is it not a marvel?'

Reluctantly, they all agreed.

'And if man could make such a thing as this,' declaimed Aaron, 'God, what wonders can he create?'

They had nothing more to say, and ate their lentil soup, bread made of barley, and a sweet cake of honey and dates and apricots.

'Will you lodge with me?' asked Aaron. 'It is a climb, but you will find it worth the effort. From my little house you can see the whole garden.'

'I will,' said Nahum, who had been stricken to the heart with longing as soon as Aaron had laid a hand on his shoulder. He had not realised how lonely he had been, until he had heard Aaron's voice, speaking the Hebrew of his homeland. He took Aaron's hand as they climbed, stopping at each of the six levels, until they reached the top.

'It is a marvel,' breathed Nahum. 'It is a miracle.'

The Garden was oblong. Each layer was laden with trees, and under them, shrubs and lattices of roses and jasmine. The gardens breathed the scent of water and leaves.

'What have you planted over there?' asked Nahum, leaning on Aaron's arm.

'That is Asher's poison garden,' said Aaron. 'Wormwood, castor oil beans, hemlock, crow-mallow, water-chestnut, nightshade, oleander, wolf's-bane. He tried to get poisonous fungi to grow, but the air is not humid enough. It makes him feel better,' said Aaron, 'we have to manage our hatred as best we can. This way, Asher knows that they cannot take him again. One mouthful of any of those, and he can die. He was very badly treated. Do not judge him harshly.'

'I do not,' said Nahum. 'Your little trees seem happier with their roots in earth. They are picking up their leaves already.'

'They will bear a goodly fruit,' Aaron assured him. 'Now, my brother, sit down, and let me draw water: you can wash, and then I will tend you.'

Nahum stripped off the dirty, torn cloth, and scrubbed his body all over with meal sewn into a clout. When he was clean, he dipped water over his head. He felt wonderful. He was a little drunk, from the sour wine doctored with honey, and as clean as he had ever been.

Aaron dried his back with the remains of the cloth, then threw it aside. He smoothed an ointment over the random stripes on Nahum's back.

'That smells so sweet,' said Nahum. 'What is it?'

'Essence of roses, bees' wax and ox fat,' replied Aaron. 'That feels better?'

'Oh,' replied Nahum, turning to his friend and leaning into his embrace. 'That feels as good as new. Will you lie with me?'

'What of Leviticus?' asked Aaron, running a line of kisses down his friend's jaw and neck.

'He isn't here,' said Nahum. 'And if he was, I'd still want to lie with you. My heart has been hollow, my brother.'

'And mine: now we shall be full,' replied Aaron. They clung close to each other, grieving and rejoicing, in the scent of the marvellous garden.

Six months later, after Yom Kippur, which even Asher had kept as a fast, Nahum noticed, amongst the harvest of figs and apricots and garlic and cucumbers, the melons as golden as sunset, the olives already in brine, a very familiar lumpy yellow fruit.

He picked it up. It spoke to him so keenly of home that tears came to his eyes.

'I thought you said it was called citron,' he said to his lover, Aaron.

'I said, as I recall, the Babylonians call it citron,' replied Aaron with his rare, enchanting smile.

'It's *etrog*,' said Nahum. 'You were planning this all this time! You ordered those trees on purpose!'

'And we have myrtle and willow and fronds from a date palm,' said Aaron. 'And we shall build a tabernacle. We will not forget. It's Sukkot!'

'I heard a poem today,' said Nahum, clasping Aaron to his

breast. 'One of the Hebrew stonemasons repairing the south west corner of the palace was reciting it.'

'Tell me,' said Aaron, kissing his cheek.

'If I forget thee, O Jerusalem, let my right hand forget her cunning,' said Nahum. 'If I do not remember thee, let my tongue cleave to the roof of my mouth, if I prefer not Jerusalem above my chiefest joy.'

'Amen,' said Aaron.

Nahum stared with great affection and admiration into Aaron's eyes. With men like this in the world, Israel would surely survive.

'Amen,' said Nahum. 'And I love you.'

'I love you,' said Aaron. 'Even above Jerusalem, you are my chiefest joy.'

THE LIBRARY ANGEL

The smoke was already trickling under the closed door. Marcus Tullius Corvinus grabbed the Homeric hymns, which he had been construing, and grappled them to his breast. Whatever the cost, these should not burn, must not burn. The scroll was heavy but he managed to seize a couple of epics as he ran past, seeking the outer gate into the colonnade that gave directly onto the sea.

The scrolls were inscribed in oak-gall ink. Even if they got soaked, they would not blur. The immortal words would not be lost to the night or war and barbarity, roaring towards scholarship and learning, knowledge and wisdom, with the fires from the burning ships.

The Library of Alexandria was a great monument and treasure of the world. The Romans probably wouldn't mean to burn it down. But they wouldn't overly care if they did.

Marcus got to the gate and a rush of flame, gusting with the high wind, forced him back. He stumbled into another scholar on the same errand, Egyptian by the look of him, a load of treatises in his arms.

'The wooden fence and landing stage is afire,' he gasped, 'and there's smoke coming under the other door.'

'Windows?' asked the Egyptian. They scanned the room. There were a few windows, but they were high up, too high for either of them to reach alone.

'Take the scrolls,' ordered Marcus. 'I'm Marcus, what's your name, fellow scholar?'

27

'Imhotep,' said the Egyptian. The kohl around his beautiful eyes was running down his face in black tears. 'What do you intend?'

'I'll boost you up, you can get out through the window,' said Marcus. 'Take the *Hymns of Homer* with you, they must not be lost.'

'But you'll die,' protested the Egyptian. 'I would not leave you to perish.'

'What scrolls do you have?' asked Marcus, pulling a table over to the wall and climbing on it.

'*Treatise on Surgery*, there's only one, it saves lives,' said Imhotep. 'All of it, eight scrolls. That, too, must not be lost.'

'This window faces onto the stone landing stage where the foreign ships come in. If we wrap them in something, make a bag, that ought to work.'

Marcus dragged off his tunic, piled the scrolls into it, and pinned it shut with his fibulae. The brooches kept the cloth close around the precious writing.

'Now, up you go,' urged Marcus. 'If you stand on my shoulders, you can reach the opening. Hurry, it's getting hard to breathe.'

Imhotep scaled the naked frame of the young Roman, dragged the scrolls to the window and shoved them out. But there was not a chance that he could fit his body through that narrow embrasure. Imhotep half slid, half fell, into the embrace of Marcus Corvinus.

'We can't get out,' whispered the Egyptian, taking them both to the cold stone floor, where there was still a little air. 'But the scrolls are safe.'

The Egyptian drew his fine woollen cloak over the two of them, so that they should not feel the teeth of the fire. Marcus Corvinus wrapped Imhotep in a fast embrace.

'It is an honour,' he gasped, as darkness crept over his sight, 'to die with such a devoted scholar'.

Imhotep prayed while he could still form words, then

snuggled into the Roman's body. To die was to return to one's mother, to go back to the source of all comfort. To die was to sleep the deepest sleep of all.

They slept. The fire roared overhead, licking up words, Greek and Egyptian and Latin, eating knowledge, consuming wisdom, leaving nothing behind but a Roman victory and a thick layer of ash.

Imhotep woke, which was a surprise. Surely they couldn't have survived that inferno! He was still lying with his Roman, under the cloak Imhotep's father had woven for him. But there was no sound or heat outside the shelter of the cloth.

He lifted one corner and exclaimed, 'Isis! Hail, Lady, Keeper of the Door of the Underworld!'

'If you wish,' replied the tall, elegant, onlooker. He had a golden aura around his curly head, a white robe and long, white wings.

Strange, thought Imhotep, Isis is supposed to be a Goddess. This is a God of some sort. I don't recognise him. And I know all of the Ennead.

'Are you Thanatos?' croaked Marcus Corvinus, waking and leaning on his Egyptian's shoulder. Odd, he thought, Thanatos, God of Death, is supposed to be a dark angel.

'I can be Thanatos if you require,' replied the figure. His voice was even and musical. And patient.

'We died, didn't we? In the fire?' reasoned Imhotep. 'I didn't think we could survive that, Marcus.'

'No, 'Hotep, we evidently didn't survive. And, if you would be so good, Honoured Celestial Being,' Marcus and Imhotep levered themselves to their feet, creaking in every muscle, 'I regret that I have no sacrifice to offer, but could you tell us where we are?'

'This is The Library,' replied the God. 'And I am the Library Angel. Come along, now, you need to bathe, and then there will be a feast in your honour.'

'A feast?' asked Imhotep, following the angel, an arm around Marcus' waist as the Roman's was around his shoulders.

'Well, of course,' said the angel. 'You saved the Treatise on Surgery and the Homeric Hymns. Naturally there would be a feast. Here is the bath. Someone will come with some refreshments and some clothes, if you would like to wear them. Then you may rest until I come to fetch you. People find the transition tiring, when it has been so,' the angel shuddered, 'violent.'

Marcus and Imhotep staggered into the bath. It was a series of large, steamy, tiled and painted rooms, where they were immediately surrounded by a crowd of nude boys and girls who stripped off the burned remains of Imhotep's cloth and sat them down on chairs to be scrubbed with a strange substance which foamed; and tasted, when Marcus tried it, very flat and unpleasant. But it smelt divine, of the cypress trees at the Serapeum, the Daughter Library where the remainder of the scrolls should be safe.

The bath creatures – Imhotep observed that they had little wings, which sufficed to lift them a few cubits above the ground – washed them very thoroughly, humming and singing to themselves in a manner reminiscent of bees. They gave off harmony, a sense of happiness and a sweet scent, like honey. But they did not speak.

When Imhotep and Marcus Tullius Corvinus were rinsed as clean as the newborn, the humming attendants ushered them out of the washing room and conducted them down the steps into a sumptuous bath, into warm water which was so mineral rich that they were buoyed up. Marcus caught Imhotep's hand and they floated together, linked, staring up at a ceiling which was made of immeasurable space, powdered by a million stars.

'I don't hurt anymore,' commented Marcus. 'All those little burns and bruises are gone. And you, my devout scholar?'

'Yes, I feel completely unharmed. Is this *your* afterlife?' asked Imhotep. 'If so, it was very kind of you to invite me to come with you. It's lovely.'

Marcus shivered and pulled Imhotep into the curve of his body.

'No, my afterlife is both tedious and frightening. Not a good place at all. And to test the hypothesis, in my afterlife you can't remember what it was to be alive. And I remember everything.'

'So do I. This isn't the Field of Reeds either, though don't think I'm complaining. And did you recognise the Library Angel? And those little winged children?'

'No, I haven't studied much comparative religion,' replied Marcus. 'But you'll stay with me? You don't want to leave me to go to the Field of Reeds?'

'I'll stay,' promised Imhotep. He relaxed in the warm water, feeling the ache of his loss dissolving in the water. 'I would not be able to go there, anyway. My body must have been burned to ash in the fire; no mummified body, no Field of Reeds.'

'That seems unjust,' commented Marcus. 'I think I like this afterlife better than either.'

'Yes. And, do you know, Marcus, even though I'm definitely dead, I'm hungry and thirsty. Can we get out and find some of those refreshments of which the angel spoke?'

'An excellent notion,' replied Marcus.

The refreshments were a fine loaf of wheat bread, a plait of honey-poppyseed cake, several cheeses, a variety of fruits and a large jug of wine. Marcus looked around for a mixing bowl and a water jug, did not find them, tasted, and smiled. He filled two cups.

'This is wonderful,' he said to Imhotep, as they sat on a pile of pillows on a warm wooden floor in a hall hung with tapestries. 'It would be a crime to dilute it. Drink with me?' he asked, looking into the Egyptian's dark eyes. 'I don't know how long this is going to last, if we're dreaming so as not to feel the fire, but I want to eat and drink, and then I want to make love with you, most beautiful of scholars. Before the spell changes. Before it all turns to ash.'

'Yes,' agreed Imhotep, biting into a red fruit which trickled juice down his chin. Marcus leaned forward and licked it up. It tasted wonderful. 'But this has a more permanent feeling than a dream. This is certainly a Heavenly fruit,' he said. 'This is nectar and ambrosia, and I would make love to you for all the time there is, until the ending of the world.'

They lay together gently, slowly, not altogether believing that each touch was real. They mouthed the divine grapes, sucking sweet juice from each other's skin, kissing through an aeon, caressing and holding. Each caress seemed to be magnified, their skin sensitised by the cleansing, and when they cried out together the winged attendants heard, and sent up a humming paean of joy.

Marcus laughed, looking down into Imhotep's face. He kissed him. Imhotep tasted of grapes and flowers.

'If it all ceases, and we go into the dark,' he told his fellow scholar, 'it will have been worth dying to embrace you.'

'I love you, Marcus. I treasure your love. And I saved the Treatise on Surgery, and you saved the Homeric Hymns, so it was worth our lives.'

'It was,' agreed Marcus. 'But I had not expected such an extravagant reward.'

Imhotep kissed him again.

Marcus elected for a tunic and Imhotep for a cloth, and they were conducted to the feast by the Library Angel. The hall was like none they had ever seen, huge and noisy, with lot of tables and chairs and hundreds of scholars, all talking and drinking and disputing. And a group of them, in one corner, were singing.

'I present them to you,' announced the Angel, and the room fell silent. 'Marcus Tullius Corvinus and Imhotep, who died in saving the Homeric Hymns and the Treatise on Surgery. The hymns inspired poets through all ages, and the Treatise educated a thousand years of healers.

'Hail!' cried the Angel, and the whole company surged to their feet and cried, 'Hail!'

'And who's that?' asked Marcus of their table-mate, Captain Elijah Raven, a grizzled old man who had smuggled Ancient Greek manuscripts out of Romanian monasteries just ahead of another purge of literature. He had one leg and a parrot called Livy on his shoulder, and Marcus liked him instantly.

'That's Pan Tzu,' said the Captain. 'He carved the Analects of Confucius on stones and laid 'em face down in a path, so that after the Tiger of Ch'in was dead, philosophy could emerge again.

' And that's Hypatia, martyred for learning, what they forbad to women. And all them women over there, they're witches, what wrote down their spells and recipes so other women didn't die. And burned for it. Good earthy company for a man like me, them witches. The singers, they're bards and troubadours; they remembered what couldn't be written down. The women over there are the storytellers – they remembered tales that would have died out, if they hadn't told 'em to the childer.

'The ones in them puffy breeks, they're Shakespeare and his pals. I like Will. He said he's here to improve his Greek. That chatty bloke, that's Sir Thomas Browne, who wrote the *Bibliographica Abscondita*, making people look for old books, and that's Mr Cotton, who bought 'em when I brung 'em. Nice old man, used to give me brandy, I used to bring 'im them fruits done up in sugar, not a tooth to 'is head but one and that was 'is sweet tooth, poor man. That's Keats, who died for 'is verse, and that's – oh, you'll meet 'em all, good fellows, most of 'em. Have some beer?'

'Do we stay here forever?' asked Imhotep.

'Forever and a day, my son,' said the Captain, 'as long as you want to be 'ere. All the lost books are in the library. If you saved a book, and you work on it, then someone in the world below will be inspired by your work. Everything we do here has its reflection in the world. Aye, somewhere some student is reading your hymns, boy, and will write a novel with a new translation that will set another soul afire. As above, so below, that's what Master Josephus says. What more could you want?

Food's good, ale's better. You've got your lover, Marcus, and your work. And if you study too much, if you tire of learning, they'll hale you out, to fly into the stars, or bask on a beach with blue sand or bathe in the light of three moons. Universe's your oyster. There's a lot of advantage in being dead, I find,' confided the Captain. His parrot Livy croaked an assent and beaked a fig, spitting the stalk down the Captain's shirt collar.

Marcus embraced Imhotep and surveyed the gathering. 'Yes,' he said. 'What do you say, my heart?'

'Yes,' replied Imhotep. A wealth, a treasury, of books awaited them. He felt light headed with joy. 'More wine, my love?'

THE GUARDIANS OF MAIDEN CASTLE

I probably wouldn't have dared; I *know* I wouldn't have dared, if it hadn't been for – well, several things: the warmth of the sun, so rare and fine, pouring down on us like honey; the sweet scent of the grass, crushed as we lay naked upon the sward; the plentiful mead and roasted meat we had just devoured; and Anest leaning over to kiss Drysi on the mouth. That was the deciding act.

We were in festival, we guardians, the painted warrior elite who kept the Great Castle safe, so that when enemies came all who could would flee within, flocks and children and possessions, and we would slam the great gates shut and bar them. There were wells and feed and shelter for all within the Great Castle.

Thereafter anyone who actually managed to toil up the earthwork would be met at the wall by us. By slingers, by archers, and if it came to it, by sword-wielding guardians. The shield of the Durotriges. Every one of us tried and tested, marked on the breast with the curling serpent, applied in one long painful session by a priest using a sharp iron pin and a strong infusion of woad.

Women and men. We were all strong and skilful fighters. Aedd was, perhaps, the best fighter. He was so light on his feet that watching him spar with a heavy blade was like observing a dance, a deadly, elegant ritual. He was a good archer, a wolf-pace runner, not fast but enduring, a pleasant singing voice, a light hand on the harp, a good poet. Oh, that was Aedd, whose name means fire, blindingly-red hair, eyes as blue as this midsummer sky. I loved him from the first moment I saw him, which was the moment he reached past me and shoved the attacker who was about to cut my throat off the earthwork.

He had come to the main gate one morning, a deserter from some tribe which did not use clan marks. The shaman sequestered him for a month, for cleansing and ritual, then inducted him, just in time for an attack by our neighbours. They said he had run to the battle, his tattoos still red and swollen.

I did not know him. But I was pulled into his arms and for a moment felt him melt against me, chest to chest, my arms around his neck. Then he smiled at me and released me, and despite sleeping near me and eating at my hearth, he had not touched me again. He would not tell us where he had come from, but when ghost stories and such were told around the communal fire, he had some dreadful tales about monsters in a place called the Teutonburger Forest. He learned our language, well enough to make puns and poems.

Why should he be interested in me? I was just Idris, brown hair, blue eyes, nothing intriguing about me. Born here; will die and be buried here.

Still, he had not taken a lover. Guardians are supposed to find a partner; thus will we fight better, having something apart from our duty to fight for. Someone to keep us warm in the winter. Someone to guard our back. Many had offered, but Aedd had refused them all. He was polite, but he refused.

And oh, I wanted him. I yearned for him. Once a year at midsummer the residents of the castle allow the warriors their own festival and feast. Shepherds and cooks guard the walls, and we have leave to bathe in the sacred pool, lie on the grass, play any game, drink too much mead and fall asleep under a tree. Or find lovers, which was what I had just seen. Anest, who is a brave woman, had just kissed Drysi, whose name means thorns, and who has always lived up to it. Rare sharp tongue and as far as we knew not interested in any lover of any gender. Anest was unarmed. I would never have dared to approach Drysi so.

And that metal-quilled maiden relented, she gathered Anest into her strong, scarred arms, and kissed her as though she had starved for her touch. Anest gave a small squeak of surprise, which made me smile.

'Aedd, would you like me to kiss you?' I ventured as he lay beside me naked in the sun. He leaned up on one elbow and regarded Drysi and Anest entwined. Then he put his hand to the back of my neck and dragged me down into a voracious embrace. We only broke apart a little when we absolutely had to breathe.

'Yes,' he said. 'I would like you to kiss me. All over. As I will do to you. Oh, my honey, Idris, my love. You were the only one I wanted, and you were the only one who didn't ask!'

'You refused all of them for me?' I gasped.

He said in his tuneful voice, 'I didn't want anyone but you. But I did not know… I didn't dare… in case…'

'Your previous tribe,' I reasoned, 'does not mate like we do?'

'No,' he chuckled, pulling me down into his arms again. 'No, they really don't. Just for lying like this, they would burn me. And you, as well. I thought it might be all right here, but not until now, when I saw Anest kiss Drysi, and no one said anything, no one raised an outcry or sent for a priest and a torch.'

'I don't think I like your previous tribe,' I said, tracing the warrior tattoo with my forefinger. 'I think I like my tribe better.'

'So do I,' he smoothed a calloused hand down my back pulling us closer together. 'Oh, Mithras, so do I.'

He had mentioned this Mithras before, but I was not minded to consider religious matters, while embracing this beautiful man, feeling his thighs part for me to lie between.

Just the ecstasy of his love, which set me alight. My Aedd.

My fire. Oh, the sweet burning. His skin smelt of autumn, his mouth tasted of honey.

We went down to the Sacred Lake to bathe, hand in hand, and were recognised as lovers thereafter. We slept together, we ate together. We were no longer single fighters, but a dangerous pair.

The alarm came, the castle filled with people and irritable goats, the gate smashed shut. We were on the walls, my love and I, when I heard him make a small, pained noise, as though he had been hurt.

'Do you see them?' he asked me. I looked. Glittering lines of men marching like ants, in order. At their head a man in a scarlet cloak, beside him a standard with an eagle.

'I must go down and talk to them,' he said. 'Quickly, before this all goes wrong. I love you,' he said hurriedly, kissing my mouth hard. 'Tell the others, do nothing, fire no arrow, wait. If they kill me, then attack if you wish. This is a foe too strong for us. Honey-sweet Idris,' he added, 'I will never regret you.'

Then he leapt down and was gone, running for the little gate by the great one and out into the road. I ran after, yelling to the guardians, 'Wait! Watch! Don't attack until we have Aedd's word! Or if you see him fall,' I screamed.

They heard me. I could not tear myself away from where I stood in the gate. I saw my dearest love walk boldly to the head of the column and say something in an unknown tongue, making a strange salute. The scarlet cloaked one dismounted. The glittering ant warriors halted.

I could not understand what they were saying! This must be the language of my Aedd's tribe. But the red-cloaked one, finally, nodded, Aedd called to me, 'Open the gate! They will not harm us!'

And against all sense, I opened the great gate and let these armoured men into the castle. Because of Aedd's word, which I had always trusted, and because I had caught the eye of the man in the scarlet cloak. A battered face, clearly an old warrior, but a calm, intelligent expression. He was not angry, greedy, or belligerent. And as the soldiers filed in, through the panicky people and angry livestock, I knew that Aedd had been right. We could not hold off this well-armed, well-clad host, all moving with one purpose. But they were men, just men. And, by the way they moved, they had been marching for a long time. There were wounded men on stretchers. The pack animals plodded, heads down.

Aedd led them to the flat centre of the castle, where there was room for all of them and their horses and their bird god. Aedd summoned me with a glance and I came to his side. He took my hand and put it over his heart, which was pounding.

'Idris, my darling, we may just have survived an encounter with a Roman Legion bent on conquest. Watch,' he told me. 'I never got tired of this sight.'

They really were ant men. In a short time, while the space boiled with activity, there were tents and horse lines and a pallisade: little fires sent up plumes of suppertime smoke, cauldrons heated, men took off helmets and breastplates and stretched out on the grass. Horses cropped. Orders were barked. It was a kind of magic. I had never seen such a thing.

Aedd laughed, and kissed me.

Our shaman Branwyn the Raven and our Prince Dyfri came to this ant warrior. He did not want much from us, just not to war against him, and we promised not to do that. He also wanted food, firing, fodder for the horses and fresh water. We agreed to supply these, and the bulk of the people went home to fetch them, taking most of the beasts back, though we guardians remained.

The name of the battered warrior was Vespasian, and the army was the Second Augusta. And they were tired. After they cooked their strange food, they lay down and slept within their fence.

'Because they are an overwhelming force, they will protect us,' observed our shaman.

'Guardians, your time may be gone.'

'There will always be need of refuge, and there will always be enemies,' said Drysi. Anest was at her shoulder, as ever.

'We will stay here for the present,' said Aedd. 'To watch them. I will send word if there is any threat. And if this goes well, I shall build a shrine to Mithras, the soldiers' god, with my own hands.'

'Those are your people,' I said to him, as we lay down in our bracken nest, near enough to the Roman camp to hear if there was any alarm.

'Once,' he said in a faraway voice. 'Once I was a soldier in that army.'

'But you ran away?' I asked, wondering how much he had missed his comrades and brothers. If he would now cover up his tribal snake with one of those tunics and return to his own clan. He must have heard the uncertainty in my voice, and rolled closer, so that I could feel his body pressed against mine, his breath on my cheek.

'You are my people,' he told me, very low. 'The guardians are my family. The Durotriges are my tribe, and you are my love, by the light of both Lugh of the shining spear and of Mithras the slayer of the bull. To whom I owe a shrine. And I will never, never leave you. What oath would you require of me, my Idris?'

'No oath but a kiss,' I whispered, and he kissed me. And we made love so sweetly that we cried aloud, and Anest in a nearby embrace told us to shut up or we would shock the Romans.

Which made Aedd laugh even more loudly.

He kept his word. The Pax Romana came, with it taxes, but taxes are better than always living on the edge of a knife. Most of us guardians stayed in the castle, in case: we still had enemies who envied our treaty, our comfort and our affluence. And we lie together every night, me and my fire, and will until the end. And when Annywn opens its gates for us, we will still be together.

ARCHAEOLOGICAL NOTES

Mortimer Wheeler, a rather excitable 1930s archaeologist, decided on finding the graves on Maiden Castle, that they had been slaughtered and flung into a burial pit by the Romans. Later examination showed that the graves were tidy, deeply dug, and had offerings set by each body, unlike a burial pit, dug merely to dispose of enemy corpses. The site is just as likely to be the cemetery of the defenders of the castle.

Amongst the dead were two men, one killed by a leaf-shaped arrowhead still lodged in his spine. They lie side by side, hand in hand, with their offering bowls of mead and their loaves of barley bread, together forever.

The people gradually left the castle and built a town in the valley. At about that time, someone built a small shrine to both Mithras and Lugh at Maiden Castle.

ESCAPE FROM HERCULANEUM

'All right, tell me another one,' urged Crassus, nailing down the crate and reaching for another bundle of scrolls. The air was smoky and harsh. He coughed as he spoke.

'Blessed are the meek,' said Piso, emptying another shelf of scrolls into his arms.

'That's just silly,' commented Crassus.

'Blessed are the poor in spirit, for theirs is the Kingdom of Heaven,' recited Piso. 'Not much more, the library's nearly packed up.'

'What does poor in spirit mean?' asked Crassus.

'I don't know,' confessed Piso.

'Look. Pisculus, this is nonsense, admit it!'

'Oh, and I suppose your Master Epicurus' sayings are divinely inspired? And don't call me that!' yelled Piso.

'You're a fish, a fish, all Christians are little fish,' taunted his fellow librarian. 'Just like the little minnows of Tiberius! Too meek to fight back!'

'I'll show you meek, Infidelis!' Piso's hazel eyes flashed.

'Swimming around in the Blue Grotto and sucking the Emperor's–'

He recoiled from a smart slap. He licked uneasily at a split lip. He hadn't known that Piso could hit like that. Or that hard. His fellow librarian was almost panting with fury.

'No time to show you proper respect for my lord Jesus Christ. The smoke's getting worse.'

'Yes, and we're leaving,' said Crassus, realising something. 'Now.'

'Why? We can put these on the cart, Pietas the donkey's outside–'

'Listen, you Christian dolt!' Crassus said. He grabbed Piso's curly hair and shook his head from side to side. Piso did not fight off the touch.

'I can't hear anything,' he admitted.

'The mountain's been grumbling and belching and shaking the earth for at least a week, right?' demanded Crassus.

'Yes, of course,' replied Piso.

'And now it's stopped. Which means that the mountain is going to erupt, come on,' urged Crassus. Piso did not move. 'Well, I'm leaving. Come with me. Oh, of course, you don't mind dying, you're going to heaven, aren't you, my not-so-meek Pisculus?'

'And you as well, if you believe,' said Piso calmly, placing his last armload of scrolls in the crate and fastening the lid. 'God will protect me.'

'Is your God willing to prevent this evil, but not able? Then he is not omnipotent,' said Crassus, dragging at Piso's arm. 'Is he able, but not willing? Then he is malevolent. Come *on*, Piso!'

'Blessed are the pure in heart, for they shall see God,' murmured Piso. It was getting very hot. Cinders were falling. Crassus hauled Piso into the lane behind the villa, flung him into the donkey cart, and freed the tether. The donkey Pietas bolted for the watergate, little hoofs ringing on the cobbles. Piso struggled briefly until Crassus sat on him. Piso prayed aloud.

'Our father, which art in Heaven, hallowed be Thy name, thy Kingdom come, thy will be done, on Earth as it is in Heaven...'

Crassus, terrified, heard the huge indrawn breath of the mountain, then Vesuvius exhaled in fire. The donkey flung herself out of the city gate and onto the plain and ran even faster. Beside her ran masterless horses and a grey flood of rats, dogs with broken leashes, goats in ragged flocks, bleating to keep the flock together.

Crassus recited Epicurus to himself as Piso prayed and the sky turned black and the earth shook. Underneath the unnatural darkness he heard huge explosions, heard a smothered shriek as Herculaneum died in lethal vapours such as issue from Tartarus. His philosophy had taken away his ability to pray, and philosophy was no comfort to him as he cowered in Piso's arms in the bottom of the cart, appalled by the violence overhead, as mindless as the running beasts, who only knew their highest imperative was to be away from the city.

'Death is of no concern to us, for he that is dead is in no way different from he who has never been born,' Crassus whimpered.

'God is our refuge and our strength, a very present help in time of trouble,' said Piso, who was sitting up, had reclaimed the reins, and was allowing Pietas her head. She was slowing. The tide of creatures had also slowed, as they came to the turn of the headland. There an offshoot of the river flowed into the sea. Pietas turned the cart and trotted inland, hoof deep in water, until she found a place where she could plunge her nose into clean water without being butted by an unnerved goat.

The air came in fresh from the land and Piso and Crassus fell out of the cart and lay in the shallows. They coughed and retched, drank more water, embraced each other and Piso kissed the blood away from Crassus' lip, very gently.

'I should not have struck you,' he said quietly. The bellowing of the mountain was somewhat damped by the ridge of stone they were sheltering behind.

'I deserved it,' said Crassus. 'I'll forgive you if you kiss me again.'

'To forgive is a duty,' agreed Piso, and kissed him sweetly.

Presently they sat up, dripping and cool for the first time in weeks, and saw that the animals had crossed the river and were still heading west.

'Shall we continue?' asked Piso.

'How is poor little Pietas?' asked Crassus, dragging himself to his feet. The donkey was restless. The cart was intact, but they need not burden her again, if she was content to walk. Piso and Crassus paced either side of her head, hands meeting over her patient neck, until they reached and crossed the next stream. There the flood of animals dropped to a slow amble.

'They feel safer here,' commented Piso.

A small village was inundated with people seeking refuge from the fury of the mountain. There was a cacophony of voices shrieking, wives seeking husbands, grabbing elbows to ask if anyone had seen a sister or a child. Dogs barked. Men shouted. Babies wailed.

Piso and Crassus attracted immediate attention. They were clearly young men of the patrician class, though somewhat singed and damp. They were swamped, mobbed by petitioners. And all they could say was that Herculaneum had gone. They said it over and over again.

Deafened and weeping and jostled, they allowed Pietas to lead them through the crowd and through the hamlet, until they were out on the road again, and even the goats had decided to stop and graze.

'What shall we do, where shall we go?' asked Crassus dreamily.

'The Lord will provide,' answered Piso.

Crassus woke up abruptly. 'Well, yes, Pisculus, because in that donkey cart, which Pietas is still faithfully hauling, is most of the Dominus's gold and the Domina's jewellery, and they aren't going to reclaim it. Let's walk along a little way, the villa of Surbita the Hetera is just over there, and we can sleep there. She's an old friend of my father's. She won't be here, but maybe some of her household might remember me. Anyway she has a very spacious stable and this donkey needs a feed of apples and oats, and I'm suddenly so hungry that I could eat a side of venison.'

'And I could eat the other side,' said Piso.

Domina Surbita's housemaster did indeed remember the young Crassus, and they stabled Pietas and rubbed her down. Her coat was flecked with little burns, and when Crassus ran a hand over his own hair, he found the same small clumps of singed hair. They fed Pietas, then were given access to the baths while a small repast was prepared.

So, to the booming of Vesuvius vomiting death and destruction onto the cities, Crassus and Piso were scrubbed, bathed, massaged and oiled. They sat in the triclinium – the great dining room was still draped in dust sheets – and wolfed down grapes and boiled eggs and bread and three sorts of cheese, chunks of roast pork in pomegranate sauce, and marzipan apples with their many cups of watered red wine. Both of them experienced an increasing sense of unreality. They had been terrified, filthy and hungry. Now they were safe, clean and replete. Crassus was fairly sure that he was dreaming again.

It wasn't until they had been escorted to a clean bed in a room painted with Dionysian orgies that they dared touch.

Piso lay down and took Crassus in his arms. They no longer stank of sulphurous fumes, fear and sweat. Crassus' scent, of green apples, had returned and Piso snuffled his neck to smell it. He was shaking with reaction, and had not realised how much he loved the unbeliever Crassus, until he had nearly lost him. Crassus cupped his friend's cheek in one clean hand and stared into his eyes. Hazel eyes, still full of fear.

'I almost fear to touch you,' said Crassus. 'We nearly didn't survive that, my Piscus, and the cities we have always lived in are wiped off the face of the earth as though they had never been.'

'We left the books,' mourned Piso.

'If we'd waited to load the books, we would all have died, including Pietas. Epicurus is a great philosopher. His books are not uncommon and much copied. They will survive,' said Crassus, kissing his friend on the chest, marking each little burn with his comforting lips. Piso's skin always tasted, for some reason, of seaweed and wet leaves and amber.

'Infidelus,' murmured Piso, 'will you stay with me?'

'There is no place I would rather be,' said Crassus. 'The noble soul occupies itself with wisdom and friendship.'

'We can work on the wisdom,' said Piso, 'and on belief.'

'I do not believe,' said Crassus, tightening his embrace.

'That's all right,' said Piso comfortably. 'I can believe enough for two.'

Outside, ash began to fall. The mountain screamed. The red light bathed the room. Piso and Crassus made love and fell asleep in each other's arms.

When they woke, later, in the midst of nightmare, they clung close and comforted each other, and were never apart again in this world. Crassus became a gentleman farmer in the Sabine HIlls, famous for his table, and Piso built a small chapel next to the villa for his own devotions.

And they never managed to convert each other. Crassus buried Piso, many years later, by Christian rites in a white marble coffin carved all over with little fish. And Crassus lies beside him in a sarcophagus of pure white, carved with grapevines and bees.

Archaeological Notes

No one has ever explained the Villa Rustica of Crassus which has a small Christian shrine. One of the men is buried as a Christian, arms crossed, feet towards the east, and the other is still a pagan. Neither of them are slaves, they are both Roman gentlemen. It is a mystery.

AELFWINE AND THE SUCCUBUS

'But why did the Devil send *you*?' asked Brother Aelfwine. 'I'm a man. I should have got an incubus, a fallen angel in the shape of a woman. Why did they send me a succubus?'

'I'm not a succubus,' replied the tall, cloaked figure.

'Of course you are,' asserted Brother Aelfwine. 'You appeared out of nowhere in my locked cell. You're naked under that cloak, I can see a glimpse of your thigh; it's bare. And...'

He consulted a sheet of vellum on which a condemnation, titled *A Warning Against Night Demons*, was written for the brothers to meditate upon before falling asleep. 'And the Warning says: "Their skin is as white as dead men's bones". Your skin is as pale as a pearl. "Their hair is as black as sin". You have dark curly hair. "Their mouths are as red and as hot as a coal in the fires of Hell." You have a mouth that begs for a kiss, and eyes like the Abbot's gem that he set in the cover of the Lindisfarne Gospels. Emerald eyes. What else could you be?'

'You are leaping to conclusions,' said the visitor, in a dark, velvety voice, with a lilting accent which was music to Brother Aelfwine's ears. He shed the cloak and was indeed naked under it. He was also the most beautiful man Aelfwine had ever seen.

'Look at you,' he mumbled. 'You are made of perfection, as all fallen angels must be. No wonder the daughters of men fell in love with you.'

'You are doing lovely work,' said the visitor, moving closer to look at the vellum laid out on Brother Aelfwine's desk. The picture of Saint Aidan, seated at his own desk, his white cat on his lap, was drawn in outline.

The white cat sitting on Brother Aelfwine's bed was clearly acting as a model. It sniffed at the succubus' extended fingers and allowed a caress. It was well known that cats were creatures of night.

'That is Pangur Ban, the Abbot's cat,' explained Brother Aelfwine. 'I borrowed him. He'll only stay as long as my supply of dried fish lasts. He doesn't really like anyone except Father Eadward. There, thank you and God bless you, Pangur, that's the lot,' said Brother Aelfwine, handing over the last of the tiny dried fish.

And indeed, the cat was standing at the door a moment later. Brother Aelfwine let him out and re-locked the door. He expected the succubus to have vanished but he was still present, looking over the other leaves on the desk.

'Your lettering is excellent,' he commented.

'Aren't you supposed to try to seduce me?' asked Brother Aelfwine. Hope was colouring his voice.

'Oh, very well,' he sighed. 'But afterwards, I want to talk to you.'

'Are you so sure that you *can* seduce me?' asked Brother Aelfwine.

'We succubi like a challenge.' He seized Brother Aelfwine by his scapular and drew him into a kiss so hot, so sweet and so long that the brother gasped for breath. The succubus' skin was so smooth, so delicate and his limbs so long and fine that the brother shed his clothes and drew his seducer into his arms, laid them down on his narrow, chaste bed, and gave himself completely over to pleasure. The only reason that the whole abbey was not aware of his forbidden liaison was that the succubus, at his moment of climax, locked mouths with Aelfwine and swallowed his scream.

Oddly enough, thought Brother Aelfwine when he could think again, the succubus had also spilled semen, which was not like the Warning at all. Possibly the Warning had been wrong. The overheated tone of the warnings about these night demons had always obscurely worried him. He said so. The succubus laughed.

'I always thought that someone should have told them to stop drooling into their ink,' he chuckled, hauling Brother Aelfwine up to lie on his chest, so that they were face to face. He smelt of sea water and musk: very earthy smells for a demonic creature.

'Oh, thou art lovely, Aelfwine! So sweet is thy love, my bones are melted with thee.'

'Thou art fair, my love, thou art fair,' sighed Brother Aelfwine. 'Thou hast doves' eyes within thy locks, and thy lips are a thread of scarlet.'

The succubus tasted some of the seed spilled between them.

'My hands drip with myrrh,' he said. 'I feed among the lilies.'

'Now that you have seduced me, succubus, and ruined my vocation and damned me to eternal torment, what is there left to talk about?' asked Brother Aelfwine, comfortably.

'You joined this monastery because they would let you spend all your time drawing and illuminating,' chided the succubus. 'You have a reputation for chastity because you do not desire women. If you were truly holy you would not have assumed that I was a succubus. If you come with me, I can take us to a prince who will employ you as an artist, and me as a singer, and we can lie together every night.'

'*Vade retro, sathanas.*' The succubus was offering him everything he could possibly want. The Warning rose to his mind again. The price would be his eternal soul. Brother Aelfwine tried to push the succubus away, but the strong arms held him tight. 'Begone, tempter!'

'No. Have some sense. You Saxons are supposed to be sensible,' exclaimed the succubus, exasperated.

There was a long silence.

'You're not a succubus, are you?' asked Brother Aelfwine, drawing the man back into his embrace. 'That should have driven you away. I made the sign of the cross.'

'And if you'll give me use of a hand I will make it myself. There. See, you stubborn Saxon oaf? I am an escaped slave of the Vikings. I came with the ships that are presently lurking just off your island.'

'What is your name?' asked Aelfwine, very gently. His exploring hands had just found the scars of many a flogging on his lover's back.

'They call me Thrall in Dubh Linn,' he whispered bitterly.

'That is not your name,' said Aelfwine. 'Thrall just means 'slave'.'

The beautiful man closed his eyes and spoke very fast.

'My mother was Welsh. A princess of Gywnedd. She called me Evan. She died young. Her master was kind enough, but she faded away in captivity. I know where her father's land lies. I will go there tonight, and I will take you with me, if you can find us some clothes and provisions. I slipped overboard naked and swam here.'

Aelfwine sat up, calculating, all action, now that his mind was made up.

'Vikings. Right. Clothes, worldly garments. And I must rescue the Lindisfarne Gospels. They are in a jewelled box. They can have that. But not Eadwin's work. I will be back,' he kissed Evan, sweetly. 'I will be back soon, my Evan.'

The candle had not burned down more than half an inch when Aelfwine was back with a bundle of garments, a sack, and something folded into an oilskin bundle.

'Dress, my honey,' he said to Evan. 'I raided the kitchen, I stole some coins from the treasury, I roused the monastery, I have the Gospels. If I leave them here, no one will think them valuable. The Danes don't usually kill. The monks will be re-housed. They will take them to their new home and make them a new cover.'

Aelfwine pulled on hose and shirt, and dragged over that a shabby jerkin and a worn cloak of dark green cloth. Evan wore much the same in dark blue, with his black cloak over all. Both wore monk's sandals.

'But the problem remains,' said Aelfwine, 'how are we to escape?'

'The way I entered. The builders left themselves a way out to the mainland,' replied Evan. 'Look.'

He pressed a corner of a lintel, and a doorway gaped in what Aelfwine had thought was a solid stone wall. Evan took his hand. Aelfwine looked back at his cell. He had been very happy there, drawing uninterrupted, with someone to feed him, and no possessions except his vellum and his paints and inks. He observed that Evan had packed up all his painter's colours and added to the box the pages he had been illuminating.

'You shall have a place,' said Evan, holding up his free hand in pledge, 'where you can write and draw, and a door you can lock. And my love,' he added, pressing a sweet kiss to Aelfwine's mouth. 'My love, always.'

'And mine,' swore Aelfwine. 'My dearest succubus.'

They left Lindisfarne, and the door swung silently shut behind them, as the crashing and shouting started outside.

Illuminated Books of the British Isles

The Princes of Gwynedd were always considered patrons of the arts. Singers and musicians were particularly welcome in their courts, or llys. However, the *Book of Merlin* is unique even amongst that royal house's treasures. It is a folio consisting of twelve twelves of vellum, stitched and boxed in oak with a jewelled inlay. The pages are lettered in oak gall ink, which has etched the vellum. Every page of text has a corresponding picture. The painter is only identified as EAE. The free pictorial style and the rich use of colours is strongly reminiscent of the best monastic work, and is dated by an inventory as being completed in A D 820.

The text is an early version of the *Mabinogion*, with only one surprising addition. This is a verse from the *Song of Solomon*. The figures are partly concealed by flourishes of ivy leaves, but appear to be a fair figure lying in the lap of a dark figure with curly hair. The verse is 'Stir not my love nor wake him till he please: he feedeth amongst the lilies'.

This may have been a make-up page to complete the twelves, or maybe a favourite verse of the patron prince, Owain the Blessed. The *Book of Merlin* has survived as a treasure of the Welsh ever since and may be found in the National Library of Wales in Cardiff.

The survival of the *Lindisfarne Gospels* through two Viking raids can only be explained by the thesis that the book was housed in a decorative box, from which the text was taken and hidden somewhere dry. It has been rebound twice, and the pages are in excellent condition, the colours as bright as when Eadwin drew them circa A D 700. Robert Cotton collected it, and it resides in the British Museum.

HAEARN-DARA

His father was a smith, so he named his fourth and last son Dara, after the tough oak knots with which he fired his furnace when he smelted the precious metal, iron.

His mother died at his birth. Sometimes such sons are cherished as the last remembrance of their wife: not so Dara. His father gave him away to be fostered with a shepherd and bade his household never speak of him again.

But Dara made sheep nervous, and he crept into the forge to watch his father at work. At first he was not noticed. Then he was driven away with harsh words and blows. But, bruised, trembling, he always gathered courage and came back, as though dragged by the wise iron. And his brothers were not smiths. One was a famous hunter, one a famous bard, one a shaman and keeper of lore. None loved the iron as Dara did. So his father, grudgingly, allowed him into the forge and began to teach him the mysteries of his craft. This colour of flame – and only this – meant that the metal could be worked. Hotter, and it could not be beaten. Cooler, and it would fracture under the hammer. It must be doused after the seventh stroke, then heated again, and beaten, and doused again. Many blows Dara endured, and much abuse, for his father still did not love him. But he was eager to learn.

The woman whom his father had married after Dara's mother had died disliked him, but he did not care. He wore the worst garments, he ate the food the pigs disdained. No gentle embrace had Dara, no kiss of friendship. He did not notice. His mind and soul were bent on the mastery of iron, and they called him

Haearn-Dara, Iron Dara, and left him alone. He grew wiry and strong from work at the forge. When he was sixteen and it came time for his shaman journey, he was as alone as the standing stone which guarded the way to the village.

He sat with the other boys to be instructed. He must go forth, fasting, blindfolded for twenty paces, then go on for another seventy paces. He must lie down without shelter and drink the potion.

Then his spirit animal would come to him and reveal itself, because the beast would speak with human voice. He must then come back to the village and declare his beast. The shaman would tell him what it all meant.

Fasting was no great trial for Dara, though the others complained of hunger. He took the cup and walked as instructed, drank it dry and lay down on his back. The night was dark. He heard an owl hooting – was that his guardian? But the owl did not speak except in the manner of owls. He heard a badger grunt as it rumbled past him. Was that his guardian? But the badger did not pause for a greeting. Dara felt the weight of the world as it reeled beneath him. The sky streamed over him, stars moving and dancing. He thought that he heard music, faint and sweet, under the ground.

'Greetings, Haearn-Dara,' said a soft voice, close to his ear. He put out a hand and felt soft fur: a pricked nose, upright ears, long, bushy tail.

'Llwynog,' said Dara. 'You are Fox!'

'Not only Fox,' said the fox, sliding under his hand so that he stroked the length of its back. 'Iron-worker. I am the only one of my people who can bear the touch of iron.'

'Are you not a beast? Are you not my guardian spirit?' asked Dara, sitting up. The fox sighed and forced his hand up again, to run over its ears and scratch under its chin.

'I have come to offer you a different life,' said the fox, and transformed into a naked man with fox red hair and green eyes, pale in the starlight.

'Why would I want a different life?' asked Dara. His eyes

were full of the beauty of the Fox. He had never seen the like.

'They do not value you,' the Fox told him. 'We would cherish you. We would love you.'

'What is love?' asked Dara.

Fox drew him close and kissed him and Iron-Dara melted like ore in the furnace, even like the red iron ready to be poured. His body was on fire for the touch of the fox, and they stroked and slid and made love in the manner of men, in the starlight, in the darkness, until Dara cried aloud in astonishment and delight.

'Thus,' said the Fox. 'Come with me?'

'Where?' asked Dara.

'There,' replied the fox. He made a gesture and a cave mouth gaped.

'That is Annywn's kingdom,' said Dara. 'You are Tylwyth Teg, an elf-man.'

'I am,' said the fox, 'and we need a smith. The world is now full of iron, which is poison to us. We must have someone who can work it, and you are that man.'

'Will you stay with me, in that dark place?' asked Dara.

'I will, and it is not dark, but full of light and music. I will lie every night in your arms until the rivers of Annwyn run dry, which is the end of the world.'

'But you are a fox and an elf,' said Dara, suddenly afraid. 'How can I believe you?'

'You must do as your heart tells you,' sighed the fox, reverting to animal form and stretching first his front legs and then his back legs, ending with a flourish of tail. 'I will come back here for three nights. After that – ' the animal shook his head. 'Then I must wait a few more centuries for another such smith. Farewell,' he said, and loped off into the darkness.

Dara fell asleep. When he woke the sun of afternoon was in his eyes and he plodded back to the village. The others were all there, proclaiming deer and bear and badger and eagle and otter: all the proper animals. Dara sat down at the shaman's feet. At last the old man noticed him.

'Dara? What came to you?'

'A fox,' he said. 'Who was not just a fox.'

The shaman saw at once with his second sight that Dara had lain with the Tylwyth Teg, and cried out, scrambling to his feet.

'Begone!' he shouted. 'Tainted! Death Marked! Cursed!'

'Then I will take my due,' grunted Dara. He walked back to the forge. His father struck at him. Dara batted the blow away. He was stronger now than his father, the smith. He gathered his own tools and a supply of iron nuggets, won by women from the bog. He took a loaf and a jug of ale and a blanket and walked away from the village he had lived in all of his life.

Stones were thrown after him. Only a few hit his bent back. He fell to his knees, got up, and went on.

When he came to the place where he thought he had met the fox, he sat down, wrapped his blanket around him, ate his bread and drank his ale until darkness fell. Then he sang into the dusk the *Song of Haearn-Dara*.

> *Outcast Dara*
> *Calls to his lover*
> *Fox or Elf*
> *Return to me!*
> *Keep your promise!*
> *I will forge for you*
> *Beautiful knives*
> *Gem-set brooches*
> *Fine strong nails*
> *If you will have me.*

From the darkness came the *Song of the Fox*.

> *Oh my iron-worker*
> *I will love you*
> *I will lie with you*
> *Until the end of the world*
> *If you will come with me*
> *If you will take my hand.*

Dara extended his calloused smith's hand. He felt a clasp, and then was blinking in a great hall, hung with many lights. Music swelled around him.

'You are home,' said the Fox, and kissed him.

At the place where the gate of Annywn had opened grew two trees: an ash and an oak. Onn and Dara. They grew tall and strong. The people of the village avoided them. Anyone who strayed between heard strange music, the bark of a dog-fox, the strokes of a smith's hammer, and enchanting, distant laughter.

Skara Brae
The Battle of the Birds

Unsteadily, Raven slipped down from the clouds, rocked on his pinions, then dropped onto the strand next to Eaven as he sat on Seer's Rock. This was Marac's Raven. He cawed weakly, and Eaven took the sacred bird into his hands. His beak was gaping. Something was very wrong with Raven.

Eaven stroked the ruffled feathers into place and offered a deep cup of cool spring water. The bird drank, throwing back its head. Wing-weary, Eaven diagnosed. Had flown a long way through adverse winds. It was late for any long journey. The Druids came back to Skara Brae for the winter, and it was late autumn. And if the bird was exhausted, where was Marac, the friend of Eaven's heart? He had been long away, in a place where they were building a huge stone circle out of Cymric bluestone. Marac should have been home weeks ago. Eaven's stomach felt cold.

'Tell me, friend, where is Marac?' he asked Raven. The bird, a little recovered, laid its beak along his jaw, preened him, and said in Marac's voice 'Come, help, Eaven.'

'I'll carry you,' offered Eaven. The bird assented by climbing up to his shoulder, digging all its talons into his flesh, and falling asleep.

Eaven called into the village that he had been summoned. Haelari, a druid with a special affinity for birds, came out, carrying Eaven's cloak and his travelling bag. She dropped the goods and ran one skilled finger along the raven's head, from beak to nape. Her rosy face paled. She thrust the cloak and bag into Eaven's grasp.

'You must hurry,' she urged. 'I shall send other winged ones to scry for Eaven. Something is very wrong. That way,' she pointed inland.

Bird Druids are seldom wrong about directions, of course; and by her own account, all of Haeleri's soul-transfers had been into birds. Swans, ducks – she said ducks had a very acute sense of humour – sea birds, a nightingale, and once, a Great Albatross. This was unusual: most druids had some experience of running in fur or slipping along in scales. But what Haelari said about bird matters was always right. It was hoped that her daughters might inherit this skill. So far they were only interested in things furry. Eaven realised that his mind was wandering, trying to distract him from the cold lump of dread which was weighing down his belly.

He called a pony, Ekka, negotiated passage, mounted, and settled his goods and his companion, who had tucked his head under his wing and was snoring lightly.

East it was.

The Druid's retreat and sanctuary, Skara Brae, lay near the two great circles of Brodgar and Stennes. Between them was the walled trading market and university which ensured Orkney's fame and continued existence. The Lord Seleven with his ships and guards kept the sea, so that any Celt could come and sell his jet, any tribesman his amber, any seeker of wisdom could find teaching, in perfect safety. The village and the sanctuary were both supplied with meat and other commodities out of Ireland, and traded for calculations for solar or lunar circles, prophecy or understanding of strange events or dreams or riddles, and the drawing of runes and Ogham script. Only a Druid could read the shadows of coming events in the stars, the leaves of trees, the movements of beasts. For had not each Druid been a beast or a bird? Did not their soul fly into such vessels, and then return, laden with knowledge of the Seen and the Unseen? Everyone knew that.

As Eaven rode through the market, many people called a greeting or patted the pony's withers, and no one found strange the fact that a Druid dressed for sleeping should be riding as fast as the pony could manage through a busy market, with a Raven on his shoulder. All called Godspeed to him, and Tauren the trader didn't even protest when the pony Ekka stole an apple from his booth as she passed. He made a mark on the tally for Skara Brae, and went back to bargaining with a tall barbarian with lint pale hair who had walrus ivory to trade, and a passion for apples. Tauren had a buyer for walrus ivory, and a surplus of apples this year, but he had his pride, as well.

Eaven and the pony passed through waves of music, as bards discussed the latest events in song. He heard as he passed a dirge lamenting the massacre of a whole tribe at a place in Cyrmu. The bard's vibrant voice fed his fear.

> *Many men went to Catttreath*
> *Only I returned*
> *To find the hearth stone cold*
> *And the hall burned...*

Eaven clapped his heels into Ekka's sides and bade her hurry, by all the gods.

After about an hour, Eaven was catching rumours on the air: pain, loss, anger, terror. The pony snorted and Eaven felt the beast's muscles quiver with fear. But Ekka was a Druid mount who had seen worse, and pressed onward, into the miasma. The first dead man had been killed running away: a red feathered arrow in his back. Several more lay dead on the short sward, hacked about with blades. Against a scrawny Orkney tree lay Eaven's heart's friend. The whole patch of murder and death was utterly silent. The attackers had gone. Haeleri's birds screamed overhead, crying out at this desecration of the Holy Island.

So they would know, at Skara Brae, and at the market, and help would be coming, and Lord Seleven's men. To avenge this outrage. Vengeance would do Eaven no good. Raven woke and flew to Marac, and Eaven flung himself off the pony and ran to take his lover into his arms. Marac was as covered in blood as though he had bled out all that he had, but he coughed as Eaven moved him, and spat out blood, and whimpered.

'Raven,' he whispered. 'You have deserved well of us. Oh, Eaven, I thought I would never see you again!'

'But here I am,' replied Eaven. 'Show me your wounds, my love.'

'It is not my blood,' said Marac. 'I had to fight. They made me fight. I bespelled them mad and they killed each other.'

'Who were they?' asked Eaven.

'They followed me from the Great River,' said Marac. 'Servants of some strange god, they believe that we are idolaters, they come to kill us all. The rest are on the Holy Island this moment, Eaven!'

'Lord Seleven will know that by now. That is his concern. Can you stand?'

Marac staggered to his feet. Then, the Raven scraping delicious blood off his face, he marked the trunk of the oak with both his bloody hands. Eaven nodded with approval. The land would know its enemies, now. So would the birds. He led Marac to a pool and sluiced him down, so that Ekka should not shy at his approach, and loaded him on to the pony's back. Marac was shaking, cold, and had been far too close to the murderous discorporation of souls. He needed food, and barley wine, and warmth. And a cleansing ritual to purge his spirit.

They passed Lord Seleven's guard on the way back to Skara Brae, leading several prisoners and carrying more bodies. Each enemy wore a mask of white and red ochre. For the moment the threat of these painted madmen was over.

Once arrived home, Eaven fed the Ekka the barley and apples that had been her fee, kissed her nose, and let her go. Marac staggered again as he entered their little house. Eaven sat him down and knelt to remove his blood-soaked hide boots. As he stripped his lover he found small injuries, bruises and welts. Marac's feet were blistered. He was far too thin. Something very bad had happened in that south country, if a Druid could be thus starved and mistreated.

Briac entered the little house, carrying a pot of hot milk in which healing herbs had been cooked. As soon as Marac was clean and dressed in a warm fleecy robe, Eaven supported Marac on his shoulder as he drank the posset. A little colour came into his face. Raven croaked his approval, and flew out the door, seemingly a beast with something urgent to attend to.

'Carrion,' whispered Marac. 'There is carrion enough for Raven and all his brothers.' He giggled, and Eaven held him close as he shuddered. Plump, dark-eyed Briac the Singer built up the peat fire. He knelt down and put both hands on Marac's bowed head. He sang gently, sweetly, his voice filling the small house, banishing pain and horror. Gradually the atmosphere cleared. Marac could smell peat and home and Eaven and barley wine. The stench of blood was gone from his nostrils. He kissed Briac on the hands as he released him, weak with gratitude.

'You are cleansed,' he told him, patting him on the cheek. 'Tomorrow you will tell us all about it. A threat from the South. Such has been predicted. All will be well. You are home and you have your heart's friend and you are safe here. I will take this tainted stuff. Sleep well,' said Briac, and took the stained garments and boots with her as she went.

'My heart,' said Marac. 'I have never been so afraid. I have never missed you so much. I will never leave you again.' He snuggled back against Eaven and accepted the flask of barley wine which they drank, sip for sip, as was their custom. The small stone house was warm, now, the firelight reflecting off the walls, the bed soft with fleeces and weavings. Everything pleased his eyes. The cupboard with the cups and plates and unusual coloured stones which Eaven was always bringing home. The carved wooden raven, made for him by a man who had been cleansed of a horrible dream. The firelighters, the skeins, the flint knives, pots of tinctures, dried herbs, bandages, a spindle, a store of dried fruit. It all combined with the steady heat of his lover at his back, always at his back. He swore he would never leave Eaven for so long again, even for a great work.

They finished the flask and turned to embrace each other. Marac twined his limbs around Eaven, burrowed into the coverings, laid his head firmly on his lover's breast, and dropped into sleep. Eaven lay awake long enough to count his bedmate's breaths, almost convince himself that all would end well.

They woke to a flat loaf of barley bread and more milk-posset, brought by Briac, who told them that the whole village was summoned to a council in the Great House. They ate, washed, donned their ceremonial garments, and walked with the other inhabitants to speak to Lord Seleven.

His round house was packed with his warriors and household. The invaders were kneeling at his feet. Seleven was a good ruler, even tempered, merciful, and young. But this was a blatant attack on the Holy Island, which all people declared to be under his peace. His countenance was grim.

'Speak,' he demanded of his prisoners. 'Most of you are dead, and soon you, too may join them. What brought you to break my peace with murder?'

'Them,' hissed a masked one. 'Druids!'

'What of them? They bear no weapons. They are learned, holy and God inspired,' said Seleven, puzzled.

'Idolators! They must all die!' shrieked the prisoner.

'Why? No, never mind. You are clearly mad. Where have you come from?'

The prisoner, encouraged by a small mental nudge from Tauren, who was skilled in such things, described a coastal settlement south of the Great River. He named his god The Masked God, The Shadow, and said that he had told them to kill all Druids, and thus gain his favour. His description of the rites of the Masked God was extensive and revolting.

Seleven shrugged, gave some orders, and the prisoners were led away. Eaven was aware that Marac was clutching him close and shivering.

'I ran from that voice for twenty days,' he whispered.

'Sit down,' said Eaven, and drew Marac to him in a crumple of unbleached linen. 'He is gone, and soon he will be dead, and his God with him. This is the Holy Island, my love. Not just any common collection of rocks. Lean on me. I must listen.'

A long discussion followed. Eaven supported Marac to the lord, to describe his flight and recount as much as he knew of this new religion.

'The Cymric people were hospitable as usual, the Stoneworkers cordial, the southern blue-painted ones as pleasant as could be, generous and wise. Only when I came north did I find this Masked God abomination. And they would have had my life, and eaten my heart. They said so.'

Seleven winced. 'Send to me as soon as the winds bring you any news,' he requested.

The druids returned to Skara Brae to summon their familiars and sniff the air for news. Trading resumed cheerfully in the market, with a free stoup of barley wine as a compliment from the lord Seleven, hoping that the market would drink his health. The market obliged.

Eleven new heads lined the stockade which faced the sea. They were masked in red and white paint. On approach, they were a sobering sight.

The autumn gales began, bringing news from the south. Marac was still nervous and Eaven unwilling to let Marac out of his sight. They were sitting together on Seer's Rock, waiting for Raven and Great Gull to arrive. Marac was fishing. He had just drawn in the third fish when Gull shrieked a warning.

A ship in Skaill bay, firing arrows at those on shore. The razor sharp flint barb sliced across Eaven's chest as he dived for cover. That was enough, he thought, before he lost all thought. He smeared his own blood across both hands and raised them in invocation. He called upon the Holy Island to defend them.

Behind him in the village he heard voices raised, feet

running: next to him he felt Marac's spell, growing like a thunder cloud, strengthening his own. Marac scored his own hand and raised bloody palms to the skies.

'Protect us, Holy Island, against these wreckers, these cruel attackers, who would defile your sweet shores with blood, who worship a devil, who burn and slay!' Briac, Tauren, Haelari and all the others encompassed the magic, uniting their powers against insanity and cruelty and unreason, the power of those men with bows in that ship.

Then the birds came. Down on the ship they fell; fulmar, great gull, sea eagle and albatross, raking talons, slashing beaks, screaming. Terrified, the masked ones tried to fight, but were smothered in a confusion of feathers until they shot each other, or fell into the sea, where leopard seals tugged them under and drowned them. Their ship, with no hand on the rudder, sailed into the sandbar and stuck fast.

By the time the Lord Seleven's guard arrived they were all dead, and not one had set foot on the Holy Island.

Seleven's men collected the bodies, hauled the ship around the point into the bay, and sent bards to hear of the battle of the birds. And Eaven and Marac went back to their fishing, to reward the warrior birds who had heard them.

'I could not let them near you again,' explained Eaven. 'We are not supposed to kill, and we killed them, Marac.'

'Good thing too,' replied his lover. 'The Holy Island killed them, and they would have killed us and all our learning and all our peace.' Marac kissed Eaven, gently. His mouth was salty from the spray. 'We survived, my heart; and wisdom and Briac's milk possets and Taurens bargains and the Lord Seleven's lordship survived. Now, pay attention to that line. We have at least one albatross to feed and you know how much they eat.'

Eaven laughed, and kissed Marac, and paid attention to his line.

SKALDIC SAGA

His name was Thord Hoskuldsson and he was the most fascinating man I had ever seen.

He came walking along the rutted farm track towards the steading late one afternoon, the season tending to winter, playing a tune on a little pipe made of bone. Every animal on the steading lifted its head and the goat I was milking tried to pull away from my hands. I heard him laugh and he stopped right next to me. He was tall and slim, with long legs clad in forest green trews, mud-spattered boots, a leather jerkin over a soft linen shirt; expensive gear, especially the sword at his back and the horse he was leading, which bore a silver mounted saddle and a tapestry blanket.

'Hush, lady goat, and yield your milk,' he instructed in his rich, seductive skald's voice. 'Or there will be no cheese, and that will not do.'

The goat stilled and allowed me to finish milking, then skipped up to him and rubbed her nose against his knee. He patted her. There were gold rings on his fingers, and more on his arm. He smiled at me. His eyes were almost green; a compelling colour and gaze.

'And your name, young Sir? To whose farm have I arrived?'

'I am Wulf Kveldulfsson, this is the steading of Unn the Deep Minded. And whose name shall I bid the houseman announce? Such finery is not often seen here. Could you be a bard, master?' I asked eagerly.

Although this was a well-run house, and we were well fed

and cared for, and there was an old man who recalled a few sagas, we were very short of entertainment. Especially in the winter.

The skald drew a relieved breath. He put back his hood and ruffled his black hair.

'That is what I wanted to hear. I have come to visit Unn the Deep Minded by request of her son Hrothgar, who says she needs a bard for the winter. I am Skald Thord Hoskuldsson. I am pleased to meet you, and pleased to reach a farm at last.'

'Go in, sir, rest yourself, I shall care for your horse, you may trust me,' I told him.

He put a hand on my shoulder. 'That is a very fair offer, but a bard cares for his own mount. Come with me, Wulf, and tell me of the house. I do not want to make any mistakes in courtesy. Or tread on anyone's toes,' he grinned suddenly, a green flash of captivating mischief, 'until I mean to.'

I was his man from that moment.

He managed Unn the Deep Minded very well. My lady is sometimes captious and sometimes hard to amuse. He bore her scolding with indifference and managed to coax her, more often than not, into a smile. Within an hour he had a place by the fire and a bed in a booth.

The old men liked him because he knew all the old stories, and eagerly listened when they told the ones they could remember. The maidens liked him because he was beautiful and could sing like a thrush. The men liked him because he showed no interest in the maidens, and could tell stirring sagas of journey and exploration.

And after Glaum, the biggest bully, had challenged and attacked him and Thord had snatched the pitchfork out of his hands and beaten him to the ground with the butt, he was not assailed.

Unn the Deep Minded praised the skald's restraint in only hitting Glaum with the butt and not stabbing him with the spikes.

And Glaum never recovered his power, since the skald made a satiric verse about him to such an irresistible tune that sailors and people farms away were singing it.

> *Glaum dung fork wielder, skald offending*
> *Takes his proud pole and boasts he will poke*
> *Bowed his pole, fallen his mast, Glaum's limp*
> *implement.*

The meaning of which was entirely obscene, and entirely deserved. I had seen that fight. Glaum was huge and strong, but the skald had danced around him, fast as a serpent. The old men had nodded with approval. And no one challenged Thord after that. It was agreed that he had, at least, made Glaum famous.

The winter came on. We were well stored and warm. We sat in the hall and wove, made rope, carved walrus ivory for sale, and the women sewed and knitted. And Thord sang or spoke, and we were entranced.

And one night as I returned from tending the beasts I paused to let my eyes get used to the dimness. Thord was sitting by the fire. He looked up as I entered, and held out his hand. His eyes flashed in the half light.

I sat next to him, and he leaned over and licked a snowflake from my cheek. I raised a cold hand to cover his. Then his mouth found mine.

We went to his booth and stripped and lay down. His skin against mine was softer than duck's down. 'Oh, my Wulf,' he said to me, very quietly. 'Would you lie with me and keep me warm? Would you love me?'

I kissed him in reply. We made love as proper men do, touching and kissing and writhing close, mouths and hands. He asked of me no mastery, he did not want to occupy my body as Trolls do. I was not used as a woman, though I felt that Unn our Lady would have words to say to any man who said that women were used. I adored him, his scent and his touch and his smooth strong back, and he caressed me as though I was a treasure. I had never felt such passion.

Unn must have been told about Thord the skald and me, but she said nothing. Comrades lying together was not uncommon. And it was a very cold winter, which lasted longer than usual, though it could not last too long for me, wrapped every night in the skald's arms.

Spring came and one day he saddled his horse and rode away, back to the lady Unn's son, to whose household he belonged. He gave me his bone pipe and bade me learn to play it before he came again.

I missed him sorely, as I would miss my own heart. When Glaum sneered and struck at me, I hit him such a blow with the broom I had in my hand that they all started singing the broken pole song again. Glaum was very angry. I think he hoped that they would have forgotten it.

The Lady Unn made me pay for the broom.

I practiced the pipe until the household banished me out with the goats to perfect my skill. Most often I tried for Thord's goat calling song. After a month, I managed it. I could summon every beast on the steading with my bone pipe.

I heard nothing of the skald Thord Hoskuldsson, though I asked every traveller and mariner. Late in the summer, one said he had heard that the skald had made a nithsong about a powerful man, and was in disgrace. A nith is a curse. The offence must have been great for Thord to risk outlawry. Or perhaps he was bored. He didn't bear boredom well.

Then visitors came singing a new verse from Thord. No one knew what it meant. Skaldic verses are very hard to understand. I was one with the lord who gave the skald a bag of gold for a poem, and said it would have been two if he'd been able to understand it.

The verses passed by word of mouth around the steadings, until someone puzzled it out. This one was exceptionally obscure, even for Thord.

> *Fanged child of Loki, fierce rainbow pacer*
> *Salt ground star scattered, sweet soft encounter*
> *Holds forth the hawk's ground, hale whole-hearted golden*
> *One-eye's son the warrior wades his brother's wide*
>   *walkway.*

Various guesses were made. At meat that night everyone talked about this new verse. I had been banished back to sleep with the farmhands, now that my skald had gone. I was lying between Olaf and Kjarten. Olaf stank of onions and Kjartan snored. And neither of them was my beautiful green-eyed skald. I couldn't sleep and told the verse over and over in my head.

Fanged child of Loki. Loki had many children, but only two with fangs: Fenris Wolf and the Midgard Serpent. Could be either. But put it with rainbow pacer, then it had to be the Fenris Wolf, because at the end of days, it will walk across Bifrost, the rainbow bridge, and kill Thor. During the Ragnarok. So, the first line meant, Wolf.

I poked Kjartan in the ribs and he rolled over.

Now, the second line: *The salt star scattered ground* was clearly the sea at night.

I did not know what to make of *sweet soft encounter* except that it reminded me of my skald's caresses.

Holds forth the hawk's ground was to hold out one's arms, as a hawk trained for hunting will land on a forearm.

Hale whole-hearted golden meant little, except that the person who was writing this verse had not fallen in love with anyone else.

By the Nine Realms. Could it be? Was this verse for *me*?

My heart beat so hard that I was sure that Kjartan and Olaf would hear it and think it a war drum. The last line made sense.

One-eye's warrior was Thor, his father Odin having only one eye. He is also a constellation in the sky, also called the Hunter. And *his brother's walkway* was the horizon, where Heimdall kept watch.

I was so enthralled with my cleverness I believe that I laughed. Then I put myself very deliberately to sleep. Tomorrow I must prepare. And that night, I would be gone.

The next day I asked leave to visit my brother, who makes rope and sails at the sea port. The steward agreed and I set forth on foot, carrying only the usual gear and my bone pipe. I was given seven little cheeses as a present for my brother. I also took my best cloak. I reached the sea after five hours walk, and found my brother's house. I gave his wife the cheeses, admired his sail loft, played with his children, sat down to twine rope with him all day, ate bread, drank ale and waited until the household was asleep before creeping out.

It was a fine night and I could see the stars. Thor Sky Warrior would be wading towards the horizon in about two hours. I sat down on the scree, above the tideline, and waited.

A ship was drawn up near me, and I could hear the mariners boasting and drinking around their fire. Time wore on. The stars wheeled.

It was cold. I wrapped my cloak close and blew on my hands. A chill wind sprung up. The night was wearing away.

I was about to stand up and stamp my feet when a rich, beautiful voice asked: 'What was the meaning of my verse, my Wulf?'

'That if I came here, at this time, I should find you again,' I replied.

'Did you never doubt me?' he asked, still behind me. I turned to see his face. He was greatly bruised. His enemies had not been gentle with him. But he was still beautiful.

'Never,' I said, and kissed him, carefully.

He sat down with me, taking my hand.

'I have to leave,' he told me. 'I have offended Olaf Peacock and I am outlawed. I am going to Orkney – there is my ship, I have a contract with Ulf the Unwashed, best mariner in Iceland. You are the only thing that I will miss, and grieve to lose. Will you come with me?'

'I will,' I said, and kissed him again. He pressed a small bag into my hand.

'Go, then, to your brother, give him the gold, tell him you are going, so that they will not lose you. I will stay here. We sail on the tide,' he said. 'Hurry, Wulf!'

I woke my brother, explained and gave him the gold. He kissed me in farewell and gave me a fine iron knife. When I returned, I found Thord sitting just as I had left him. He looked up at me.

'Yes?' he asked.

'Yes,' I said.

Orkney is a good place, hospitable, also warmer than Iceland. The Lord of Orkney was so pleased with Thord that he allowed him to build his own house. Thord entertains around the island. I travel with him. When we are home we farm a few sheep, a goat or two, a hive of bees for Thord's favourite winter drink, goat's milk and honey. Thord sings love songs to me in our shared bed and I still summon our flock with that tune on the bone pipe.

Our household will bury us together when we die.

And so ends this story of Wulf and Thord.

THREE WISHES

Ari dragged in his net for the third time. The first two drags had been empty of anything resembling food, though he had a good harvest of shells, seaweed, and puffer fish, which had to be picked up very carefully with gloves and tipped over the side. And there was nothing biting on his lines, either. One more trawl and he would have to row home and have bread and cheese for dinner. Again.

The net came back weighted with inedibles, one of which rolled and clanked as he set the net down in a tangle on the bottom of the boat. It was a vessel of some kind, heavily decorated and firmly stoppered. Ari turned it over in his callused hands. Probably gold, inlaid with stones, must be worth a fortune. But why would it be stoppered? Some kind of very precious wine? It felt strangely warm. Nothing metal that had been in the sea ought to be that warm.

Then he set it gently down, gathered his net, and rowed for the shore. He had heard about finds like this. Two stories were presently warring in his head.

One was the story about the fisherman who opened the bottle, talked to the genie, and got three wishes – which he wasted; but the three wishes were true. The other was about a genie who was trapped in a bottle at the bottom of the sea and who, for the first hundred years, had vowed three wishes for anyone who let him out. Then he got progressively more bitter until he vowed that he would kill the person who released him. That unlucky man had been an innocent fisherman.

Ari dragged his boat up onto the beach and spread his net to dry then carried the bottle to his little house. There he put it on his table as he prepared his flat bread and goat's cheese, with a handful of bitter herbs drizzled with oil. He ate his supper, looking at the bottle. It made no move, said no word. What a banquet he would order, if he had a wish. Roast peacock, sherbet, strange fruits and vegetables, exotic wines; served by gorgeous semi-naked slaves–

'That doesn't look like a very lavish dinner,' remarked the bottle. Ari suppressed his jump.

'No, it isn't, but the fish just aren't biting today,' he replied. 'Are you angry?'

'Why would I be angry?' asked the bottle. 'Just because I've been stuffed into a bottle and flung into the sea?'

'Well, I thought that–'

'You mean, why should I be angry because I've been looking at a lot of fish for 38 years?' The voice was as beautiful as a flute and getting louder by the moment.

'And not good conversationalists,' said Ari. 'Fish seldom have much to say.'

The voice laughed. It was listening to a chime of silver bells.

'No, very tedious, especially sharks. Eat, swim, eat, swim, eat, swim. So, are you going to let me out?'

'Depends. Are you going to kill me?'

'No,' said the voice. 'Not unless you really annoy me.'

'I'm supposed to ask for three wishes,' insisted Ari. The bottle sighed.

'You'll be sorry. But, all right, three wishes it is. And I expect the first one will be about food.'

'Maybe,' said Ari. 'How do I get you out?'

'Really, don't people tell stories anymore? Get a cloth and rub the vessel.'

The voice muttered various uncomplimentary things as Ari found a cleanish neckcloth and rubbed the bottle.

There was an odd bubbling noise inside.

'Good, now cut the seal,' instructed the bottle.

Ari cut the seal. Then he dropped the bottle.

A great cloud of bright green smoke appeared. Out of it came undulating the most beautiful man Ari had ever seen. He moved to the window, looked out at the sea, spat indelicately and pulled the curtain across. A sea view was not going to recommend itself to the genie any time soon. He leaned back with his hands on the windowsill, hips thrust forward, inspecting Ari.

Never before had the fisherman been ashamed of his small and poor house, his shabby clothes, his scarred hands. Under the scornful gaze of this bejewelled houri straight from Paradise, he felt grubby and ordinary.

'Well, at least you're handsome,' sighed the genie. Ari's mouth dropped open. He was an ordinary man from a family of ordinary men. This genie was long-legged, silk-skinned, with long black hair with a faint reddish flame in it, soft hands, untouched feet. All Ari wanted to do was to fall to his knees and kiss his belly, where a star sapphire was fixed in his umbilicus.

That was not all of the genie he wanted to kiss. In fact there wasn't any of the genie he didn't want to kiss. It all looked delectable. Edible.

'So, I am your first wish?' smiled the genie. 'Have you got a bed?'

'No,' said Ari sadly. 'You wouldn't be able to say no. That wouldn't be just. Not that you aren't beautiful, you're gorgeous, you're a dream, but no. I'll think of something else. Can you eat? Would you like some bread and cheese?'

'I can do better than that – off the record,' said the genie. He seemed astonished. 'I don't drink that vinegar. Pick up the bottle and lie it on its side on the table.' More green smoke issued forth, and the table bore dishes and bottles of wine. 'Tip out that stuff, you'll curdle your insides. Drink with me?' asked the genie.

'Thanks,' stammered Ari.

The wine tasted like honey. The small dishes were all different, all marvellous. The genie picked and tasted.

'Roses from Lebanon,' he remarked. 'That was a good year for roses. Try some of this, the spikenard makes it so fragrant.'

'Wonderful,' said Ari, with his mouth full. The genie laughed again, with a chime of bells. 'Have you a name?' he asked. 'Or should I just call you genie?'

'My name,' the genie stared at Ari for a long moment. 'My name is Mahu. Have some more wine. Have you any idea how long I'll be here?'

'What?' asked Ari.

Mahu sighed. 'I mean, are you likely to make up your mind quickly? I have to stay here with you until you do,' he explained.

'Then I never will,' said Ari. 'If you will stay with me forever.'

Mahu kissed him on the cheek. His lips were hot. He smelt like frankincense.

'Aren't you sweet,' he cooed. 'Right, then a little decoration. I like to be comfortable.'

Green smoke filled the whole of the little house. When it cleared away, the walls were hung with silks, the floor covered with carpets, the plain table and chair transformed into such as would not disgrace the palace of a sultan.

Ari looked into the other room. His bed had been changed into a huge padded couch hung with gold-embroidered azure curtains.

'Much better,' said the genie, flinging himself supine.

'Blue looks good with your skin,' breathed Ari. 'You are so beautiful!'

'Wish, then?' Mahu patted the couch.

'Not like that,' said Ari, with great effort.

He took himself firmly back to the other room and opened his new, tapestry curtains.

'Wind's picking up,' he observed. 'Do you want some clothes, maybe a blanket? It's about to get cold. Or would you rather go back into–'

Mahu shuddered. 'No,' he said firmly. 'I do not want to go back into that bottle.'

'How did you get stuck in it?' asked Ari.

'The usual way,' Mahu shrugged his shapely shoulders 'Summoning spell, bound for a period of years or until someone releases me. And then...'

'Then?'

'I can't tell you the rest,' said the genie.

'There's a way to disenchant you?' asked Ari.

'Yes, of course, there's always a way out of spells, but I can't tell you what it is.'

'And if you are disenchanted, where do you go?'

'Wherever I want,' said the genie. 'I miss Persia most. And flying. In fact I cannot convey how very boring it is to be stuffed into a bottle and have no one to talk to except fish.'

'Terrible,' sympathised Ari.

The wind blew harder. Waves crashed the shore. Mahu conjured himself a warm cloak of azure fur, into which he beckoned Ari.

'Come and be warm,' he invited.

'Daren't,' replied Ari.

Suddenly there were voices crying and women screaming. Ari looked out of his suddenly glazed window.

'It's Tanesh's boat. Gods, they'll smash on the rock. Do something!' he yelled at the genie.

'This is your first wish?' asked Mahu, shrugging out of the cape and raising his slender hands.

'Yes, please, save them!' cried Ari.

The genie clapped his hands. In that moment, the wind dropped. People on the shore yelled that Tanesh was coming in unscathed. That it had been a miracle.

Ari grinned at Mahu. 'That was amazing!'

'No, the thing that is amazing is you,' replied the genie. He dropped the cloak and paced around Ari, inspecting him from all angles. 'You seem perfectly common,' he mused.

'Thank you very much, I could have told you that!' exclaimed the fisherman.

'But you are not,' concluded Mahu. 'Let's have another cup of wine. At the rate you are going, I might not be here for long.'

'Don't say that,' begged Ari. 'I'll be more careful. I won't wish another wish in all my life.'

Mahu crooked an eyebrow.

They spent a fascinating evening in conversation, and Ari slept uneasily next to the immensely seductive body of the genie. He could have his wish, but then he would be within one wish of never seeing Mahu again.

And that would not be bearable.

Ari went out fishing at the usual time. The sea was full of storm-debris, but he managed a reasonable number of fish. He sold most of his catch when he reached the shore, then carried the best home.

Mahu was lying on the couch when he came in from the outside. The little house was warm and scented. Ari cooked the fish and Mahu sat up, tasted and approved.

'Lemon juice,' he conjured, and the fish tasted even better. 'Keep the pips,' he instructed. 'Plant them somewhere green and warm, and you will have lemon trees. Perfect with fish. Which seems to be your usual diet.'

'Yes,' said Ari with heavy irony. 'I'm a fisherman. My father was a fisherman. My grandfather was a–'

'I see,' said the genie. 'Fish. I understand.'

Again they spent the evening talking. It was very late at night when someone came banging on the door, and Ari lurched out to answer it.

'Come, Ari, your sister is dying and the baby with her, she wants to say goodbye,' said his nephew.

'Wait,' said Ari. He went back inside.

Mahu had heard the conversation. 'If she's already dead I can't fix it,' he warned.

'Try,' said Ari. 'Please.'

'This is your second wish?' asked Mahu formally.

'It is,' said Ari heavily. The genie stood up and clapped his hands.

Ari went with his nephew to find his sister recovering, and the baby crying loudly enough to take the roof off the hut. He kissed his sister and his new niece and went back to Mahu.

'Wine?' asked the genie.

Ari nodded. He sat and drank a cup of ambrosia, slowly, his hand on the genie's shoulder. Then he stood up.

'This is my third wish,' he said.

Mahu grabbed his hand. 'Think about this,' he urged. 'I like you. I would like to stay with you.'

'I like you, too,' said Ari, tears sliding down his face. 'I love you. I want nothing more than to lie down in your arms and stay with you forever. But I can't. So, my third wish, is that you should be free.'

'This is your third wish?' asked Mahu, ritually.

'It is,' said Ari.

The genie clapped his hands together. There was a flourish of green smoke. The bottle shattered. Mahu vanished. The hut reverted, instantly, to its shabby former appearance. Ari staggered to his chair, sat down, and buried his head in his folded arms. He wept as though his heart was broken.

Gradually he became aware of something happening. Something was pushing at his sandalled toes. He lifted his feet and a carpet shot past under them. He lifted his elbows and his table grew a tablecloth and an array of dishes, cups and bottles. His windows curtained themselves. The huge couch reappeared. Arms wreathed around him from behind.

'Mahu?' he whispered.

'Free!' exulted the genie. 'Have another drink. I shall have one too. Several. You freed me! No one has ever done that before. Ever. I knew you weren't ordinary.'

Ari drank. He was far too afraid to speak, in case he would shatter the illusion.

When the genie guided him, sometime later, to lie down on

the huge couch, Ari slid his hands at last up those sculptural thighs, kissed the star sapphire in that belly-button, felt the satiny skin against his cheek. The genie drew him up to lie flat on his body, pressed together from forehead to knee. He had never been so aroused, so surrounded by sensuality. They began to move together.

'But,' stammered Ari, 'I don't have any wishes left.'

'Ah,' purred Mahu into his ear, making him shiver with delight, 'but this is *my* wish.'

Snow White

His pregnant mother had pricked her finger while sewing, looked at the blood drop on the snowy windowsill, and wished for a child with lips as red as that blood, hair as black as the ebony window frame, and skin as white as the snow.

She bore the child, named him Karadoc and died in bearing him; and the King never forgave him for it.

Because he grew up startlingly beautiful. Karadoc was bright, deft, clever at all the skills of a prince: fencing, dancing, conversation and law. But he also was fascinated by languages. He wandered into fairs and sat at the feet of market women, learning their speech and their skills. He consorted with the rough men who rode in from the plains with their rough horses, and sang and drank kermiss round their fires. He sat in the kitchen and distracted the maids and learned how a kitchen worked. He made clay figures and carved wood.

And the people said, 'Here is Karadoc, a pearl among princes!' and wondered to which beautiful princess his father would marry him.

But his father Kerrigan was proud of his own beauty, and had a magic mirror to which he spoke every day, as he preened, combing back his golden hair, sleeking down his fine moustache. Every morning he asked, 'Mirror, mirror, on the wall, who is the handsomest of all?

And every day the mirror would reply, 'You are the handsmest man, Your Highness.'

And the king would go about his royal duties, his vanity appeased.

Until the day he discovered a strand of silver in his golden hair, and the mirror replied to the usual question

'Mirror, mirror, on the wall, who is the handsomest of all?'

'The Snow White Prince is the handsomest man, Your Highness.'

The king roared with wrath and summoned his best huntsman. This was Gahan, son of an old retainer, who had recently taken his father's place. Gahan's father and the king had been boys together. His father had always impressed on Gahan how much he ought to love the king, and it was to the king that he owed his whole duty. He stood easily in the king's chamber, brown of skin, hair and eye, dressed in his wilderness clothes of deerhide and green cloth, armed with his bow and his short sword.

'I command you to take Karadoc the Snow White Prince into the forest and kill him,' said the king, his eyes dark with hatred, his own hand on his sword. 'And I order you to bring me his heart.'

Gahan's own heart thudded in his chest. But if he refused this despicable order the king might kill him, and would find someone else to carry it out. So he stood up straight and bowed.

'As my lord commands,' he said, and went to look for Karadoc. He found him in the kitchen, where he was being fed bites of gingerbread by the cook as she instructed him in the proper basting of roast boar.

'Come out with me,' coaxed Gahan. 'Bring your cloak and a few useful things, we might stay out all night.'

The Snow White Prince caught something in Gahan's voice. So he collected a bundle of clothes and a heavy cloak, his belongings and a firelighter and a bottle full of fiery spirit. He took his weapons and followed Gahan out into the forest. They travelled a long way before Gahan stopped and said, 'Let's sit down.'

The Prince agreed and they sat down on his cloak. He put a hand on Gahan's shoulder, saying, 'What troubles you, my friend?'

'Oh, my dear prince,' Gahan replied. 'The king has sent me to kill you and bring back your heart. His envy and pride have overthrown his reason, Karadoc. '

Th prince withdrew his hand and laid it on his sword hilt.

'And do you mean to try to carry out his wishes?'

Gahan's face flushed with shame. He embraced the prince, saying, 'No, no, my lord, I would rather die. But you cannot go back to the castle while your father is alive. We must contrive an escape. I haven't got much time. I must be back with your heart before darkness.'

'Come with me,' urged Karadoc. 'There are miners within reach, there are the horsemen. We can both go – don't leave me, my dear Gahan.'

'My family are in the kingdom,' said Gahan miserably. 'If I do not come back with your heart, the king will kill them. I must go back. So, I prefer the miners, they stay in one place. I will l know where to find you. Let's walk that way. I need a young boar. If you give me your scarf, I will wrap the boar's heart in it, and thus prove your death.'

'So, we go hunting,' said the Snow White Prince. 'But do not forget me. I will stay, if you think I should, with the miners, and learn their language and their trade, but do not forget me, my Gahan, or it would be better if you took my heart indeed, cut it out of my breast with your steel knife and fed it to my father.'

'I can never forget you,' swore Gahan, and kissed him fervently.

They found and killed a young boar, and Gahan wrapped the bloody heart in the Prince's scarf. Then they carried the boar to the encampment of the miners, who hacked precious stones from the deep mines for the king.

It was almost a village. They spoke their own language and kept themselves to themselves. The custom of that folk was for all bachelors to live together. With the gift of meat, the miners were convinced to allow the Snow White Prince to stay. He found a place in a longhouse with ten others. And Gahan went back to the castle.

He was allowed into the king's private chamber and knelt before his murderous lord. He held out the bundle in his cupped hands.

'This is the heart you commanded me to take,' said Gahan.

The king unwrapped the bundle and stared at the bloodstained relic. Leaving Gahan on his knees, he ordered the guard to bring him the head cook. She came in, breathless, having been hurried away from her preparations for dinner.

'Cook, what is this?' demanded the king. The cook looked at Gahan, remembered that he had left with Prince Karadoc who was still not home, recognised the scarf, and was about to shriek when she realised that Gahan and the prince had always been very close friends and that this was the heart of a pig. So she put her apron to her eyes and murmured, 'That is the heart of a man, my lord.'

'Cook it for me,' ordered the king. 'Out, all of you. Gahan, take this,' he threw him a bag which chinked, 'And never let me see you again.'

The cook received the heart into her shrinking palms and both of them were hurried out again.

The king folded the silk scarf which had contained the heart and locked it in a coffer with a silver key.

Gahan and the cook returned to the kitchen. Once there, she ordered a scullion to scour the smallest pie dish. Then she set about making pastry while her helpers chopped onions and sage. She had an excellent recipe for boars' heart pie.

'I must go soon,' Gahan told her. 'He'll kill me if I stay.'

'Margery, make up a basket for the huntsman,' ordered the cook. 'Take another blanket from that pile, some clean shirts, linen. Take as much as you can easily carry. And you take care, do you hear me?' demanded the cook, kissing Gahan on both cheeks. Then she leaned very close and whispered, 'both of you.'

Gahan took all that he was offered and the guards saw him

out of the castle. Something must have been guessed as to the dreadful deed he had done, and some soldiers yelled insults at him as he went.

He arrived at his family's house, split the bag of gold with his mother, and told her what had happened. He did not tell her that Karadoc the Snow White Prince was alive. What she guessed was always hard to tell. She was a widow and could live quite well on this money, until her younger children could work. She kissed her son goodbye, and his little brother cried.

Then he went out into the forest again. He did not mean to go straight to the miners' village, in case someone was following him. The king was an enchanter, and had ways of knowing things. Some folk said that he had a magic mirror. So Gahan travelled only as far as the edge of the kingdom, crossed the border, and found a place to sleep in a barn. The farm wife gave him a dish of eggs for his supper. He slept well, breathing in the warm smell of the cows.

Karadoc the Snow White Prince knew that he would only survive if no one knew him, so he tied back his hair under a hood and smirched his face and hands with soot. The next day he would make a fast brown dye out of walnuts which would colour his skin for at least six weeks. He had learned a lot in the kitchen, and talking with the market women.

Meanwhile he had to earn his place amongst the miners. He watched the way they lived, what they ate, and how they were clothed. They seemed to manage well enough, though they ate mainly bread made of beans and spicy stews: almost no meat and no fruit.

Then he watched a man bend silver wire as a mount for a glittering stone, and found his metier. He sat down with the jeweller and was allowed, after he managed to say a whole sentence in the gutteral, strange language, to try a little smithery on his own account. He knew he could do this. And might eventually experiment with sandcasting and moulds. The jeweller grinned and patted his back. They gave him a name, Daragh, which means, snow.

Day dawned. The king rose, took his usual bath, had lotion massaged into his skin, was attended by his barber and his coiffeur, donned his finest garments and stood before the mirror.

'Mirror mirror on the wall, who is the handsomest of all?'

But the mirror made no reply. The king thumped his own image, but no voice issued forth to tell him how beautiful he was. He snorted and stormed into his library, searching his books. He had made the magic mirror many years ago. It contained a minor demon, which could not refuse to answer.

Gahan woke and was about to take to the road again when a raven flew close to him, croaked, and sat on a tree branch.

'Good morning,' said Gahan. 'Might I be of some service?'

The raven made no answer. Gahan negotiated for breakfast, and began on his journey to the miners' village. The raven followed his every step. Gahan knew that the king used ravens as spies. This one was not behaving like an ordinary raven. The king had not entirely trusted Gahan, as indeed, he had broken his oaths in letting the Snow White Prince escape. So this raven would follow him, until the king was satisfied that all was as it should be.

Gahan sighed, put down his bundle, and went to ask the farm wife for a day's work. Fortunately she had wood to be chopped. Gahan worked all day on the woodpile. The raven did not leave him until he had been fed, and was back in the barn for the night. Gahan ground his teeth. But he could not make his way through trackless forest in the dark. He would have to work on a raven trap. The prince would think that Gahan had abandoned him. And that would break both their hearts.

Daragh stained his skin brown the next day, and learned more about the setting of stones. He was interested in his new craft, and wondered where Gahan was. He was deeply concerned that Gahan, an honest soul, had not been able to persuade King Kerrigan with that pig's heart. Karadoc did not know what he would do if Gahan never came back.

The king summoned the demon of the mirror, threatening it with dreadful pain, and demanded again, 'Who is the handsomest of all?"

And the demon, cowering, whispered, 'The Snow White Prince is the handsomest of all.'

He struck it and it fled, howling. The king mastered his rage. Then he sent for his second huntsman, and ordered him to scour the forests for the Snow White Prince. Then he gathered all his skills and his power, and he ordered the servants to prepare a great silver bowl, to be filled with water and ink, and he scryed for his son.

He caught a glimpse of the prince's hands, deftly attaching a loop to a silver chain, and knew where the Snow White Prince was. Then he brewed in his cauldron a poison made of the skins of toads and certain fish, which would kill with one bite. Into it, when it was completed, he dipped a perfect red apple. The apple seethed briefly, then resumed its shiny appearance.

The king cast a glamourie around himself and was transported by his arts to the miners' village. He saw his son crouched over a smith's fire, his skin brown, his hands marred with little burns. Then he realised that even so, Karadoc the snow white prince was the more beautiful, and he wafted into the miner's longhouse and laid an apple by every bed. The poisoned one sat next to the pile of blankets on the floor, where the prince must be sleeping, as he would never fit into a miner's bed. They were a small people.

The king returned to the castle. His raven reported that Gahan was still at the farm just over the border.

The king went to bed happy.

The next morning, when the raven returned, Gahan netted it despite its squawking and penned it in a cage.

'There you stay, my dear, as a penalty for being a spy. The wife will feed you. I have a place to be, and one where I do not want the king's eyes upon me. If you are an honest raven, forgive me. She will let you out in a week's time.'

Gahan set off into the forest with his burdens. It was a long walk. It took all day. When he came to the miners' village, he heard wailing, and ran towards it. The little men were tearing at their beards. The Snow White Prince, brown now, lay on his blankets in a longhouse. Gahan dropped to his knees beside him. He laid his head on Karadoc's chest, breathing in the sweet scent of his skin. The body was warm and flexible, but there was no heartbeat. No pulse in the elegant wrist under Gahan's despairing fingers.

'It was the apple,' wailed the small man in passable Common Speech. They appeared and we all ate them but he – he just fell down. And now he's dead!'

'No,' said Gahan, 'No, he can't be dead. When did this happen?'

'This morning,' they told him.

'A corpse would be rigid, cold, he's warm; it's some magic, some venom. Some spell of the king's. Oh, my love, Karadoc my prince,' pleaded Gahan, gathering the body into his arms, 'I swore never to leave you, I promised never to forget you. If you are dead, I must follow, or be foresworn. So if there is poison in your mouth, share it with me.'

And he turned the Snow White Prince's face towards him, and opened his mouth for a lethal kiss.

A chunk of apple dropped out. Gahan kissed his prince. There was no response at first from the soft lips, then gradually he felt life begin to return to the body, a tongue seeking his own, a hand sliding up to grip the back of his neck, until Gahan was holding his prince in his arms and the prince was embracing him as though he never meant to let him go. The small miners backed away, awed. Then they retreated outside.

'I'm so cold,' whispered the prince. Gahan wrapped them both in blankets, and the prince laid his head against Gahan's neck, surrounded with the huntsman's familiar smell of forests and dogs and iron, his own scent.

'You will soon be warm,' said Gahan. 'You're alive. I trapped the king's raven, so he doesn't know you're not dead. We'll have to leave here.'

'In the morning,' said the prince drowsily. 'The spell is broken. You broke it. Death spells have a strange quality.'

'What's that?' asked Gahan, settling the prince to lie comfortably against him in their cocoon.

'They have to kill someone,' responded the prince, 'And this one hasn't killed me.' and he fell asleep.

Gahan lay awake all night, listening to him breathing.

The king died that night.

When men came searching for Karadoc the Snow White Prince, who was now king, they found him sleeping in a miner's longhouse in the arms of his huntsman. They were never parted again while they lived. And after that, who knows?

THE CRUSADER'S HEART

Selim bin Daoud was fairly sure he was not dead. There were no green meadows, sherbet, or virgins. And in paradise, he had been informed, there was no pain. Selim felt as though he had fallen from a horse onto a hard surface.

This was, he discovered, because he had fallen from a horse onto a paved courtyard. He paused a moment to listen. No sound but the wind. He sat up, groaning.

Everyone who wasn't dead was gone. The battle at the oasis had been short but sharp. Twelve bodies lay on this tiled forecourt; fallen, with garments rolled in blood. But a magnificent crusader's horse was stamping uneasily, not wanting to leave his dead master, perhaps. With that mount, he could easily catch up to the others. Selim got into a crouch and then stood. He was pleased to find that he had broken no bones.

He threaded his way through the corpses to the horse, talking to it soothingly. Horses hated the smell of blood.

'Oh my dove, my beautiful creature, oh, nuur 'eni, light of my eyes, soon we shall find you some water, and then we shall be away,' he said. 'Come now, come to hand, rohi, my soul.'

He caught at the dangling rein and suddenly found himself on the courtyard on his back again.

A young man had lain there, the horse's leading rein tied around his wrist. Now he was straddling Selim and he had a knife in his free hand.

'Yield,' he demanded.

'I yield,' said Selim instantly. 'Who are you?'

'Richard of Devon,' said his assailant. 'Is anyone else alive?'

'I don't know, I must have hit my head, I just woke up.'

'Let's find out. Come along, Tonnere,' he said to the horse.

'You speak my language,' Selim noted, following his captor into the mess of bodies.

'I've been here for three sodding years,' said Richard of Devon. 'Squire to Sir John– ah, here he is: dead as a stone.'

He kicked his fallen lord in the ribs. 'And got his deserts. I hope the devil likes him. I hope he's screaming in a lake of burning pitch.'

'Your master was cruel to you?' asked Selim.

'Aye, he was,' said Richard. 'And yours?'

'He's away,' said Selim, shivering. 'I have no desire to see him again.'

'Ah,' said Richard. 'Roll these bodies over there, shall we, and throw sand over all this blood. Then we'll find this poor beast a drink, and one for us, too. And some food would be nice. Bastard kept us half starved. What are you doing?'

'Looting,' said Selim, matter-of-factly. 'We are going to need some money, more food and something to carry water in. It's nearly twenty miles to the next oasis, and nearly eighty to the sea.'

'Oh, ah,' said Richard. 'I think you'd better call me Dickon. That's what my friends call me. '

'Dickon,' said Selim. 'Good. Habiibii,' he added, and held out his hands.

Dickon took them and they kissed formally.

They put Tonnere into the caravanserai for the moment, with a pail of water, and then arrayed and stripped the bodies of all valuables. They piled up the loot on Sir John of Devon's shield. It was a reasonable haul. It included two waterskins and various coins.

'Excellent, now us, I'm as dry as a chip,' said Dickon, and they drew more water from the pool and washed themselves clean, donning better clothes from the saddlebag. Dickon sighed as he sipped another cup of cool water.

'Not a lot of food, But we can cope as long as there is water. What about Tonnere?'

'There is grain in my pack, my master made me carry it. He rode and I walked. I'm not going to miss him at all, Habiibii.'

'You are not like those filthy Franks, you are cleanly,' observed Selim, sipping in turn from the one cup they had found.

'I'm an Englishman,' replied Dickon.

'You need not lie to me, I yielded to you, you owe me truth,' protested Selim.

Dickon stared at him. 'I am English, as was John of Devon, and I won't miss him, either. Why do you think I am lying? We are allies; friends, perhaps. You said Habiibii. That means, friend.'

'It is well known that all Englishmen have tails,' said Selim, stiffly.

Dickon chuckled. 'We'll you've seen I have no tail. And we can strip my late master and he hasn't a tail either. And I swear on any god you care to name that we are both English. So–'

'I was wrong,' said Selim, humbly. He took up Dickon's hand and kissed it.

'No matter,' said Dickon. 'Is it true that– no, never mind. So, Habiibii, what are we going to do now? Two young men riding a cavalry horse are going to be a bit noticeable. And you said it's eighty miles to the coast. Then we can take a ship to England, if you care to come with me.'

'I would like to see England,' replied Selim. 'My father, Sieur Daoud of Applegate, he was an Englishman. That's why I'm not welcome here, they call me a mongrel.'

'But you're beautiful,' said Dickon. 'You've got olive skin and blue eyes and that curly brown hair, shot through with silver, like the silk we bought in Persia– what was it? Tabbi, that was it.'

'You are beautiful too, though scorched by the sun. Your eyes are as blue as mine,' said Selim, and kissed him. Dickon kissed him back. They embraced.

'Wait,' said Selim, putting Dickon aside a little.

'No, I want you,' he assured the young man.

'As I do you. But we had better do the horrible thing first, and then we can wash again and lie down together in the caravanserai. I have thought of a plan which will get us through without interference, all the way to England.'

'What?' asked Dickon, nuzzling his Habiibii, kissing down along the beautiful throat to a beautiful shoulder.

'We have to cut out your lord's heart,' replied Selim.

Dickon sat up abruptly, shoving his friend aside. He was about to exclaim in horror when he understood. Selim saw comprehension bloom across Dickon's face like sunrise in the desert. It was an honest, plain, snub-nosed face, and Selim adored it.

'Brilliant, most delightful son of Saladin! Yes, quick, my knife might be better. How did you know about the heart quest?'

'My mother told me. She met my father Sieur Daoud when he was taking his own lord's heart back to England to be buried in his own church. He wanted her to come with him, but she would not leave her own mother, who was dying. He said that no one would interfere with the heart quest, it was holy, and both sides admitted this. We need some kind of box to put it in. I shall search the caravanserai. Can you do this?'

'Of course,' said Dickon. 'I hated him enough while he was alive. He isn't going to hurt me anymore, now that he's dead.'

'You do not need to saw through the ribs, slit the diaphragm and you will be able to feel it with your hands. Then you can draw it out and sever the vessels,' directed Selim.

Dickon did not ask him how he knew this.

A messy and uncomfortable interval later – Dickon had had to cover Sir John of Devon's face before he could manage the surgery – he had his master's heart in his cupped hands. He washed it in three changes of water, and put it into a box which Selim had found. It fitted well enough. Then Selim packed the box with sand and they wrapped it in string and then in Sir John's surcoat.

'We'll have to take his shield, and his signet. We drape the shield in – this shirt will do – as a funeral hatchment. And all we need to do now is to wash again, and then–'

'Ah, yes, please,' said Dickon, and reached for the bucket.

They washed each other, carefully, lingeringly, and then lay down naked on three of the less bloodstained cloaks in the dimness. Tonnere munched and stamped. They kissed.

'Do you want my, I don't know if the English…' Selim scrabbled up onto his knees and presented his rear. 'That is what my master wanted. He hurt me, but it will be different with you.'

'No, nuur 'eni, danaya, sweetheart,' soothed Dickon, 'come back into my arms. My master demanded that of me, too. We never have to do it again. Let me touch you. Let me look at you! I was curious.'

'About?' asked Selim, almost weeping with relief, kissing all the parts of Dickon that he could reach.

'Are you circumcised?' asked Dickon, blushing. 'I have never seen...'

Selim laid himself out flat for his lover to investigate, which he did with hands and mouth, and then allowed Selim to do the same. They were both very pleased with their educational experience. They lay together, panting, sweating, delighted, exhausted.

'We sleep here tonight,' said Dickon. 'If anyone comes, we have our story and our quest. Did you learn any English, umri, my life?'

'Some,' replied Selim, pillowing his cheek on his lover's chest. 'But I don't think that *Die, dog of an Infidel* is going to be of much use in ordinary conversation.'

'Then you stay silent, I shall say you are mute because of a vow. You will not speak again until we have carried our master's heart home where it belongs. You can explain most things with a vow. You will have English clothes and you are with an Englishman, riding an English warhorse. And if they worry you, glance at them with your dazzling blue eyes. They will forget what they were saying. No Saracen ever had such eyes.'

'You admire my eyes?' asked Selim, kissing Dickon's jaw.

'They pierce my heart,' replied Dickon.

'We can stay together?' asked Selim.' It is a long journey, but I cannot bear to lose you, rohi, my soul. I will not go forth if I must farewell you at the end of the road and find myself outcast in a foreign land.'

'On the way I will teach you English, my darling,' said Dickon in English, then repeated it in Arabic. 'Then you may greet your father, Sir David of Applegate, in his own tongue. He lives near my own village. But if he doesn't want you we shall find other lodgings. But we stay together,' said Dickon firmly. 'Say, I love you,' he said, in English.

'I love you,' repeated Selim.

'I love you, too, nuur 'eni, light of my eyes.'

CHRONICLE OF APPLEGATE ABBEY

23rd of Aprille in the Year of Our Lord 1191
Being the feast day of Saint George.

On this day two devout squires, Richard of Devon and Stephen of Applegate, son of Sir David, reverently brought to his grieving widow the heart of pious Sir John of Devon, who died on crusade in the Holy Land. Masses for the repose of his soul were endowed in perpetuity by Sir David.

The two squires have been taken into the household of Sir David of Applegate, who dotes on his son Stephen. It is said that his mother was a Princess amongst the Saracens and a Christian woman, who was killed by her sire for loving an Englishman. The two squires, the said Richard of Devon and Stephen of Applegate, have lately rid the countryside of a monstrous boar, to the thanks of all the people. They live together in Sir David's gatehouse.

Word has come of a prodigy in Yorkshire, a woman has given birth to a serpent, which it is said portends that Jerusalem will soon be freed. So we all pray.

A GESTE OF ROBYN HODE

Lyth and listin gentilmen
That be of freebore blode
And I shall you tel of a gude yeman
His name was Robyn Hode.
The Geste of Robyn Hode
(anon)

He was tall and handsome and commanding and Will Scathelock hated him on sight.

They had stopped Scathelock in his miserable journey through Sherwood Forest, offering him a drink and a bite of venison in exchange for news or any song. He was by then tired of his own company, had recited the whole of Aristotle, was hungry and thirsty and – perhaps – lonely.

He had enjoyed university. He had loved the cut and thrust of debate, the sea of ideas. Then he had cut down one professor too many. They had withdrawn his scholar's privileges and flung him out, to wander the roads, seeking a little employment as a scribe. Will Scathelock wrote a beautiful hand. He hated every farmer, every silly boy, every dry clerk who demanded that he write down their trite, foolish words.

But he had done so. Even scholars have to eat. These bandits did not seem hostile, though he had no doubt that he could annoy them sufficiently to cast him out when he was sick of them.

For the moment, however, he allowed himself to be led off the road into their camp.

It was well-ordered and clean. A deer was roasting over a proper charcoal fire. Dishes, cutlery and a barrel of wine were all arrayed correctly. Will's stomach rumbled. That venison smelt delicious. A young man was mending hose. A tall woman was braiding the hair of a small, rebellious child. Various men sat on sawn logs, cleaning weapons. A fat cleric was staring into his cup as though the mystery of his lost sanctity lay in its depths.

'Who have we here?' asked the tall handsome man.

'Will Scathelock,' Will allowed the tall man to engulf his hand. 'Scholar.'

'The reward for learning hasn't been rich,' commented the tall man. 'I am Robin Hood, and this is my forest. If you mean us no harm, sit, there will be meat soon and there is wine and bread now.'

'I thank you, and I mean you no harm,' said Scathelock.

Robin sat him down on a log and fetched bread and wine. Scathelock dipped bits of bread in wine and ate slowly. He was very hungry. He did not want his treacherous stomach to revolt and shame him under the regard of those penetrating brown eyes. This Robin Hood understood about men.

The strange thing was that he also liked them. Robin adopted Scathelock, partly because he was so acerbic.

No one else argued with Robin. Scathelock argued with him all the time. He was not only annoying, but often right. Robin was prone to leap into situations. Scathelock was a planner. Together they made a formidable, bickering, difficult team, but a team nonetheless.

Robin had many lovers, Scathelock none. He was not interested in the maidens, or the young men, who cast amorous glances his way. After a few wounding rebuffs, they stopped trying. His virtue was his armour, they said. He would never endure another person close enough to touch that cold heart.

Will Scathelock opened his eyes. It made no difference. It was still dark.

In this cell it was always dark. Not black night but deep dusk. He clenched a dirty fist on his bare knee and heard the clink of his manacles. He was firmly attached by ankles and wrists. He knew the attachment was firm because he had spent days hauling on it with no result. In all the time he had been in the cell, he had not been able to move more than four feet from the wall. He was naked. He was blind. He was filthy.

Chained just out of reach, Robin Hood seemed to be sleeping. Will Scathelock could just hear his ragged, soft breathing. Sometimes he had to strain to hear it and gulp down his own fear, his own pulse drumming wildly in his ears, when he thought that Robin had died and he was alone.

Robin Hood was still breathing. Will Scathelock was not alone. He was, however, perilously close to breaking point and he wondered coldly what form it would take; he hoped that he would not scream or beg, but he was no longer sure. It was not that he was more afraid than usual; Scathelock was always afraid, it was part of the background radiation of his consciousness. It was, perhaps, the darkness, which stripped away one sense he relied on to warn him and made him more vulnerable both to assault and to loneliness. He could hear and speak, but he could not touch Robin and he could not see. This drove him down into the depths of his own mind, and he feared the monsters who swam there more than any real enemy. Only when he could speak or listen were they kept at bay, and he knew where they were lurking. Not even following the army to Jerusalem had shown him such darkness, such loneliness, such terror. Even in the desert, there are always stars.

The others of their company were far away, alwatys watched by the Sherrif's soldiers. Even if they returned the crew would not be able to find them and perhaps would not try. Robin and Scathelock had been scouting for news about a gold shipment which might be travelling through Nottingham. They had foreseen that they might be away for days: it was possible that no one had missed them. It wasn't unusual for Will and Robin to become interested in some mystery and sleep out for nights.

Their capture by the silent guards of a strange priesthood was sudden, brutal and puzzling. Unspeaking, they had shoved Robin Hood and Scathelock into this dungeon underground and left them there. They had been in the cell for so long that Scathelock had given up what hope he had, which was never so much as to incommode him. What kept him alive, he considered, was how much he hated Robin Hood. For Robin Hood had not despaired. Robin Hood kept telling him that someone would come. If he had not been manacled Will Scathelock might have strangled Robin Hood himself. He had screamed at him into the dimness to stop hoping, that hope was false, that there would be no rescue, that they would die in the darkness, in the filth.

Then Robin Hood had fallen silent, and silence was worse.

At irregular intervals they heard other cell doors open. Still the guards did not speak, but they could hear what happened to the other prisoners. Woundingly loud in the underground stillness came screams and the thud of falling bodies. Then, always, a choking gurgle followed by a hollow silence in which a whisper started echoes.

The Priesthood of the Holy Name had come for the others, one by one. There was chilling evidence that others had inhabited their cell before them. The floor was stamped earth, soaked with old blood which sprang up as a stench when water or urine softened it. A lot of blood had been spilled near where Will Scathelock was lying and his skin crawled as his naked torso and buttocks came into wincing contact with it. Even the manacles which confined his wrists and ankles were black with old stains.

No one had come for Robin or Scathelock, though they knew that one day the dark soldiers would stop at their cell door and they might be allowed to fight for their lives. To judge from the fate of the others whose death rattles they had heard, they would lose. Once a day a hooded priest opened the door, put in a dish of water and a loaf of bread, replaced their bucket, then closed the door. He never spoke. After a few days they shrieked at him to respond, but he never replied.

'Will? Are you awake?' asked Robin Hood. The scholar answered, valuing precision as usual.

'I'm awake, or perhaps I should say, I am now awake.'

'How long has it been, do you think?'

'No way to tell the time down here. We cannot tell day from night in this eternal blackness. But they've fed us twelve times; I've scratched a tally on this wall, in case it should be of historical interest when the King takes over this disgusting castle and finds our bones.'

'Twelve days then.' Robin Hood's voice was still rich and deep.

'Probably,' said Scathelock. 'I'm hungry, but I have been since they threw us into this hole. And I observe that my beard has grown and so have my nails and my hair. We are probably not imagining this, Master Hood. The chances of us sharing a Vision of Hell as a result of drinking a dish of Mother Hammonds disreputable ale is as likely as Friar Tuck taking up Abstinence and abandoning his old cup-mate, gluttony.'

'Very witty, i'faith. It must have been awhile. The scrapes I gave myself trying to get one handcuff off have scabbed over and started to heal.'

'Remarkable, i'faith,' the voice was scathing. 'Considering the number of people who have died and rotted down here, you'd think you'd have gangrene by now.' Will Scathelock's cut-glass scholar's voice was husky with thirst and loathing.

'Well, I'm glad to have all my limbs.'

Will Scathelock exploded into rage. 'Must you be–'

'Cheerful?' Robin Hood was angry and suddenly Will Scathelock was wary of annoying Robin so much that he retreated into muteness. Silence gnawed at him in the darkness.

Robin Hood went on 'I'm chained in a cell underground. I've been listening to what sounds like constant murder happening outside. I'm dirty and thirsty and I've got no one to talk to but you, Will Scathelock. Why shouldn't I be cheerful?'

Will Scathelock was about to snarl a retort when the cell door slammed open. Two cowled men came to Robin Hood.

They stooped, unlatched the manacles and hauled him to his feet. Robin could barely stand. The guards dragged him roughly upright between them.

Will Scathelock observed that the one with the crossbow kept well back and his aim never faltered. He leapt up, staggering as his limbs cramped at the sudden movement. 'Where are you taking him?'

'Peace, perhaps we can barter for our lives,' Robin said, and staggered as he was struck across the face.

'Silence,' hissed the first guard, the first word they had heard any of them say. The door clanged shut behind Robin Hood.

Will Scathelock was too furious to slump into the hollow his body had worn in the dirt floor. Instead he stood with his back against the wall, as he felt he had stood all his life. Time passed. He scuffed his bare feet in the dust, scratched the wall with his black rimmed nails, combed back his hair with his fingers. They had taken everything from him. First, the weapons. Finally clothes. He had never felt so acutely naked and vulnerable. Years appeared to have passed since Robin Hood had been taken from him. For the first time he admitted to himself that he needed Robin Hood exactly as much as he hated him. The darkness pressed closer. He swallowed dryly.

All Will Scathelock had ever wanted was to be safe. He had always known that Robin Hood would get him killed, though he couldn't pin down any action of his which had not been taken in the interests of keeping Will Scathelock in one piece. Now it had come, he felt strangely empty. There is an advantage, he thought, in the worst having actually happened. This is what I was afraid of, dying alone in the dark, and now I have come to it, for Master Hood is dying even now, and then they will come for me.

The door slammed open and a body was thrown inside, impacting with a grunt of pain. Not dead, after all. Will Scathelock dropped to his knees, stretching to the extent of the manacles.

'Robin!'

'I can't see,' mumbled Robin Hood. 'Blood in my eyes. Will? Where are you?'

'Here,' Will Scathelock felt around in the darkness. 'You can follow my voice; turn toward my voice. I'm here, here. Robin. This way.'

He saw a dim shape crawling across the filthy floor, smelt a human scent, then touched Robin Hood's arm and dragged him close. Robin sagged. His face was sticky. Will Scathelock smelt blood and felt gently for the source. A small cut on the forehead. Someone had hit Robin Hood with an armoured fist. A kick would have done more damage. The bone underneath felt whole. He drew a sharp breath of relief and wiped some of the blood away.

'What did they do to you?' Scathelock attempted his usual precise diction and heard his voice quaver shamefully.

'They called us unclean,' mumbled Robin Hood. 'Going to kill us tomorrow. Unclean. Heretics. Their chief priest says we have to die. Tomorrow.'

'No rescue, after all,' murmured Will Scathelock.

'You always said there would be no rescue,' said Robin Hood.

Chains clinked as Scathelock hauled Robin Hood into his arms so that he lay as close as he could, his bloody brow against Scathelock's neck. 'You stink,' chuckled Robin Hood weakly.

'So do you. I'd give everything I've ever stolen for a hot bath. We're going to die,' said Scathelock, and kissed Robin Hood on the mouth.

Robin's hands fumbled up to clutch bare shoulders and missed, sliding down to the flat belly, cupping and stroking. The kiss went on. Will Scathelock tasted salt and dust. Their mouths meshed like a gear. The kiss broke only when Robin Hood gasped as Will Scathelock with dirty hands began to caress him.

'This is mad,' commented Robin Hood. 'You're still chained. We're going to die.'

'Don't talk,' Will Scathelock recaptured his mouth.

They were breathing faster. Sweat broke on their skin and puddled to mud in collarbone and groin. Straining for purchase on the dirt floor, they grappled like wrestlers. Their embrace was rough. Strong heartbeats throbbed in the throat where Will Scathelock's mouth clung and then bit. This was no sweet mating of lovers but a breaking of restraints, a hard contest, long-denied, gripping with fingers like talons.

Perhaps it was the dark. They could not see expressions, only hear the short fast breathing, feel the touch which grasped the penis, stroked the balls now hard with sperm. Robin Hood, who could move, buried his face in Will Scathelock's thighs, taking his penis into his mouth, tasting the skin. The clasp of the strong, sucking mouth was so piercing that Scathelock threw back his head and groaned with something close to pain as he came. He shuddered the length of his manacled body. Robin Hood lifted his head and Will Scathelock kissed his saturated mouth, sliding hands now wet with sweat and blood along and around the erection until he felt Robin's thighs tremble and the hot spurt of semen onto his belly.

'I always loved you,' gasped Robin Hood, gathering Will Scathelock into his arms.

'I love you,' responded Scathelock. 'I'll never leave you.'

When Little John and the others fought their way down to ransack the dungeons of the Holy Name and Marion found them, they were asleep so deeply and curled so closely together that she ordered them bundled up and hauled out still in their embrace.

Marion never forgot the sight of how they lay, pitiable and beautiful. They were breast to breast and belly to belly, legs intertwined, Will Scathelock's head on Robin Hood's chest, their arms wrapped around each other as though they had meant to die so. They were so painted with mud and blood and sexual fluids that the only similar sight she could recall was a holy image of two martyred saints, Cosimo and Damien, who had gone to their heavenly reward wrapped in each other's arms.

It was obvious that they were not badly injured, and she could not bear to wake them and watch the image break apart – it seemed cruel, almost irreligious. Because of this, she rode in the back of the cart with them and when they had arrived in the camp, ordered them carried to the pool of sweet water, warmed by the sun, to bathe. She left a flagon of wine and a loaf of bread and some cheese – not too much, for they had clearly been starved. Then she ordered the whole camp to leave them alone, to wake as they would. She had wounds to tend and roasting to supervise.

Therefore they woke in sunlight. Robin Hood opened his eyes and found that he was held fast in a cage of limbs. He was holding Will Scathelock, who questioned him, nagged him, complained, made his life difficult, and whom – it seemed – loved him, as much as he loved Will.

And by some miracle, they were lying on soft grass in sunlight. Real sunlight. He raised his head to look around.

'Will, wake, we're either in Nottingham Forest or in heaven. Which is how I expected Heaven to look, it seems.'

He flung himself flat on his back in the grass.

Will Scathelock woke with empty arms to see Robin Hood lying supine entirely covered with mud and filth. His eyes were bruised, his hands, his body bloomed red and black. He looked like a casualty of some forgotten war, left unclaimed on a battlefield.

'Robin Hood,' murmured Will Scathelock, trying to rise to his knees and failing. 'Master Hood. Rouse yourself. Robin Hood! Don't you dare die before you can remind me that I should never give up.'

'Will?' Robin Hood shifted shoulder and hip and flinched. There were black shadows under his eyes, Will Scathelock saw, possibly matching his own. Some scars would take a long time to heal. Robin Hood shook his head. He opened his eyes and Will Scathelock saw him smile.

Robin Hood saw Scathelock's hair falling over his brightening eyes and wonderingly reached to touch his lover's wet face. A tear tracked down through the mire. Will Scathelock, weeping? That cold, philosphical student? Rescue from prison was always possible, but to see Will Scathelock crying was unthinkable. But then, unless he had indeed been granted a Vision, Will Scathelock was his lover now. It had taken twelve days in the dark and the certainty of imminent death to make him declare himself, which was also, he reflected, like Will Scathelock. Robin Hood dragged himself up onto one elbow.

'This is Nottingham Forest,' he said. 'We're home.'

'Evidently,' Will Scathelock replied. 'You were always one for the statement of the obvious.'

'And there is your bath,' commented Robin Hood, hauling himself onto all fours. Will Scathelock coughed and sat up, shedding filth. They crawled, neither trusting their feet. It was only a little way to the sun warmed pool. They fell into the water with a splash and Will Scathelock sobbed as the warm water stung his new skin. He opened his mouth and drank, and it felt like his whole abused body sucked in moisture as it birthed clouds of mud and blood into the fluid warmth. He ducked under, feeling the drag of the water on his hair, watching Robin Hood roll like a dolphin in delight. So clean. So bright. After twelve days underground, the water reflections hurt his eyes. He closed them and floated, weightless, stripped, newborn. For once, he was possessed by joy, not analysing, not thinking. He heard Robin Hood laughing aloud as he surfaced, spouting like a whale.

Their mouths met and they kissed, cradled in the kindly water. Robin Hood lay beside him, Will Scathelock's head in the crook of his arm, anchored by one foot. The waves subsided around them and grew still.

'Did you mean what you said?' asked Robin Hood.

'Did you?'

'Yes,' said Robin Hood.

'Yes,' said Will Scathelock.

THE SAMURAI

The road was dusty, the hedges withering, the sun was burning. He wanted a destination and he really, really wanted a drink.

But when the attack came he whirled on one foot and narrowly avoided putting a blade through an unarmed young man's throat.

'Fool!' he snapped, sheathing the sword. 'Never startle a Samurai. Who are you?'

'My unimportant name is Takeshi,' faltered the comely young man, bowing. 'I was about to speak to your magnificence... your reflexes are amazing–'

'Thank you. Go away,' said the Samurai.

'I want to be a Samurai,' insisted the young man.

'You don't,' snarled Samurai Chiba no Suke Taira Ichiro.

'Oh, but I do,' repeated Takeshi.

'The rewards of being a Samurai? Regard me, and tell me what they are,' said Ichiro softly.

He stood still as Takeshi looked him over. Shabby robes which had once been fine, dirty hair, dusty feet. No attendant. No horse. His only valuable possessions were his sword and the small eating knife at his waist. No rings on his fingers. No coins in his belt. Tired and in need of a bath. And not as young as he had been.

Ichiro let the young man stare. Then he made a dismissive gesture. 'Off home, you. You don't want to wander the roads, hungry, unrespected, unrewarded, to find an unmarked grave.'

The young man bowed again. 'It pains me to say so, but I have seen you, noble lord, and I still want to be a Samurai.'

'Then you are a fool indeed,' Ichiro resumed his steady pace. Takeshi fell in beside him. 'I did tell you to go away,' Ichiro reminded him.

'Yes, lord, you did,' agreed Takeshi.

Without warning, Ichiro aimed an irritated slap at the back of the young man's head, to find himself, exceptionally, brought to his knees by a couple of lightning fast blows. Then Takeshi stood back and bowed again.

'Will you stop bowing!' yelled the Samurai. 'That was curious. Fast! Remarkable. Come and help me up. That was karate, eh, the empty hand? Do you know how forbidden that is?'

'I do,' agreed Takeshi, hauling Ichiro to his feet. 'There is a bathhouse just along this road. I think we need a wash.'

'And that's the truth,' grumbled the Samurai.

The sento was just like all other bathhouses in the Shogunate. Clean, spare, and to be had for 45 ryo, a fixed fee for the whole island. Takeshi paid for both. They left their clothes with the attendant to be washed or brushed and sat down on stools on the slatted wooden floor as attendants began pouring buckets of hot water over them, lathering and scrubbing them with oatmeal. The Samurai indicated that he wanted his hair washed, and almost groaned with pleasure as all the grime was scoured off his body, his nails cleaned, his foot soles pumiced, his hair washed clean and combed and dressed high on his head.

'You, boy, you're staring,' he grunted.

'Honourable scars, noble lord,' replied Takeshi.

The Samurai was muscular, with the swordsman's broad shoulders, solid arms and scarred hands. His body tapered to a small waist, the perfect shape. Takeshi could not take his eyes off this pure, beautiful masculine form. He was striped and slashed with scars, one across his chest, one which must have almost taken off his leg at the knee, one glancing blow which had sliced across his belly. He shifted uncomfortably under the young man's gaze.

'Battered,' he said. 'Damaged. Not like you, Takeshi. You are quite perfect.'

Ichiro examined the young man. He was built like a dancer. All slim, long musculature, golden skinned and untouched. Takeshi blushed.

'You are beautiful, lord, and your body just proves your life of service,' he replied. 'Will you tell me of those battles, while we recline in the pool?'

'Boys always want to hear war stories,' grunted Ichiro.

But he took Takeshi's hand as they went down the steps into the pool of mineral water, warm and clean, and as they sat together, Takeshi insinuated himself under Ichiro's arm like a snuggling cat. The Samurai chuckled and hugged him.

'You're very determined, aren't you?' he asked. 'Tell me, Takeshi, have you done this before? Sought a Samurai as a lover?'

'Never,' said Takeshi, sitting up straight in horror. 'Never!'

'Then, why me?' asked Ichiro. 'No, come back, I did not mean to offend you. My apologies. Look at me, I am thirty and battered and no object for a young man's dream. Why me?'

'I saw you defeat six bandits with your sword still sheathed,' said Takeshi, still withdrawn from the embrace. 'They had oppressed my parents and robbed and stolen, and you reduced them to porridge. You didn't even pause in your walking. I thought, that is the man for me. I had been waiting for you.'

'Oh, yes, those bandits,' Ichiro recalled. 'I did encounter some minor resistance as I came down the road. Nothing serious. Not worth getting my katana out. What do you mean, waiting for me?'

'The monk said...' Takeshi returned to Ichiro's arms and touched his face with a careful forefinger. 'A monk told me that there was a karmic string, a link, between me and a samurai, and that I would know when he came along. And you came along, and I knew.'

Ichiro was silent. Takeshi wanted to throw himself on that broad chest, but stayed still. Perhaps he was wrong. Perhaps this samurai felt no such connection. He wondered if he could actually die of the shame.

'Yes,' said Ichiro. 'I feel it, too. So; this is shudo. You know this is serious? As serious as a marriage. I will belong to you, and you to me, for life. There are vows.'

'I will take them,' declared Takeshi. Ichiro laid his cheek beside that of the young man's. Takeshi's skin was smooth and smelt of jasmine tea and spices. The oil that the bathhouse had used on the samurai's hair, Takeshi found, smelt delightfully of dry grass. And Ichiro smelt of strength, earth and iron.

'I have never sworn myself to anyone but the Shogun,' murmured Ichiro. 'But I will swear myself to you. But you should consider this carefully. The poets say you should test me, to find if I am worthy.'

Takeshi was about to reply when he heard running feet and voices shouting. The peace of the bathhouse was disturbed by several peasants, screaming 'The Samurai! They say there is a Samurai here! Where is he? Where is the Samurai?'

'Here,' groaned Ichiro, hauling himself out Takeshi's arms and subsequently out of the bath. A sudden, heavy dread settled like stone in his belly. This was the last fight, then, and just as he had discovered the man of his heart. Fate had always disliked him but this seemed unutterably cruel.

'The ronin has taken Kimicho!' shrieked an elderly man. 'He just seized her! You must help us!'

'Where is he?' asked Ichiro, allowing himself to be dried and dressed in his clean clothes and robes, retrieving his swords.

Takeshi was there, tying on his sandals, holding out his gown. He settled around the Samurai's neck a broad, flat, metal pendant on a chain. Ichiro raised a questioning eyebrow.

'My token,' he whispered. 'You are mine now. You can't get killed.'

'I'll do my best,' replied Ichiro, and kissed the young man. Takeshi's lips were thinned with fear. He embraced the samurai fiercely, briefly, and released him.

'And I am coming too,' he declared.

'Atsusi,' murmured Ichiro. 'Faithful.' He touched the boy's shoulder. 'Where is this ronin?' he asked, and the peasants led the way.

The ronin had the young girl by the hair. He was in the process of trying to subdue her frantic struggles when he heard someone ask, in a pleasant tone.

'Greetings, ronin. Your lord is dead. Why are you still living?'

Snarling, the man released the girl, who fled, and turned to face the Samurai, who had drawn his sword.

'The old eagle,' he sneered. 'Is it you, Chiba no Suke Taira?'

'As you see,' replied Ichiro. 'Why not leave? I have no wish to spend an hour cleaning your dishonourable blood off my precious sword.'

'Sato,' yelled the ronin. 'Where is your lord?'

'Quite healthy and ruling the realm as usual,' returned Ichiro.

Without warning, the ronin attacked. Ichiro fended off the wild blow, then another, without much effort. Takeshi and the peasants watched, agog. One of the old men said, 'It's as good as a play!' and Takeshi bit his lip so hard that he tasted blood. No one but he, himself, would care what the outcome of this fight might be. The peasants had their girl back unharmed. And fighting evildoers was what Samurai were for.

They circled each other, the ronin and the Samurai. Ichiro recited a verse. Takeshi realised it was a death-verse – his last words, if this duel went the wrong way. And the ronin had called him the old eagle.

'Snow showers scan tipped wings
Blue clouds draw strength of will no more
Rise wings: above all storms.'

The endless circling continued. Then the ronin stooped, grasped a handful of dust and flung it into the Samurai's face. He stumbled back a pace, and the ronin's sword slashed across his chest.

Takeshi suppressed a scream.

Ichiro leapt forward and with one magnificent, deadly sweep, sliced the ronin's sword arm from his shoulder. The ronin fell to his knees. He said:

> *'Had I not known*
> *That I was dead already*
> *I would have mourned*
> *My loss of life.'*

Then, as blood spouted from his wound, he fell face down and did not move again. The peasants cheered, and fetched a hurdle to remove the corpse.

Takeshi rushed to Ichiro and bore him up as he staggered. He tore at the Samurai's robe, parting the front. To reveal his own love token cloven in half, and a mere scratch on the precious skin underneath.

'You know that you said that I should test you?' asked Takeshi, pressing close to the samurai's side. 'I have. You're mine, Ichiro-san.'

'And you're mine. I think I need to lie down.'

'Come,' said Takeshi, and led him to the inn, where he laid him down on a tatami and lay down beside him, kissing him feverishly.

'First kisses,' groaned Ichiro. 'Then food. Then sake.'

In the morning, Ichiro woke entwined with his lover, slightly sore and bewildered. There had been a fight, he had managed not to get badly killed, again, and – karma had given him Takeshi. His golden young man was wrapped around him, fast asleep, with his loose hair tickling the samurai's nose.

'Praise to Buddha,' said Ichiro, and fell asleep again.

'Where are we going?' asked Takeshi, shouldering the bundle of clothes and trying to imitate the Samurai's even, easy pace.

'To the Abbot of the Temple of Heavenly Clouds, to register

our vows, Takeshi-chan. Then I think we should head towards the capital. I need to report to the Shogun.'

'The Shogun will see you?' gasped Takeshi, taking the Samurai's left hand. Ichiro grinned.

'Yes. I'm his half-brother. He sent me out to find my heart. And now I can go home, because I have found it.'

> *Dancing in the air*
> *Twin butterflies*
> *until, twice white*
> *They meet, they mate.*
>
> *Ichiro and Takeshi*
> *Iron and Brave*
> *They meet, they mate*
> *Together. Forever.*

MERLIN

Finally, a tree was returning his song. Phillip Beckford, 2nd Earl of Doveton, had been playing to the oaks, which were the oldest trees on his estate, for several hours. In truth, he had been studying the nature of tunes sung by birds and seals for three years and was only now applying his knowledge.

Plato had suggested that the universe began because of heavenly harmony and even the Bible said that the morning stars sang together. Close research into Ancient Greek Orphic hymns had disclosed what the Orpheans thought were the notes which Orpheus used to charm man and beast alike. And so it was reasonable, Phillip surmised, they ought to work on trees.

So he'd been playing his syrinx – an instrument of his own invention – all morning. Perhaps trees just took longer to react than forest animals. These oaks were 800 years old; 300 years growing, 300 years living, 300 years dying, that's what the country folk said about oaks.

By the time that they replied, it might be a year later. He began to wonder if he should seek out some saplings; they might be more responsive.

But at last, this very old and beautiful oak was singing in return. A modal song, the Myxolidian, sad and sweet. The tune resembled *Long A-Growing*.

Phillip stared into the trunk, playing his syrinx; a high, sweet piping, harmonising with the tree's voice. And as he played a figure began to emerge from the dark, wrinkled, iron-hard bark. A full-grown man – hair swept back, high nose, deep eye sockets – was slowly coming into being like a grey cloud picture.

Oh, how Phillip longed for someone to love him, to stay close to him, to lie next to his heart. His great love, Georg, had died young of a fever in Germany and Phillip knew he could never truly love again. Or rather that he never wished to love anything mortal again.

And yet he burned and wept in his solitude.

The Earl was also virtuous, and cautious enough not to consort with the dark powers, but legend said that the people of the trees, the *hamadryad,* were faithful, beautiful and kind.

Perhaps an understanding tree spirit would be enough; a faithful companion who did not ask the world of him.

For even with servants and relatives in residence, life in his great house was lonely; more so since he had lost the Queen's Favour and had nothing at all to do.

But Phillip could not, in all concience, marry the woman who had been chosen for him. Poor Bess was a kind girl and deserved a good husband. As a consequence, Her Majesty had icily advised him that his presence was no longer acceptable in her court.

And so, Phillip played his soulful melody, and the tree sang with him, and the tree spirit continued to emerge. The great oak and tree spirit were almost separate; the *hamadryad* gaining colour as his skin struck the air.

And Phillip almost wept, for the tree spirit was beautiful: pale skin, waist-length hair the colour of oak-bark, eyes as green as new leaves, and a mouth as red as holly berry.

The man, now flesh, wreathed his new arms around Phillip's shoulders and kissed him, breathing a first breath into Phillip's mouth. The Earl kissed him back, and then sobbed and slumped to the ground. The tree man followed and somehow Phillip was naked too, and they were lying together on a purple cloak that had not been there before, making love so passionately and generously that they cried out together.

When they finally relaxed into each other's embrace the great oak tree fell silent.

The magnificent tree-man, however, chuckled as he gazed

into Phillip's eyes and stroked his cheek with one smooth forefinger. He was young – perhaps in his 20th year as his body was muscular and unscarred, and his face unwrinkled – but there was a depth of age and wisdom in his eyes which made Phillip almost afraid.

'You freed me,' said the tree man. His voice was deep and rich and strongly accented. 'What is your name, my love?'

'Phillip Beckford,' he stammered. 'Do *hamadryads* have names?'

'Not generally,' replied the tree man. 'I, however, am not a dryad, but a prisoner, and you have freed me. A very long time ago a wicked woman sealed me into this tree, and it and I have grown old together. When I was a man I was called Myrddin Ambrosianus.'

Phillip sat up in surprise. 'The wizard Merlin?'

Merlin raised himself a little on one elbow and bowed. 'The very same.'

'They said that Nimue sealed you in a cave because you threatened her virtue,' said Phillip.

Merlin reached across, slid a hand around the back of Phillip's neck, and drew his head towards him. There he kissed the young man's mouth until he was close to swooning, as bees swoon in midsummer in the clover fields. So sweet, so sweet!

'Do you think I am a threat to any woman's virtue?' Merlin laughed. 'Yours, perhaps, but it was your longing that brought me forth; and your tune.

'No, Nimue wanted power. And with me gone, she got it. And, I have no doubt, she misused it and brought ruin on the kingdom and the death of the King.'

'Yes,' said Phillip.

'Thought so,' grumbled the wizard, pillowing his head on Phillips naked chest. 'A long time ago?'

'More than a thousand years,' Phillip told him, stroking the silky hair back from the sorrowful face.

Merlin sighed. 'How did my poor Artos die?'

'His bastard son Mordred killed him – or so they say,' Phillip explained. 'But Artos ordered his knight to throw Excalibur into the water. And then three ladies came and took him away in a boat, to the Isle of Avilion, to wait for a change of days.'

'Ah, yes, the prophecy,' murmured Merlin. 'I made it myself, you know. *Rex Quondam et Rex Futurus* – the Once and Future King. So, Artos will be at rest then, these many centuries. Lie down with me again, my Pip,' he said gently. 'It has been so long since anyone loved me.'

'Yes,' breathed Phillip, as wise hands touched his body.

Merlin tasted sweet, like oak flowers, and the scent of his skin was mossy and woody, deep and musky. Phillip sank into the magician's embrace, already bewitched, and almost weeping with delight.

Phillip woke and turned drowsily in the young man's arms. He had been half afraid that Merlin would have vanished, but he was still there, lying on their purple cloak in the warm dappled shade under his parent oak.

'I listened, you know,' said Merlin in his woody, tenor voice. 'All the time I was enclosed. In the winter the tree and I slept, we woke alert in the spring, enjoyed the summer, and dozed again in autumn. And although I was captive I was not in pain: I had no body but the tree's. Mostly I drowsed. But I listened to the passing humans, I heard men making love under my boughs.'

'What did you hear?' asked Phillip, kissing the chest on which he was pillowing his cheek.

'I heard the Saxons coax *hunig* to their lovers; then the Normans – they had more words. 'Mon brave, mon ame, mon amour, mon cher, mon p'tit chou', and then came the English who speak as you do, my honey, my heart, my dearling, myn lyking. I would say all these words to myself, thinking that if ever I was released and found a man to love, I would say every one of them. And I would never stop saying them.'

Phillip smiled hopefully. 'Sweeting, will you stay here and use these words on none but me?'

'Oh, yes,' Merlin replied. 'If you want me.'

'Never doubt that.' Phillip stretched. 'But suddenly I am very hungry. Will you come into the castle? I would show you your new home and perhaps find you some clothes.'

Merlin laughed, then stood up with his hand against the tree. He made a small gesture, and was clothed in his long white robe and purple cloak. He watched as Phillip re-assembled his own wardrobe: stockings, breechclout, trunk hose, codpiece, belt, shirt and doublet.

'What are those?' he asked.

'Trunk hose,' said Phillip.

'Your clothes are strange and interesting,' commented the wizard. 'I shall have to examine them more closely before I can produce copies. But will this do for now?' he asked.

'Certainly,' said Phillip. 'You look beautiful. Now take my hand, or I shall believe that I imagined you.'

Merlin took his hand. It was a definite clasp, fingers and palm. Phillip's imagination was good, but it was not *that* good.

At a late dinner, Merlin tasted new fruits and complimented the cooks and drank a little red wine of Portugal, well diluted with spring water. Phillip had never had such an interesting guest but soon found himself telling Merlin about the court of the Great Queen Elizabeth, by Grace of God, Queen of the English, and how she had come to the throne and the trouble with the Spanish and sometimes the French, and the many voyages of discovery undertaken by her great sea captains.

Merlin chuckled. 'Women, like men, love power. This one seems to be a better bet than her father or her siblings. At least she loves the country. Countries know if they are loved; particularly England. It is no common earth, the Island of Britain. She knows her friends.'

'Was Artos her friend?' asked Phillip.

'He was,' said Merlin.

'Merlin, how much magic can you do?' asked Phillip.

'As much as I ever could, my heart. Why do you ask?'

'Don't you want to bring your Artos back?' asked Phillip,

biting his lip on a surge of quite-unbecoming jealousy.

Merlin took his hand and kissed it. 'Artos is gone. He was of his time and cannot be summoned out of it. But you are here, and so am I. And that is where we should be.'

Phillip smiled. 'So it is,' he said, and poured more wine.

Three hours later, when it was fully dark, the lookout's boy rushed into the hall, fell at Phillip's feet, and gasped 'Master, Master, the beacons are lit! The Spanish fleet is sailing!'

'Is our beacon afire?' demanded Phillip.

'Yes, Master,' panted the boy.

'Here, drink this wine and sit while you catch your breath.'

Phillip turned to Merlin. 'Will you come with me?'

'Where else should I be?' the wizard said.

And so Myrddin Ambrosianus, the great wizard Merlin, followed Phillip Beckford, 2nd Earl of Doveton, as he strode through the hall, calling, 'Turn out the guard! Tom, my armour!'

Phillip stopped suddenly and turned to his lover. 'My dear, can I get you a weapon?'

'I need none,' Merlin said. 'But I will meet you outside.'

Aware his great hall now bustled with the noise of men preparing to defend the castle – or indeed the country – Phillip's attention was nonetheless on Merlin who took a sharp knife, a draught of wine and a napkin and went out into the darkness, moving surely on his hard bare feet.

Then the multifarious tasks claimed him for an hour. When Phillip walked out of the great house to mount his horse, Coalblack, he found the wizard standing, waiting for him. He was still clad in white and purple, but he had a bloodstained napkin trussed around his left arm. And in his hand he held a long, strong oak staff.

'The tree required a sacrifice,' said the wizard. 'It is nothing. Where is your enemy?'

'Mount and ride,' ordered Phillip. The wizard sat as easily in a saddle as a chair.

An hour later, they stood on the edge of the cliff high above the small village of Amberly, and looked at the huge array of ships sailing towards the coast. Phillip had never seen so many vessels. The full moon picked steel and silver from their decks and masts.

'They do not mean to go ashore here,' said Phillip's armour bearer, Tom. 'That's good, isn't it, Master?'

'And if they invade, my boy, what place will be safe from the Inquisition? They will light the fires of Smithfield all over England. And the ocean's as flat as a plate! Oh, for a witch who can whistle a wind!'

'Why should you need a witch?' asked Merlin in a low, amused voice. 'I was a tree for many winters and know winds as only a tree can.

'And their ships,' he said, lifting the staff, 'are made of wood. Tell your brave men to fall back, myn lyking, and get the horses far from the edge. And you go back, as well.'

'No,' said Phillip. 'I just found you, I'm not leaving.'

He dismounted, gave the horses to Tom, and ordered the castle guard down to the grain silo in Amberly, where they could shelter from any storm.

'My love,' said Merlin, fondly. 'You have your syrinx?'

'I have,' said Phillip.

'Then we shall play such a song as the winds will answer,' said Merlin, and raised the staff, beginning to sing in a low, rumbling monotone. Phillip followed the notes, shrill and high, and, now summoned, the air began to thicken and keen as a wild wind rose and roared.

Down in the village the sound of the storm was terrifying but even so the guard, safe in the silo, could still hear the high piercing melody of their lord's syrinx, and the low vocal notes underneath it.

As the gale picked up the waves responded. Into the song and the howl of the wind was woven the grinding of sand on shoals and the crashing of the flood and splintering timber on cliffs and rocks. And all in the village of Amberly heard the screaming of sailors and the smashing of ships. There would be a fine harvest of broken keels tomorrow, for the gleaners to feed their fires.

Sometime later – when the storm had quietened and the moon had gone down – the guard ventured up onto the cliff. They found their master and his strange guest, locked in each other's arms, lying soaking and freezing on the rocks. They carried them home in the pelting rain.

Phillip woke, warm and dry and cosy, in his own bed. At first he wondered if he had been fevered and dreamed, but then he sneezed and brushed a tress of oak-bark hair from across his nose. Merlin was there, deep asleep.

Someone had brought them home, dried and put them to bed; together. The fire in the room was just burning down. It was late afternoon.

'Master?' asked Tom, who was bringing in more logs.

'Tom, my boy, how goes the day?' whispered Phillip.

'The Armada is mostly wrecked, Master,' Tom told him. 'It was that God-given storm, Master, that's what we are all saying. That you prayed to the Lord and our Heavenly Father, He sent the storm. And Saint George. Some people are saying they saw him, marching over the waves.'

'That's a good thing for you to say, Tom,' said Phillip.

He looked around the room. Merlin's staff and his own syrinx lay shattered on a purple cloak. That did not matter. Both could be replaced. And Merlin was lying beside him, sleeping, his leaf-green eyes closed; a lover who would not leave and would not die. That oak tree still had a good hundred years left.

It was probably just a coincidence (though there has never been a better-informed monarch than Elizabeth Regina) that when My Lord Phillip of Doveton was awarded a Royal Mark of Favour for his readiness and defence during the Great Armada, it was a medallion with Saint George on the face, and, on the obverse, an oak tree.

THE HIGHWAYMAN

ST ALBANS, THE GREAT NORTH ROAD, 1740

'Stand!' cried a voice. 'Stand and deliver!'

The horseman pulled on the reins and the mare halted. The rider turned his head and found that a flintlock barrel was being brandished far too close to his face. The masked highwayman was wearing a felt hat which had seen better years and a red handkerchief across his mouth. Tendrils of golden hair curled out from under it.

'Very well,' said the rider, 'I'm standing. What would you like me to deliver?'

'Purse, rings, gold,' said the highwayman.

'Oh, no, I don't think so,' drawled the rider. 'I really don't have time to be robbed by an amateur today.' Swiftly, he grabbed the barrel, forced the gun from the highwayman's hand, and struck him across the temple with the stock. The hat fell off and the rider was faced with a very pretty young man, clutching his head and about to burst into tears.

'God's nightgown, cully, what made you take to crime?' demanded the rider. 'You've precious little talent for it! Come along, there's an inn near here, I'll buy you a pint and you can tell me about it. Up we go, Dowsabelle, my love,' he said to his horse. 'There's a bran mash waiting for you at the Silent Woman.'

'Ain't you going to turn me in?' asked the young man.

'Tare 'n 'ounds' boy, don't you know me?' asked the rider, exasperated. The boy looked at him. Hawk-featured, black hair in a queue, streaked with silver, long hands with a flawed emerald on the forefinger, horse called Dowsabelle. Oh. He blushed and hung his aching head.

'You're Matthew Benjamin, the Famous and Notorious Highwayman?' he asked in a small voice.

Matthew swept off his feathered hat and bowed. 'The very same. Delighted to make your acquaintance, my dear.'

'Oh, I am such a fool,' whispered the young man.

'Come, take heart, we all make mistakes. What's your name?'

'Jeremiah,' whispered the boy. 'They call me Jem.'

'Then come along, Jemmy, 'tis a tolerably sharp day and Dowsabelle wants her bran mash.'

Jemmy came quietly.

The Silent Woman was a busy coaching inn on the Great North Road. The sign was a woman holding her head under her arm. "If she be silent, why should men dispute?" the caption asked. It was locally considered to be a fair question.

Matthew Benjamin was evidently known here. He led Dowsabelle and Jem's farm horse into the stable, rubbed her down, made sure that she had her bran mash, and reached a small parlour by way of the kitchen. There Matthew sat down, doffed his hat, and put his feet up on a hassock. There were pots of beer on the small table and several new clay pipes. Jem shifted from one ill-shod foot to another. He was not used to the company of gentlemen. Especially masterful, handsome gentlemen who had taken possession of his life so suddenly. Matthew waved at him.

'Sit down, cully, don't loom. Have some beer and pass me a pipe and the tobacco. There. All right?'

Jem gulped, blew foam off his nose, and nodded.

'Now what has caused a good yokel like you to take to crime?' asked the highwayman. He had an educated voice, sharp and quick, and it was impossible not to answer his questions. Jem gulped more beer.

'My brother, Isaiah,' he said. 'In the holding cells, taken for poaching. Gaol delivery's two days away. I can bribe him out, but I need palm-oil.'

'So you thought you'd take to the High Toby?' asked Benjamin, puffing a cloud of white smoke.

Jeremiah blushed again. 'I'm sorry,' he muttered.

'Tol-lol, Jem, it's just fortunate that you decided on pointing that barker at me. You might have had to shoot someone if they'd panicked. And you don't want to do that,' said the highwayman softly. 'So, how else can we raise the gelt for your brother? I haven't a tosser to my kick.'

'We?' asked Jemmy.

Matthew Benjamin blew more smoke and smiled at Jemmy. He was very good looking, this stout yokel. This curly hair was just the shine of guinea gold, and his eyes were as blue as hyacinths. Matthew was greatly taken with him.

'Ay, both of us, I've conceived a fancy for you, Jemmy. Most brothers would not go to such lengths. Especially now, when you could get forty pound reward for me. And it hasn't even occurred to you to turn me in.'

'O' course not!' protested Jem indignantly. Matthew patted his shoulder.

'My point exactly. So, where are they holding your Isaiah?'

'Lock up on Squire's land,' said Jem. 'With all the others.'

'Right. How many guards?'

'Two, but one goes off to buy ale at about seven, and for his supper; and then the other in turn, so there's only one on duty for those two hours. And the one I had a mind to bribe is Jacob Harkness, a fat greasy pig, mistreats the prisoners. But he has a ready palm.'

'Sounds like he has a pate begging for a blow,' observed Matthew. 'A little crack might let in some ethics.'

'You think we can break Isaiah out?' asked Jem breathlessly. 'But what of the others?'

'They will run away too, and create a great number of false

trails,' replied Benjamin. 'Where are you sending your brother if we can release him?'

'Into Scotland,' replied the young man. 'Got relatives. He can put on a Scotch voice, too. There's a coach. I've got the gelt for the ticket.'

'Well, then, let's us have Molly the landlady put up a nice little basket for him, and go load Isaiah on the Edinburgh coach for freedom,' said Matthew Benjamin. Jem snatched at his immaculate sleeve.

'If you can do this,' he said, leaning up so that he could see into Matthew's eyes. They were green and very bright. 'I will do anything, anything at all, for you.'

'Agreeably unconditional, by God,' said Benjamin, and caught the young man's chin, pulling him up into a deep kiss. Jem flushed and pressed closer. It was clear that he wanted this encounter. So did Matthew.

Therefore, he must rescue this delightful countryman's brother, and then take Jem back to the inn to ravish him senseless.

That sounded like a procedure. So he carried it out.

The dishonest guard went down without a sound. Matthew harvested his keys and opened the door. The miasma which flooded out would have turned the stomach of a crocodile. Matthew took up the guard's gun, though by the look of the rusty barrel, it would be unlikely to fire anywhere but possibly backwards.

'Go in, Jem, find your brother, urge these poor people out, tell them to carry anyone who cannot walk. And shift your arse, we don't want no hullabulloo.'

Jem put his handkerchief back over his nose and people began to issue forth, coughing, weeping, moving always away towards the forest. Jem came out dragging his brother by the hand.

Matthew dropped the useless gun and retreated with his

prize. He wiped Isaiah's face, dusted off his hat, put the basket in his hand, and, clad in Jem's coat, escorted him onto the Edinburgh stage. The last he saw of Isaiah was an astonished face, already delving into the basket for bread and cheese and stuffing food into his mouth.

'Back to the inn,' said Matthew. 'Someone is going to notice that the birds have flown about–' a trumpet call and a halloo! broke the silence, '…now.'

He took Jem's hand and led him swiftly through various stairs and tunnels until they emerged into a small suite of rooms. By the feel of them, Jem thought, they were underground. Air came in through vents in the roof. A barrel of water stood by a tin bath, which held a dipper and French soap scented with lavender. A grate drained the floor. A hearth was provided with a large kettle, and a small fire was already burning on it. A sumptuous bed was spread with quilts, and the highwayman's wardrobe was folded into chests, on which reposed his boots. A table held food and wine.

'A wash,' suggested Benjamin. He stripped unaffectedly, soaped, rinsed and dried his body, and donned his silk dressing gown. Jem, blushing, did the same. Matthew had been slim, muscular and graceful. Jem felt like a heifer compared to a deer.

'Or shall I help you?' asked Benjamin, smiling wickedly. Jem took his hands away from his body and stretched out his arms.

'I'm all yours, master,' he said, and Benjamin, washed him very gently, every touch electric, until Jem was writhing for release and begging for more friction. He slid his hands in under the dressing gown, catching nipples in his calloused hands, and finally, at last, Matthew laid him down and proceeded to ravish him senseless, as he intended.

'Matt?' mumbled Jeremiah.

'Mmm?' replied the highwayman, who was drowsing in luxurious splendour.

'Don't send me away. I'm yours now.'

'I won't,' murmured Matthew. 'I can't, not now. Even though you're likely to get me killed, or I'm likely to get you killed. We'll both be riding the horse foaled by the acorn, Jemmy, if you stay with me.'

'Aye, maybe,' said Jemmy, nuzzling his neck. He was a beautiful, solid armload of pure animal heat, scented with French soap. 'But until then, there's us.'

'There is,' sighed Matthew Benjamin, and kissed him again.

RED RIDING HOOD

ENGLAND, 1812

The child looked cold and lost, so Hal leaned down and asked, 'Where are you going?'

'To Grandma's house,' she piped. 'With this basket.'

'That would be Grandma Boone?' he asked. 'You're Robin?'

'Yes, who are you?' asked the child, looking up at the tall solder in his battered, splendid uniform and red cloak. She liked his deep voice and when he smiled his kind brown eyes sparkled.

Hal was a little surprised the girl could understand him, so sure he was that he'd shed his country burr from being so long away, fighting on the Iberian Peninsula.

'I'm Hal Baker, your cousin. Is it not a bit late for you to be out? It's getting dark and I think it's going to snow. But as I'm going that way anyway, why don't you give me the basket.'

Robin looked dubious and Hal realised she might be reproved for giving away a valuable basket stuffed with goodies to a random stranger. He smiled and added, 'And tell your mother, my Aunt Chloe, that I'll call tomorrow and tell her how her mother is managing.'

'Thanks, Cousin!' squeaked the child, and ran away, back down the path to her house.

Hal hefted the basket and walked on, with his easy soldier's stride, into the darkening wood. The full moon was already riding high, silver as the coins he had grabbed from a certain baggage train.

It was getting colder, presaging snow, and the ache in his

leg, wounded at Salamanca, intensified. He really wasn't used to the English climate anymore, he thought. I had better get where I am going. Grandma Boone use to live – where? Down this path? I don't remember this wood anymore, he thought sadly. I used to know it so well. I played here with my friends, with dear Tommy and Danny. I wonder where they are now.

He stopped trying to map the forest in his head and just walked, coming upon the small thatched cottage almost where he thought it might be. Snow started to fall as he pushed at the back door and found it, as usual, open.

There was no light but the fire. A shawled and lace capped figure sat in the big bed.

'Well, Grandma Boone, how are you this cold night?' he asked, but she did not reply.

Hal dropped his pack, deposited the basket on the kitchen table, and threw an armload of kindling onto the dying fire. Then he swung the kettle onto the hob and shed his red cloak over the settle. He sat down and sighed, rubbing at his aching thigh. He had been happy in the army. He was sorry not to be there, at the triumph he was sure would take place. He would never see Wellington ride into Paris. He had seen many things in Portugal and Spain, and now he was home, he did not know how he was going to stand the loneliness. No one knew what he knew, had been where he'd been. And with this injured leg, no army would have him back.

He shook himself and unpacked the basket. Small fruitcakes, a pot of milk, a pat of butter and some sugar in a screw of blue paper. Hal found the tea and the teapot. He poured boiling water over the leaves, inhaling with pleasure. Tea was something he had certainly missed. He poured a cup for the old lady and approached the bed.

'Grandma Boone?' he asked. The lace capped head tilted a little. He could see the gleam of dark eyes.

'Why, Grandma,' he commented. 'What big eyes you have.'

'All the better to see you with, my dear,' came a voice which might have been a very old woman's. He looked hard at the lace cap. It was lumpy.

'And, Grandma, what big ears you have!' he exclaimed.

'All the better to hear you with, my dear,' said he old woman's voice.

'And what big teeth you have,' he observed, 'putting down the cup.

'All the better to eat you with, my dear!' growled the figure, and found itself grabbed, mid leap, and pinned down by hands which had been lethal on many a battlefield.

'You shouldn't play with your food. Didn't your mother tell you that?' The wolf struggled. 'Lie still, wolf, or I will snap your neck,' growled the soldier. 'What have you done with Grandma Boone? Where is she?'

'I don't know, she wasn't here when I came in,' protested the wolf. 'Ouch,' it added.

'Hoping for little girl for dinner?' asked Hal, one hand fisted in the wolf's ruff and one slamming his hindquarters flat.

'They're tasty,' admitted the wolf. 'You would have been a fuller meal. I might have had to store a few bits of you for a few days, to soften.'

'But now?' asked Hal.

'I am at point non plus,' admitted the wolf. 'You're not frightened of me?'

'No,' said Hal. 'I have seen *loups garoux* before.'

'Where?' asked the wolf, sounding a little muffled, nose in pillow.

'Portugal, in the mountains. They attacked our camp. A musket ball restricted their ambitions, as it will do for you. '

'I really don't know what to say,' said the wolf.

'If I let go, will you attack me?' asked the soldier.

'No, I'd really like to talk to you rather than tear out your throat. Though that remains a possibility, you understand.'

'Good,' Hal gradually released the wolf, who shed the old lady's garments, shook its fur into order, and sprawled on the bed.

Hal sat down beside him and took up the cup. 'Please refrain from tearing out my throat until I have finished this tea,' he instructed.

The wolf nodded, taking in Hal's uniform and almost offensive lack of fear. The soldier emptied the cup, then took the other which he had prepared for himself and sipped with great pleasure. Milk *and* sugar. Pure luxury.

'That's where this happened to me,' the wolf told him. 'Where I was bitten.'

'Portugal?' asked Hal.

'Yes. I was sleeping in my tent, the next moment, teeth were in my neck. I thought that it would kill me, but I was rescued. Unfortunately. The French attacked. They sent me to a surgeon, he stitched me up, I was a happy enough prisoner until–'

'The next full moon?' guessed Hal. The wolf sighed.

'Yes. I escaped the prison easily enough, slunk aboard a fishing craft, slunk ashore somewhere on the coast, and slunk all the way home.'

'You're from here? Do I know you?' asked Hal.

'Who are you?' asked the wolf, tilting his head to eye the soldier more closely.

'Hal Baker, late Corporal of the Northumberland Fusiliers.' Hal stood up and saluted. 'Invalided out after Salamanca. Shot in the leg. It's serviceable 'nough, but I can't march. I slunk home, too, my wolf. And now I don't belong here. I don't belong anywhere.'

'Try having paws and fur and fangs and a terrible desire to tear out throats. I don't belong anywhere, either. My name was Tommy, and you were my friend.'

'God, Tommy, Dammit, I was so looking forward to meeting you again!' Hal dragged the wolf into a close embrace. After a startled moment, the wolf nosed him, huffing into his neck, absorbing his scent. Hal lay down, and the wolf curled up almost in his lap, licking his hands.

'You joined the army, too?' asked Hal.

'Just after you. And, as I said, in Portugal the loups got me, and here I am.'

'And here I am, too,' said Hal. 'I loved you, my Tom.'

The wolf licked his hand again, then reached up and licked his face.

'I love you, too. But there isn't much I can do to prove it at present. In any case, you need to shoot me. If you have a silver coin you ought to be able to beat it into a pellet which can be fired out of your musket.'

'Don't be foolish, wolf. How many little girls have you actually eaten around here?'

The wolf looked ashamed. He hung his head and licked a paw nervously.

'Er, well, none. I haven't eaten any people. Just deer. Human blood smells delicious, but I think I came in here to try to be a real werewolf. I don't know if I could have done it. I'm a failure at being a werewolf, as well as everything else.'

'No, listen,' urged Hal, scratching the wolf's ears. 'How much news of the war have you heard?'

'Not much,' confessed Tommy.

'There was a great battle at a place called Salamanca. We captured the baggage train and found a lot of gold coins. The others went straight for them, but I knew there'd be trouble about gold, so I collected a knapsack full of silver. I was wounded and waiting for the surgeon, so I sewed my coins into an ammunition belt and put it back around my waist. I changed them in London. I've got enough money to buy a house and to live on for the rest of my days. Come and live with me.'

'But I turn into a wolf for three days at the full moon!' protested Tommy,

'I limp on my left leg,' returned Hal. 'We all have our problems. Can you change back into a man at all?'

'I only have to be a wolf in direct moonlight,' said the wolf. 'I can turn back into a man if you want me to be a man.'

'Do you agree? Live with me? Think of what successful hunters we could be! I can put a collar on you so that no one will think you are anything but a dog, though you are a beautiful, silver-furred animal of great magnificence,' added Hal, as the wolf seemed insulted. 'If you agree, bring my dear Tommy back to me. I have missed him for a whole war, over the seas, through Portugal and Spain, fire and smoke, blood and death and fever and very poor rations.'

There was an eye-tearing moment, the air blurred, and lying in Hal's lap was a naked man of great magnificence, his hair silvering in the firelight. Hal leaned down and kissed him, and was kissed and then licked in his turn.

'Build up the fire, take off those military rags, and come to bed,' said Tommy. 'Oh my dear fellow. It's snowing. Without my fur, I'm cold.'

Hal did as he was bid, barring the door of the small house. When he padded back to bed, his feet icy on the stone floor, the wolf and Tommy both dragged him into their arms and they fell into each other's embrace with gladness.

In the morning, Grandma Boone returned, having been detained at a lying in. She sold Tommy suitable clothes and even a pair of her late husband's boots. Hal introduced him as a soldier overcome with fever, having torn off his garments and thrown them away in his delirium. Grandma Boone, who needed the money and didn't need the clothes, did not question the story.

When the woodcutter, who had followed wolf prints to the very door, burst in to rescue the inhabitants, they had to give him quite a lot of money to go away.

The Old Bullock Dray

Roll up your swags, boys, let's make a push!
I'll take you up the country and show you the bush
You know you won't get such a chance another day
So come and take possession of the old bullock dray

GEELONG, AUGUST 1841

Just past the long dry plain, near a shaded gully with a sparkling little brook running through it, Miss Drysdale called a halt.

'Have a rest, boys,' she said in her clear, clipped Edinburgh accent, much like my own. 'Water for the bullocks, if you please, Mr Grahame.'

As I summoned a couple of other convicts to slide down to the water with the buckets, I heard Miss D soothing her companion, Miss Newcombe, who found the motion of the dray unsettling. 'You shall have a cup of tea, presently, my honey,' I heard her say. 'And then perhaps you might like to get out and walk, now the heat of the day has passed.'

Miss N made a murmuring reply, and I smiled to myself. That was the most passionate of passionate friendships. In fact, you could call this journey to their new agricultural lease an elopement. Miss D had been staying with the Rev Alexander Thomas, en route to her leasehold, with a hundred sheep, miscellaneous animals and stores, twenty convicts (including me) and her huge tabby cat, Nimrod, swearing in his basket. When she left she had some useful advice, more stores, more tools, a group of goats, a house cow in milk and – Miss Caroline Newcomb, the Rev's governess, who had quite thrown her bonnet over the windmill for her commanding, dark-eyed older lady.

I liked Miss Drysdale fine. She was exact, just and sure. She knew what she wanted, and meant to get it. She had already sent one guard back to Geelong for mistreating a convict. With only two others, she ought to have felt unsafe, just herself and her lady, and us fierce lawbreakers.

But we were promised a ticket of leave by the Governor La Trobe himself, if we gave no trouble and established Miss D's sheep farm and built her house. I wouldn't be a lot of use in that, being crippled, but I could stitch, weave, sew and mend. I could also cook. And I got on very well with the bullock team. So Miss D had made me a bullocky. I did not shout and swear and lash them. I coaxed and sang and talked to them. I noticed that they liked conversation. I had given them names, and they answered to them: six fine animals, Isaac, Aaron, Job (the creature always looked put-upon, even when nose deep in hay) Mari, Delphine and Elijah. I was fond of them.

Little fires had been lit in the shade. Tea was brewing. Miss D did not stint. She wanted us to work, and that meant she had to feed us properly, and she even had some tobacco for the evenings, issued per man. No, if I had to be out here in this Godforsaken country, instead of home in Edinburgh, I was happy enough with my situation. Miss D liked my voice, and sometimes joined in the long discourses with the beasts as she walked beside us with her long, hill-woman's stride.

I added some warm water from a billy to the bullocks' drink and attended them all, in order. First my lead beast, Isaac, right down to the smallest, Delphine. Then I accepted a cup of tea myself. With milk, for the redoubtable Miss D had milked the cow. I sat down on the dray and looked around.

This was good sheep country. Wide, grassy plains, golden with kangaroo grass. Water from the Barwon River and from all these little burns. It was a pity that the place was infested with more stinging flies, mosquitoes and dangerous serpents than Satan had ever devised. The men knew enough to beat the banks of the little stream with branches, to frighten them away.

The sheep came up and collapsed in the shade. Tom Davis ran out the canvas trough to water them all. August was only spring in this upside down place. God alone knew what summer would be like. I was glad of my calico shirt and my wide cabbage tree hat. That sun would cook those foolish enough to strip off their shirts. The dogs drank, moving the sheep aside so that they all got a place at the trough.

'We'll spend the night here,' decided Miss D. 'Get the dray off the road, Mr Grahame, if you would be so good, and we can unpack the tents. Muster your men, Guard.'

I drove the wagon into the middle of a flat field, released the traces and tug girths, and allowed them to walk out. They would not stray. Neither would we, because, indeed, where was there to go in this vast and empty land? And how far would I get, on my crutches?

I settled the bullocks inside their temporary fence, washed in the refilled trough, and found my own tent. I cooked myself a damper and ate it with some Portable Soup. I smoked my tobacco ration, and put myself to bed. The dogs and shepherds were ranging out around their flocks. We would have warning if anything happened. The stars blazed down. All was calm.

I woke abruptly as someone dived into my little tent. A hunted thing, panting. I put out a hand in the dark and felt bare flesh, ribs and hip bone: a man. I clenched a fist to strike when he whispered 'Oh, Jock Grahame, mercy, let me hide here!'

'Tammas?' I whispered. I had noticed him, a good looking Hebridean, curly red hair, tallish, could sing like a bird in the Gaelic. A sweet nature. He brought fresh grass to the bullocks, because he had never seen beasts so great. I patted him.

'What's come to you, man?'

'They found out,' he fell on my bosom and wept. 'I was transported for sodomy. They found out and were minded to–'

'I see,' I said. 'There, there, Tammas, lie down, lie still. I'll not harm you. Catch your breath, now. Who's hunting you?'

'Rob, Nobby, the Cockney, that bastard Jones.'

This was bad. Rob was a moron who would follow anyone; Nobby was a grey Liverpool oaf, the Cockney gave Englishmen a bad name; and the red-faced bully called Jones was a guard. The other three could be dealt with easily enough. But Jones was Official. I thought about our predicament as poor Tammas' heart hammered against my breast.

'I see a solution,' I told him. 'Now, have a sup of this from my bottle, Tammas, and tomorrow I shall tell Miss D that I need an offsider. You shall ride in the wagon with me. That way we don't need to peach. There, now. You're safe. Sleep,' I soothed.

He fell asleep in my arms. I felt a response in my treacherous body. But such a thing was not to be thought of. Finally, the shouting and barking died down and I fell asleep, too.

I had never slept so well.

I woke as Miss Newcomb's rooster announced that it was morning. I left my bedmate sleeping, made tea and crept to the dray, where the ladies reposed in one bed. I said, very low, 'Miss Drysdale, I have made you some tea, may I speak with you?'

She emerged clad in a long flannel night shirt, took the tea, and sat on the dray, legs swinging. At this time she looked like any lass, out on a picnic. Her severe features had softened, her hair was loose, her eyes sparkled. Miss Newcomb's company was tonic for her, that was plain. She took the tea and swigged.

'Will you allow me to take an offsider from amongst the convicts?' I asked, still very quietly.

Her eyes bored several holes in me. She must have heard that hallooing after my Tammas last night. Not much got past Miss D.

'It is customary,' she answered me. 'If you tell me it is necessary, I will grant it.'

'Oh, indeed,' I said. She gave the empty tin mug back into my hand.

'Very well, Mister Grahame,' she smiled suddenly and clapped me on the shoulder. 'It's a grand morning and we shall reach our destination today.'

Nimrod leapt up onto the dray, carrying something feathery. His hunting had been good. He had brought Miss Drysdale what looked a little like a quail. He was a paternal cat. He chirruped at her to eat it while it was fresh. She laughed and crawled back into the dray. I heard Miss N give a soft, sleepy giggle. I thought they might understand about Tammas.

Thereafter, Tammas rode with me, learned how to drive the beasts, and shared my tent. Once it was clear that we had outwitted them without informing on them, Jones and his cronies stopped harassing my Tammas. We went along very pleasantly, with Elijah and Aaron, especially, appreciating the sweet Highland songs with which Tammas, released from terror, serenaded them.

We set up camp as usual, and now – as Miss D said to Miss N, we were home. No one kissed me as I said it, but that was not unusual. Who would want such as me? Tammas was affectionate to me, but that was only because I was his protection from that gang of rapists. He had a gentle nature, that was all.

We were organised into groups. Tammas and me for the house, and to take the bullocks to the timber cutting and drag the logs home. Jones and his mob were sent to the sawpit. I suspect that Miss D had deduced what we hadn't told her. It would be a solid but modest house, and we could stay under canvas until it was finished. It wasn't going to rain any time soon, if it ever did.

McAlister, a Tipperary man transported for some political crime, took charge of the goats, and the sheep had their own shepherds and dogs. Miss Newcomb cared for the poultry. For the moment, we drove them under the dray at night, and netted the wheels. Nimrod would give an alarm if anyone came near. He objected to the wild dogs they called dingoes. And he positively delighted in killing serpents.

He dragged his latest prize into the camp as I was setting up my baking oven. It was a really big snake.

Miss D asked, 'I wonder what it tastes like? I'm a mite tired of endless bully beef and unidentified small birds.'

'I shall cook it for you, Madam,' I bowed from my crutches, 'if Tammas will bring me a pot and a skinning knife.'

'And I,' said Tammas shyly, 'can make you a belt of the skin, Ma'am.'

She smiled at us. I assembled vinegar, salt, and my best small pot. Tammas skinned and gutted the snake and cut it into sections.

'It's not one of the poisonous ones,' he commented. 'See,' he laid the mouth open over his knife. 'Just ordinary teeth, like. I reckon it'll cook up nice, like eel.'

'Best give a bit to Nimrod,' I remarked, as the cat put a clawed paw on Tammas' knee. Tammas obliged. Nimrod had a lot in common with his mistress. They both knew their due. And meant to have it to the last scruple. The snake tasted slightly fishy, but quite pleasant and a change from tinned beef.

The dimensions of the house were laid out, the first lot of logs sawed, and a more permanent camp set up, privies dug. A large shelter was made with spare canvas, the kitchen was established and the dray parked in the middle, with the bullocks all round, grazing.

We should have been comfortable, but I was uneasy. First, because I had fallen in love with Tammas. Sleeping next to him every night was torture of the most refined kind. He was so beautiful to me, under the odd light of those strange stars. He would turn confidingly to me in his sleep and lay his head on my shoulder. I burned for him.

And the next was, those four were plotting. I could see them together as we lay around the fire, smoking our tobacco and drinking tea. Every now and again Nobby or Jones would speak, stare at Tammas across the fire, and return to their conversation. I wished I had a gun. I swore I would shoot them down to welter in their blood before they laid an unclean paw on my dearie.

And considering that I had been condemned and transported for forgery, and could hardly stir a step without my props, that was an absurd thing for such as me to vow. But I vowed it by Heaven. Tammas knew something was in the wind, as well. He stayed close by my side.

The attack came as we were hauling a huge log back to the camp. Tammas was at Elijah's head, urging him on, I was behind, leaning on the log. It was very heavy and we shoved and sweated and swore – I was compiling quite a lexicon of Gaelic oaths – when someone hit me from behind and I fell, face first, into mud.

Jones cried out, 'Grab him, boys, and we shall have him, one after the other, the little Scotch whore! We just need to get shot of his minder!' I was rolled in the churned-up earth, the four of them kicking me, and I commended my soul to God when I heard a shriek of rage such as I had never heard before. Tammas loosed the chains from the bullock with a deft twist, turned him, and bore down on my attackers, his red hair flaming like his ancestors, screaming a war cry. It was *Buaidh no bas*! And it sounded like nothing on earth. No wonder the Romans had been so afraid of the clans.

With fast, merciless slashes and flicks of the stock whip, he lashed one, two, aside with red wounds on their faces, hauled me onto the bullock, then beat the others without pity or cessation, screaming Victory or Death!, until they turned and fled.

I don't recall the journey back to camp, but they say that Miss D stared at Tammas and the whip, me lying over the bullock almost dead and half stifled in mud, and then she fetched her Brown Bess. Miss Newcombe stood beside her, shoulder to shoulder. They were a formidable pair.

When Jones, Nobby, the Cockney and stupid Rob raced back, demanding justice and accusing Tammas of having attacked them, she held them at gunpoint against the tent wall.

'Justice, is it, you would have?' she asked, very clear and cold and clipped. 'Mr McIsaac, take the bullock down to the shallows and wash your master, care for him, I would have him able to speak. I will take the whip. You,' she addressed our attackers, 'Stand still. I acknowledge that I have only one shot, but I will not miss. Who wants to die today?'

They didn't move, displaying unexpected wisdom. I came back to myself as Tammas lowered me into the river and scraped and rinsed until I could see again. His battle rage had left him. He propped me up on his arm and gave me water. Then he kissed me, very gently and tenderly. His lips were soft and unbearably sweet.

'You are my master,' he told me. 'Miss D says so.'

'And you are mine,' I answered, and we kissed, in the dazzle of the light on the water, or was that my tears?

Miss D knew the truth of the matter without any more words. She instructed two of the other convicts, MacKenzie and MacLeod, stout Scotsman like myself, to chain the four, and sent them back to work in the sawpit.

Jones protested. 'I am a soldier, I cannot be chained!' he said.

Miss D smiled a small, cold smile. 'You are no soldier,' she said with devastating iciness. 'You are a disgrace to humanity. You will work in chains like the felon you are. Did you think me a fool, not to see that you have been dogging that young man's footsteps, conspiring to injure him? Or, if you object, you may go to Geelong. It's that way,' she added. 'Quite a long walk. But if you leave, and I see you again, I will shoot you through the heart.'

Jones hung his head. My fellow countrymen heaped him with the heaviest chains. There was no one that he hadn't hurt with his endless little cruelties. Jones was not going to have a happy time amongst the convicts.

Miss D dismissed Tammas and I to collect some provisions, go to our tent and recuperate. We obeyed. He helped me halt along, arm over his shoulders, and when we lay down together I knew that no man could have greater happiness than mine. And he said the same, nestling into my embrace, stroking and caressing me.

'I always wanted you,' he whispered. 'Why did you think that I chose your tent for refuge when they were hunting me?'

'Oh, my own dear,' I sighed.

We're old now. I have surrendered the dairy to a maid, the kitchen to a cook, and the bullocks ended their long lives, dying of old age, in these green meadows. I would not let them be butchered, but buried them under their own gravestones, near the stone which marks the resting place of that mighty hunter, Nimrod.

Miss D and Miss N have a fine house, now, and live together in great harmony. Miss D runs the farm, and Miss N the house. Miss D says we should stay here until we die. We have a little house of our own, Tammas makes and repairs furniture, and I make shirts for the household and mend the fine linen.

My Tammas's fiery hair has faded. Mine is white. But never once, not once, in all the time we have lived together, have I forgotten that shriek of pure, naked rage, *Buaith no bas!* as Tammas declared his love for a crippled man by driving into a mob which meant him terrible harm.

I have never wavered in my love for him, or he, for me. We are much blessed. God be praised. Amen.

THE PIPES OF LUCKNOW

BRITISH INDIA, LUCKNOW, UTTAR PRADESH, 1857

Eighty days since the beginning of the siege. The air thick with smoke and the stench of death. The sepoy guns never stop.

'There are 8000 attackers and we are the only defenders,' said Colonel Inglis. 'There are 900 of us. There are over two thousand wounded, sick, women and children. We cannot cut our way out to Cawnpore, as General Havelock suggested in his pigeon message. We have to stay. If we leave our non-combatants here to be cut to pieces, raped and mutilated, we have lost India and we deserve to lose it, along with our honour.'

There was a general murmur of agreement. News had come through about the well at Cawnpore, where the bodies of the women and children, murdered under a safe conduct, had been thrown. After atrocities about which the spy would not speak, but went pale and trembled. No. We could not move. If we evacuated them we could not protect them. Therefore, we had to stay.

Besides, I had promised the friend of my heart, my dearest Tammas McIntosh of the 78th Highlanders, that I would meet him here. My Tam would be coming. I did not doubt his will. But I did wonder if he could possibly get here in time.

The engineers reported their saps and tunnels going well, though they would have to be very long to extend past this huge army. As I looked out across the valley, all I could see were the linen garments, the plumes, the tents, the little cooking fires and the ranked flintlocks of the enemy. Our flintlocks, our

143

training. Our ammunition, too, in some cases. Our own army gone rogue after a mad mullah. And me, Evan Davies, aide to the commissioner Thomas Kavanagh, who had gone forth three weeks ago dressed as a sepoy, to find Havelock's army and lead it to our rescue.

He was a wonderful man, Kavanagh Sahib. I had dressed him from the skin out as a common sepoy soldier, loincloth and much washed dhoti, mended shirt, unadorned turban, with the scarf around his arm which marked him as a holy warrior. He had taken nothing that would identify him, not even his wedding ring. I had had to rub his finger with soap to get it off. He had given it to me to mind for him as he tied a rag around the mark. 'Until I come back, Evan lad,' he said, patted my shoulder, and walked quickly into the crowd outside the wicket gate, vanishing into the throng of traders and soldiers and bazaar women. He spoke flawless Hindi and the local dialect. Even his body looked right – meek, lowly, trying to avoid official attention. The sepoy armies were composed of many different forces. He should manage it.

I hoped. I prayed. Because Col Inglis had just distributed to us the bullets which we would use to kill the women and the non-combatants if the sepoys broke in. I had only one – my loader, Eileen McLaren. The others were detailed to kill each other's families. Their fate was bitter. Mine was not noticeably sweet, either, indeed.

I joined a sortie. We frequently slipped out at twilight, when the sepoy changed watches, and set a few little explosive surprises for the enemy. We had been successful. This time, too, we slipped out and slipped back, and nothing blew up until we were safely back in Lucknow.

The 'Bang!' was heartening and destroyed the muezzin tower from which a sniper had been making killing us his holy mission. But I stood watch that night looking at the mountains and wishing with all my heart that they were my own mountains, and that I had never left Yr Wyddfa. Eileen stood beside me.

'They look a little like my own Grampians,' she said.

'I was just thinking that,' I answered. 'Snowden, Mount Snowden, I was thinking of. Eileen, I have to tell you this. Today I had dreadful news and a dreadful task laid on me.'

'I know,' she said calmly. 'We all know.' She's a pretty girl with a mass of blond hair and blue eyes, much to Indian taste. The thought made me shudder.

'And?' I asked. I wanted her to speak, to give me her permission. I am no strong, silent Englishman.

'You can hardly miss me at this range,' she said, smiling. 'I've no taste for violation and torture. I'd like fine to live, but that fate really is worse than death. Just put the pistol barrel into my breast, Evan dear, close your eyes, and pull the trigger. It will be all right, I promise. And for me it will be over in a moment.'

'If it comes to that, for me, too,' I agreed, and we embraced. I never met the limit of her courage. No one else would have comforted her murderer for having to kill her.

'The Colonel's lady is cross with me,' she laughed, taking her place a little behind me as usual, next to the rank of flintlocks, the powder and patch and ball. We had run out of cartridges weeks ago.

'That is not news,' I said. The Colonel's lady did not approve of the girls acting as lookouts and loaders, but she had no choice – there were not enough males to patrol all the walls alone. 'What dreadful crime have you committed now? Has she found out about your Robbie?'

'No, no, Lord bless us and keep us,' she fanned herself. 'My Robbie's away with the 78th Highlanders, like your ain Tammy. No, I took off my corsets, and she disapproved. Especially when I told her I could be raped and murdered just as comfortably wearing corsets as without. It's too hot up here to wear a corset.'

'Indeed, I've abandoned mine entirely,' I said, straight faced. She giggled.

It was quiet for the next hour, and then we were fired upon and returned fire, joining the crackling fusillade, Eileen loading each gun and passing it to me. We worked very smoothly together. We had been doing this for eighty days. Eighty-one.

Then we slept, woke, ate, washed not at all, because there was not a lot of water, then we stood guard again. And another night and another day. I was remembering my Tammy, reciting Burns to me, while we lay wrapped up in his plaid. He was one of the dark Highlanders who recall a Spanish heritage – perhaps someone very attractive swam ashore from a sinking Armada; dark eyes and black hair and swarthy skin, so unlike my scrubby reddish hair and pallor. But he liked the contrast, my Tam, laying his bare chest beside mine, white skin and olive skin.

> I will love ye still, my dear
> Till all the seas gang dry.
> Till all the seas gang dry, my dear
> And the rocks melt wi' the sun:
> And I will love thee still, my dear
> While the sands o' life shall run.

I could hear his sweet Highland voice reciting to me, punctuated with kisses from his mouth, which tasted of honey. So deep in love was I.

It looked like the sands o' life had nearly run through. Our life, at least.

The siege was 87 days old when we got up that morning and knew that today, everyone at Lucknow must die. We were running out of ammunition. The near-constant sepoy firing, which drew our answers and wasted our ammunition, had reduced us to sniping, though some of the inventive boys had made slingshots.

On my battlement I had an attack of *hiraeth*, of longing, yearning. I wanted so badly to be lying in my Tammy's arms, anywhere, even a cowshed, even in deep snow, so that at least we could die together. His blood would mingle with mine, and they could bury us in the same grave. Even more I longed to be back in my own land, listening to the Welsh voices outside the window, stretched out in the same bed with my love, close enough to kiss, close enough to feel his breath on my mouth. While the rest of the world walked to market outside, in the spring, with the daffodils flowering.

Eileen leaned beside me. 'I should ha' lain wi' my Robbie when I could,' she mourned. 'I pushed him awa and prated of my virtue. Fine use my virtue has been!'

'They'll come,' I said, suddenly feeling sure.

'And so will Christmas, but we will no' be here to see it,' she scorned.

I loaded the pistol and laid it on the wall. 'Not yet,' I said. 'Not until they break the doors. Then we can die. Not before then, all right, girl?'

'Not until they break the doors,' she agreed. Our hands on the stone met and clasped. I thought she was going to kiss me, in lieu of her lost Robbie, but then she exclaimed and leaned forward, dangerously far. I grabbed the back of her dress.

'What are you about, you mad wench?' I demanded.

'Listen, you deaf Taffy,' she snarled. 'Can you no' hear it?'

I listened. The rumble of the camp, the sepoy voices, dogs barking, camels, donkeys, cannon, a scatter of shots, usual noises. But she had heard something. I tried to sharpen my hearing. I swallowed and spat. I remembered the psalm singers in the halls of my youth and listened so hard I nearly made my ears bleed.

Then I heard it. Pipes. Highland pipes. Who would have pipes but Havelock? I dragged Eileen into a hard hug. No one played pipes but Highlanders. It must be Havelock. And the 78th Highlanders. And Robbie. And my Tammy at last.

'They're playing *The Black Bear*!' she said.

Then I kissed her.

They were within a mile. They only played *The Black Bear* when they were within a mile of their camp. It was a sprightly little tum-tum-tum tune, meaning, pick up your feet boys, we're nearly home. It grew louder. We heard the brrm brrm brrm of the drums.

Then we screamed our good news down into the Residency and the sepoy heard it too, and the besieging camp erupted into confusion.

It was fine to watch them run like ants, trying to find their commanders, who had retired with their concubines for the night, and we helped along by using some of our scarce ammunition to snipe down into the crowds, spreading confusion and panic, most enjoyable. It was not virtuous, but it made my heart glad, God forgive me.

It was a fierce fight and Havelock lost near five hundred men, but the sepoy died in heaps and ran and scattered, leaving their goods and weapons, and we were saved. Kavanagh had got through and led Havelock by careful ways almost into the enemy's lap. For which he got a Victoria Cross, quite right too. I slipped down into the army camp, following my Eileen. She hunted like a hound, casting about, asking, casting again, until she fell into the delighted arms of her Robbie and cried into his shoulder with joy.

And I searched, further, further, a dreadful fear gripping my heart. Where was my Tam, my dearie, my own dear love? I came into the surgeon's area, where the ground was wet with blood, loud with groaning men, and did not find him.

I had lost heart and was turning to go back into the Residency when someone grabbed me from behind and hugged me so hard that I lost all breath and could only gasp, 'Tammy? Alive?'

'Evan, my dear, and you live too,' he said into the back of my neck. 'Come wi' me, I've a wee heathen tent to myself and a bottle of the good stuff and I must have you, I must, I was so afraid, it was such a long march and...'

I dived into his wee heathen tent, which was hung with tapestries and must have belonged to a minor princeling, took a long gulp of his scotch whisky (where had Tam found Scotch whisky? I decided not to ask) and we tumbled down, me in my rags, him in his bloodstained kilt, both filthy with grime and gunsmoke and the stench of fear, to rut like beasts, biting, bruising, fast and hard until we collapsed on each other and wept until we had no more tears.

'I kept thinking of you,' he said to me. 'Murdered like them at Cawnpore.'

'And I thought of you, shot or speared on a battlefield,' I told him.

'I've got a sackful of gems here,' he said. 'I found them. We'll finish this Mutiny out, my dearie, and then I'll buy mysel' out of the army, and you come wi' me and we can go hame. Wales or Scotland, as you like, as long as I'm wi' you.'

It's a good solid stone house we have, a thorny hedge of red oses, Yr Wyddfa in the distance, a few acres for a cow, and a small treasury still sewn into my East India Company shirt.

It's been 20 years since the Indian Mutiny. They say things are better there now. But I have no wish to return.

Even now, sometimes, particularly during a thunderstorm, I wake screaming and sweating in terror and Tam takes me into his arms and kisses my brow and very quietly hums the tune which means rescue and safety and Tammas McIntosh: *The Black Bear*, as played by the 78th Highland pipes at the Relief of the Siege of Lucknow.

The Last of the Navajo

I was about to start my pre-flight checks when I felt something poke into my back. I assumed it was my co-pilot celebrating the first banana, as he always did at this time of year, until I turned and noticed that the person who was poking me was a strangely-painted, hooded man and the thing with which he was poking was, in fact, a Dreyse needle gun.

And 1868 had started so well. I was happy with my position as Flight Lieutenant Eugene Woodford, in charge of the aerostat Her Majesty's Air Ship Victoria Victrix. We carried cargo, in a long near continuous line of airships, all the way across the Atlantic to The Colony of America, largely self-governing but with 30 members in both Commons and Lords, the same as Australia, India, Canada, South Africa and New Zealand, all part of the British Empire on which the Sun Never Set. Our Queen was Victoria Plantagenet, newest of the ruling house descended from the semi-Divine Richard III. She was small and dark and graceful, like her ancestor. Her younger brother Prince Michael was one of the tall, hefty, blond Plantagenets. Charming fellow. He was Aviator in Chief and often walked down to the yards to speak to the pilots.

And now someone was pointing a dangerous weapon at me on my own flight deck.

Now that I looked at him, rather than the weapon, I realised that he must be one of the Indians, a southern tribe. He was wearing warrior paint, a tricolour stripe across each cheek. Not

an Apache, with their ghost faces. More South, more West. Aha!
I remembered my studies in Ethnology at the famed University
of Atlanta, Georgia.

'Ya-ta-hey,' I greeted him, correctly, with open palms.

He stared at me, mouth dropping open. He was beautiful in
his confusion, his hard face softened.

I waited without further speech. My professor had told me
that the Navajo valued silence. In any case we weren't going
anywhere until he decided whether he really wanted to shoot
me. This gave me licence to examine his face – young, perhaps
the same age as me – smooth, unscarred. The cloak had fallen
open to reveal a smooth body, just the colour of new-fired
bronze, long thighs in deerskin breeches, a neat waist bound
with a concha belt. A bare chest, hung with necklaces of teeth.
This lad had been a scourge for the local predators. That bear
must have been as big as an omnibus. Or possibly it was a lion,
or a huge wolf.

Then he lowered the gun, sighed, replied 'Ya-ta-hey', which
means, 'Very good,' and asked in a small voice 'How do you
speak my language?'

'The same way you speak mine. I learned a little. My name
is Eugene. And you are–'

'White men call me Tommy,' he replied, sullenly.

That wouldn't do at all.

'And amongst the Dineé, what is your name?'

He gave me another startled glance and said, 'Wolf fighter'.

'Nice. Now, would you like to tell me why you held me up?
What have I that you want?'

'Your airship,' he grimaced. 'A terrible thing has been done
to my people, and I must go to your Queen and tell her about it.
Everyone knows she is merciful. She must not know what is
being done in her name.'

This was a distinct improvement on being shot. I smiled at
him.

'Oh, well, if you just need a lift, my dear, make yourself

comfortable. London in three days, and there's no one here but me. And it's time I got on with my checks, so have a seat. By the way, what have you done with my co-pilot, George?'

'I gave him money and he went away,' said Wolf. 'He said he was going to a house.'

'That would be Madame Sans Gene's. Again. Oh, well, then you will have to be my co-pilot. We'll be off in a moment.' He sat down and I signalled my tower.

And up we went. The only time anything really serious can happen to these airships is in rising and descending. Once you're up, as my instructor used to say, you're up. The hydrogen is packaged in such strong packages, inside the airtight aluminium skin, that nothing much will penetrate it. Lightning will not explode it. And mostly it's a smooth ride.

My Wolf Fighter hadn't flown before. He grabbed the arms of his chair until his knuckles turned white as the ground slid away. But the weather gods were kind. The air was blue and still, the engine puttered away, and the wide windshield allowed him to see clouds and birds. We never flew very high over land. Just above the shear of the ground winds. Ahead, there was another areostat. Behind us, there was a further aerostat, continuing along. We are much faster than any other method of flying. And I like being isolated, up in the clouds. Soon I saw that Wolf Fighter was enjoying the view, as well.

I put the controls onto automatic and left my seat.

'Would you like coffee?' I asked. 'I have tea as well. And perhaps you might shed the cloak. We aren't going anywhere until we get to London.'

'Coffee, please,' said my kidnapper, staring at the other airships. 'They are just following along like sheep going through a stile,' he added.

'Marvellous, isn't it? I never tire of the sight.'

We drank coffee amicably. The best coffee still comes from the Spanish kingdoms in South America. I always bought some whenever I landed in the Americas. In fact *HMAS Victoria*

Victrix was carrying a load of the best coffee beans, destined for the Palace. And that might prove useful. Prince Michael was very particular about his coffee.

'Wolf Fighter, why did your chief send you on this mission?'

'They can spare me,' he shrugged the cloak off his satiny shoulder. 'I am a shaman, Third Sex, and a story speaker. There are many they value more: men and women they need to continue our tribe. If any survive this captivity to bear and sire.'

'And you chose me because?' I was instantly suspicious. His bronze cheek mantled with a blush. Aha! Someone had been gossiping.

'They said you were – as I am. I thought you might understand.'

'I do,' I told him. 'More coffee? We are alike. Accepted but not approved. Tolerated, barely. Have you left a husband behind?'

'No one,' he shrugged again. 'And you?'

'No one,' I repeated. It sounded rather desolate. I decided to break out my sealed tin of the very best tablet chocolates, given to me by the man who shipped the coffee for expediting the loading. They were as black as night but tasted like heaven, pressed into moulds marked with the Inca jaguar mask.

I gave him one and put mine upon my tongue. Bliss! I don't know who reached out to whom, to share the chocolate in a deep kiss. After a few minutes, I didn't care. We lay down in my nest of quilts, naked, shivering with desire. All my previous amours were revealed as mere dalliances. I was drunk on his kisses, his touch, the slide and rub of his body on mine, the strong embrace of his arms.

I surfaced from an impromptu nap as the alarm sounded: it was time to adjust the rudder. I rose from my delight to make sure that we were back on course. Wolf Fighter had woken and was watching me, his dark eyes unreadable.

'You have had lovers before,' he commented.

'So I have,' I slipped down into the cocoon, gathering him

into my arms again. We fitted very well together, like one of those picture puzzles that are all the rage in London.

'So have you.'

'I have,' he replied, kissing my shoulder. 'But they were not like you. Lying with them was not like that.'

'No,' I agreed. 'This was much better.'

'Ya-ta-hey,' he said into my mouth, claiming another kiss. 'Good. Very good.'

We spent the night making love and sleeping, and the morning eating and washing and drinking more coffee. The appointments of my gondola were small, but acceptable. My Wolf Fighter was a cleanly creature who washed all over every day. Those who consider the Native Americans savages, might contemplate their own hygiene; or the lack of it. The last time I had been forced to take a train I had longed for a pomander to cover the stench. My Wolf smelt of desert, sand and salt, and a fugitive sweetness from the oil he used to dress his hair. I took down his black tresses, fine as silk, and combed them as we flew through the sky. He noticed the birds, exclaiming at his first albatross, and I plotted.

How to get my Wolf Fighter in to see the Queen? The events which he had imparted to me were inhuman, foul and disastrous, but probably legal. I would need to present to Her Majesty something new and interesting. It was well known that she was most concerned for the welfare of native peoples in the Empire; especially the clean, pretty ones who spoke excellent English.

But my beautiful Wolf was too plain to catch her eye. His hair was knotted in a bun at the back of his neck. He wore no feathers when everyone *knew* that Indians wore feathers. He was too modest and too simple.

But that could be amended. I had sewing supplies, I had clothes, and if I took apart a souvenir, I had feathers. He had his own paints in the bag he had concealed in my airship before he tried to kidnap me.

That night, as we lay down in each other's arms, I explained my plan. I had to pin him down and kiss him into submission before he would let me finish.

'You would make me into a doll!' he protested, struggling feebly.

'I would make you into a prince,' I riposted, kneeling between his thighs and holding him flat with my torso. 'A prince fit to speak to a monarch. This is the best chance you have, my Wolf. Think about it! The actions against the Navajo are legal; ghastly, but legal. To get them even examined we have to go over the heads of the whole government of the Americas. That means we need the Queen, God bless her, and she likes beautiful men. Exotic beautiful men. As does Prince Michael.'

'No,' he said, lying as still as a bolster beneath me. 'I am no whore!'

'Don't be foolish!' I snarled. 'I do not sleep with whores. You are my lover, no other man's, and I belong to you. Is that clear?'

I released him and sat up. He blinked at me. He rose on one elbow.

'Yes,' he said. 'We belong together. So, what would you have me do, Eugene?'

'Let me dress you so that everyone will know that you are an Indian, which means plaits – yes, I know that Navajo don't wear plaits – and a suitable costume. You have your shaman's drum? Play it and chant and dance. Dance confusion on the whole Empire, if you like, if it will make you feel better about the whole farce. Then fling yourself at her feet and speak your grievance. It's your best chance. Going through channels will take months, and your people don't sound like they have months.'

'I will think about it,' he conceded.

That was good enough for one night. We renewed our bonds of love. I didn't know what I was going to do, without him. I was intoxicated with his touch, his scent, his sweet lips. I did not know how I was going to sleep again, when I could not sleep nestled in his arms.

Prince Michael came to inspect his coffee and I was ready. I escorted the hooded, cloaked figure out of my aerostat as the royal personage ran his fingers through the delightful, aromatic beans, and said to him

'Your Royal Highness, I bring a petitioner to the Queen.'

'You, Eugene? What have you picked up in the Americas?' he chuckled. 'My Lady is in the palace at present. Who is he and what is his petition?'

I pulled back the hood, revealing a magnificent figure. My Wolf Fighter's eyes were ringed with kohl, his plaited hair danced with bright feathers (my sister would have to wait for her new hat) paint emphasised his high cheekbones and, as he swept back the cloak, the supple, beautiful lines of his oiled, largely naked body. He wore only his deerhide boots and a long loincloth, heavy with beads. Prince Michael caught his breath.

'I am Wolf Fighter,' said my dearest love. 'I come from a great injustice, and I wish to beg the Queen's mercy.'

'Come,' whimpered Prince Michael. My informants had told me he was very susceptible to male charms. 'You had better come too, Eugene, tidy yourself up a bit. Guard! Escort these men to the Audience Chamber.'

As we began to march away, Wolf Fighter perfectly upright and dignified in the middle of the red uniforms and brass helmets, the prince turned back to his adjutant. 'And see about getting my coffee delivered, Jones, will you, there's a good chap?'

We marched through the park. Then we were through the golden palace gates.

I had never been into the Audience Chamber before. Prince Michael left us, with the escort, at the door, and hurried in to speak to the distant figure on the throne. People moved away, leaving Wolf Fighter a clear path to the Queen.

I exchanged one glance with him as he tapped his fingers on the small skin drum, and then he began to chant and to dance.

I don't know what he was saying. It might have been 'confusion to the Empire' for all I knew. But he was mesmerising. No one in that huge, ornate hall, even the people who had been put aside for this savage, said a word or took their eyes off him for a moment. I couldn't even move. And as he danced, he approached the Queen, who was sitting forward, her small feet barely touching the floor, eyes bright and focused – drinking him in.

He reached the foot of the throne, flung himself to his knees with his arms spread wide, and declared in a deep, thrilling voice, 'I am Wolf Fighter, your Majesty – last of the Navajo, unless you can save us.'

He couldn't have said anything better. Victoria had been firm on the proper treatment of native peoples. The Commission she had ordered set up in India had broken several Nabobs. Although she was a constitutional monarch, she held a great deal of sway. No one wanted to offend this tiny, dark, bright-eyed queen.

Victoria gestured and Wolf Fighter stood up. They spoke together for some time. I could not hear what they said. Prince Michael whispered in her ear. She gestured at me. I hurried to Wolf Fighter's side and fell to my knees.

'You are an airman, my brother tells me.' Beautiful voice, tuneful as little bells. I dared to raise my eyes to her lovely face. Intelligence shone from her dark eyes.

'I am. I brought Wolf Fighter to you, most gracious lady,' I replied.

'How quickly can you return to the Americas?'

'Three days, your Majesty,' I faltered.

'Then I give you a task, Flight Lieutenant. Carry Wolf Fighter and the proclamation you will be given to the person I appoint. You may stay until the matter is concluded properly. Will you accept?'

'Gladly,' I breathed. She extended a hand for me to kiss.

Her soft skin was scented with attar of roses. Wolf Fighter and I were collected, escorted into a small but exceptionally-ornate room, served with a very opulent lunch, and Wolf Fighter was required to speak to Prince Michael as we ate. I was tempted to stuff some of the food into a handkerchief, it was so delicious and there was so much of it. Someone must have noticed this – the Plantagenet are very acute – because when we were escorted back to the *HMAS Victoria Victrix*, which had been cleaned, re-stocked and refuelled, the equerry handed in a large hamper; and grinned.

Within an hour we were in the air again, still out of breath, joining the long trail of airships, on our way to Washington, to find a certain general, and transport him south to a place called Bosque Resando.

'Did you expect that to happen?' demanded my Wolf, slumping into the co-pilot's seat.

'Yes, but not that fast,' I admitted.

'I want to kiss you,' Wolf told me. 'But first I have to wash off all this paint.'

So he washed off the paint. Then he kissed me.

'And you thought that this was a humane solution to the Indian problem?' enquired the Lt General, in a deceptively quiet voice.

'Indeed, they were raiding, they were even raiding each other, and the settlers were at risk,' bleated some benighted civilian who was shortly about to wish he had never been born.

I saw General Sherman take a deep breath.

This treaty conference was expected to last two weeks. With Sherman in charge, it wasn't going to manage a second day.

I had not spoken to Wolf Fighter since we had arrived. He had plunged into the miserable, starving mass of his people. The chief who had sent him on his errand had died on the journey. Ten thousand Navajos, children and women and old people, sent on a punishing march through desert to this paltry wilderness, stinking, infertile, forced away at gunpoint from their burned hogans and the land which meant everything to them, even who they were. The Lt General was barely keeping his outrage buttoned under his greatcoat.

'We will have a treaty,' he announced. 'No one raids anyone, for anything, is that agreed?'

Heads nodded all around the table. Sherman had a magnificent presence.

'Indians are protected citizens, do we agree? If you murder them, you will hang. If they murder you, they will hang. Clear?' he bellowed.

They all nodded.

'We will provide seeds, tools, and restore their livestock. Agreed?'

Again, no one dared to disagree.

'We will provide a teacher for every thirty Navajo children so that they shall learn English, agreed?'

Everyone nodded. Everyone signed.

'Right,' said Sherman, and stood up so abruptly that his chair crashed over. 'You, Manuel, bring out all those stores you've stolen. Right now. Equip all the families for the trip. I want all the horses you have for the infirm. Have you no humanity?' he yelled. The walls echoed. 'We need to get these people home!'

Everyone jumped to it. The chief of the Apache and the chief of the Navajo stood. Wolf Fighter approached Sherman, his pot of paint in his hand. Sherman inclined his head so Wolf could reach. Wolf painted the three lines of a warrior on the leathery skin of that sensitive, suffering, poet's face.

When Sherman stood up again he did not look ridiculous, like a clown. He looked like a chief. And in two hours we were leaving.

Things really did happen quickly; at least in my life, lately. I fell in behind the general. After all, I had Royal permission to stay until everything was concluded properly.

And I hoped I might talk to my Wolf again, if only to say goodbye. My heart was bleeding freely. And I had only known him for seven days. Only a week; and my life would never be the same.

This was going to be a slow, unforced march. No one was hurrying. Everyone was settling down, after a few hours, to make small fires and cook some of the rations which a furious Manuel had reluctantly distributed. I sat down with the general and ate cornbread and some sort of mutton stew. The General was still too furious to easily converse. I wandered away into the desert, not too far from the fires, feeling as miserable as I ever had.

I heard a drum, tapping softly. I went toward it. There sat Wolf Fighter, singing a strange, sad little chant. When he saw me he froze.

'Have you come to farewell me?' he asked, very quietly.

'You will want to stay with your people,' I said stiffly. 'I understand that. But I wanted to say... I wanted to ask, would you come with me – sometimes?'

Then he was in my arms, solid and real and scented with pinyon smoke. His hair flowed over my shoulder.

'I want to come with you,' he whispered. 'I thought you didn't want me anymore!'

'We shall fly,' I told him, holding him close, breast to breast. 'We will mount into the sky in my airship, and sleep and make love, all the way there, and all the way back.'

'Yes,' he gasped. 'All the way to where?'

I made a broad gesture with my free arm, making him a gift of the immeasurable sky.

'Anywhere,' I told him.

'Ya-ta-hey,' he murmured into my neck. 'Good! Very good!'

STEAMPUNK'D

GREAT BRITAIN, 1868

'Sorry, Sir, you can't come in,' the guard told him.

'I am Engineer Tolhurst, of course I can,' said Max, and brushed past the guard.

The guard tried to bar the Engineer's way with his musket, but Max had always moved fast. What was going on here at the Rendell Steel Works, that he was sudeenly not allowed see?

There had been some odd rumours flying about, all about how wicked the people of neighbouring Astonia were; and how they ate babies, apparently. Max didn't like it. He also didn't believe it. This was all very suspicious.

When he was gently but firmly ushered out again, he turned on his heel and stalked back to his office. He was alone as he always was. He flung his top hat at the stand, sat down, drank a cup of now cold tea which he had made earlier and forgotten, and said aloud 'What on earth is going on?'

'You will have to ask the dragon,' said his cat, Monsieur. Max scritched his stripy ears. Monsieur turned his head to indicate the exact spot which needed attention.

'Oh, yes, Cat, very funny,' he said. 'Everyone knows that dragons can't talk.'

'Like everyone knows that Astonians eat babies?'

There was a brief silence, in which Monsieur washed a front paw in a very significant manner.

'Point to you,' replied Max. 'Which dragon and how can I talk to him?'

'The Rendell dragon; his name is Powys,' said the cat, sitting down very exactly, all paws in a precise group and tail folded over. Only the very tip twitched. 'You can talk to him through me. But I don't know if I feel like helping you. You keep him captive.'

'I do?' asked Max, scratching him behind the ears again.

'Your kind, do. He is bricked in, under this city, and he cries for freedom, and for mercy, and for the skies you have forbidden him.'

'I had no idea, really,' Max said. 'It's not as if we need him anymore. I thought steam generation from coal is universally used. Why is he still there?'

'Letting things slide. It's easier than thinking,' said the cat dismissively. 'Most humans don't think, if they can avoid it.'

'That is also true,' sighed Max. 'What do you think they are making at Rendell Steel?'

'I can ask. And he might tell me, rather than instantly eating me, if I can tell him that you will set him free.'

'I don't know if I can,' demurred Max.

The cat sniffed. 'It's easy. You walk along the tunnels, find the Seal which the Old Ones put there, smash it, and Powys will be released.'

'And when he is released, how is he going to get out?'

'Dragons make their own paths,' said the cat, evasively.

'And is he then going to munch his way through the whole population of Melonia? Because if matters are as you say, I don't think he'll be in a very good mood.'

The cat laughed. 'Eating will be the last thing on his mind. A female dragon has been calling him for months. He will fly straight to her.'

'Where's she?' asked Max, putting on his coat again and settling his hat.

'Astonia – that way,' said Monsieur.

'Very well,' said Max. 'If you would care to hop up on my shoulder, we will be going.'

'I'm sorry, Sir, you can't come in,' insisted the guard. The door to Rendell Steel Works was firmly closed.

'But I'm Engineer Herbert, of course, I can come in!'

'Director's orders, sir,' said the guard, and barred his way with a pike. And a pike is not a weapon with which to try conclusions.

Andrew stalked back to his office, placed his top hat very carefully on its stand, and slumped down at his desk. Absently, he drank the cup of hot tea his secretary brought. It was just as he liked it, and he gave the young man a pleasant smile.

The secretary batted his eyelashes, but Andrew didn't notice. It had been six months since his employer's lover had run away with that airship captain. The secretary sighed and left the room.

'What's going on?' Andrew asked his black cat, Madame.

'You will have to ask the dragon,' she said. '*Juste comme ca, oui*. Prrr!'

'What dragon? I didn't know we had any dragons left in the city, since we switched to solar power.'

'There is one under Rendell Steel Works. She is walled in and screaming for rescue. Her name is Gwynedd. I can talk to her for you. But you will have to agree to free her.'

'Certainly, poor creature, that's terrible, she should be freed immediately, but I don't know how to accomplish that feat.'

'*Je sais, moi*. You break the seal, and she is free.'

'Then what will she do? Demolish Astonia? Or perhaps fly into Melonia. The papers are saying that they eat babies.'

'Pfft,' said the cat, with infinite scorn.

'My view entirely. All right. Now?'

'Indeed, before it is time for my afternoon snooze. *Allez-hop!*' said Madame, and sprang to his shoulders, settling herself comfortably with one set of claws buried in his neck, as usual.

'Anything I ought to take?' asked Andrew Herbert.

'Some rope, a hammer, and maybe,' she cocked her elegant head, 'maybe a shorter hat.'

Andrew changed into a trilby and they went out, stopping at the equipment shed on the way.

Maximilien Tolhurst paused at a junction. The tunnels under the Rendell Steel Works were airy, competently constructed and evenly lit. Rails ran underfoot. He asked, 'where now?' and Monsieur woke from an impromptu nap.

'That way,' said the cat. 'He is crying, can't you hear him?'

And whispering along the tunnel came a sad, high keening. How could anyone listen to this all day and not feel something? Max's heart, which he thought was pretty obdurate, was breaking. He had to hold back tears because he knew that Monsieur would be cross if cried upon.

'Can we get to him?' he whispered into Monsieur's ear. 'Is he bricked in?'

'This way,' insisted Monsieur, and directed Max to a blank wall in which was a round, prettily edged window. The keening was loud enough to sting the ears.

'Hello, Powys,' he said. 'I've come to get you out.'

There was an interval where Monsieur made some very odd sounds. Some of the conversation was either super – or sub – sonic. Max could see the cat's mouth moving, but hear no sound. Then Monsieur spat and fluffed up all his fur.

'They have his female captive in Melonia,' said the cat. 'And they are making guns and cannons and things like that. They intend war.'

'Tell him to wait a bit, I have to break the seal,' said Max, disgusted. The two kingdoms had avoided conflict for almost 500 years. 'And can you ask him please to try not to kill us when he breaks out?'

Another silent conversation.

'He will take us with him;' said Monsieur, pleased. 'We just have to sit in his mouth, so he doesn't accidently destroy us.'

'You're willing to do this?' asked Max.

'Of course,' said the cat.

Max went to the elaborate terracotta seal, picked up a lump of road metal, and shattered it.

Instantly a giant head, dusty with mortar, smashed through the wall and opened its enormous mouth. Max and Monsieur stepped in over the picket-fence teeth, and sat down on a tongue like a mattress.

The mouth closed, and sounds of complicated destruction started to be heard in the Rendell Steel Works.

There was plenty of air in the spacious mouth, so Monsieur, and eventually Max, lay down and went to sleep.

'Are you sure about this?' asked Andrew Herbert. Madame flicked his nose with a lightning fast black paw. '*Certainment*,' she said. 'Get on with it! *Allez*! I am wasting time which could be spent in beauty sleep!'

Andrew smashed the seal with the hammer he had provided, and a massive green head broke the bricks and opened a gape like a train tunnel.

Andrew and Madame entered, made themselves comfortable on the tongue, and listened as the dragon Gywnedd stood up, stretched, and smashed the Rendell Steel Works into smithereens. She broke through the pavement and stepped up into the air, shedding glass and stone and broken building. There were screams but no wailing over the dead. The breaking of the seal had triggered a dragon alarm which evacuated the whole Works in a matter of moments.

Andrew and Madame were bounced this way and that, but the walls were soft. Gwynedd opened her mouth and allowed them out.

'She says, climb on, we're going to Melonia,' said Madame. 'Ooh, *ecoute-moi,* she has a lover! And she is going to him. His name is Powys.'

'All right,' said Andrew, who was feeling more alive than he had for years – and hadn't thought of his broken heart for hours. 'Where should we sit?'

'She is wearing a harness, idiot,' said Madame affectionately. 'Climb up there, put your foot there, good, and here we are.'

Andrew found himself sitting comfortably in a species of howdah just behind the dragon's glossy green neck. Her wings were bronzed and caught the light like a peacock's tail. She was still a little dusty, but not at all injured as far as Andrew could see.

Then she took off. She rose into the sky with ease and grace, and Andrew laughed aloud and kissed Madame on the nose. She purred excitedly into his ear.

Max was riding a dragon. An actual real authentic *dragon*. He had Monsieur wrapped round his neck like a scarf and his top hat had blown away, but he was laughing.

And Powys was magnificent; redder than blood, redder than apples, and edged and flecked with gold.

Monsieur grabbed Max's earlobe in his teeth and said, 'Powys says his lady love is free and flying this way! So we don't have to rescue her, too. We'll meet her and then fly home.'

'Which home?' asked Max.

'Wales,' of course,' said Monsieur scornfully. 'That's where dragons come from. I thought everyone knew that. And I don't think we'll be really popular in Melonia, eh? We just wrecked their war.'

'Good thing too,' muttered Max. 'They say Wales is nice at this time of year,' he agreed.

The howdah arrangement included a very old picnic basket. The sandwiches and cakes had been eaten by rats, but the flask of brandy had improved with keeping.

'Gwynedd says we're going to meet her lover and then go to Wales!' exclaimed Madame. 'And there he is! *Quelle beau gars!* He is as handsome as she said,' she commented.

'He is, indeed,' said Andrew. And then he caught sight of the red dragon's passengers: a lovely man bearing a stripy cat around his neck, his brown curly hair slicked back by the wind. 'Oh yes, he's gorgeous.'

The dragons moved until they were sailing through the air, side by side.

'Impudent!' said Madame. 'He is a very impudent Tom cat!'

'They're like that,' soothed Andrew. 'What's the man's name?'

'Maximilien, he is an engineer, like you, and he– No, let him tell you, he likes you. He likes you very much. And I quite like him even though his cat, he is impudent.'

'Oh, what a beauty,' said Max, of the magnificent green dragon and then at her passengers: a blond man wearing a contrasting black cat. His previously unaffected body reacted. *Oh.*

'His name is Andrew Herbert and he is an engineer, and he thinks the same of you,' Monsieur informed him briskly. 'And his cat – oh, she is delightful!'

'She just snarled at you,' said Max.

'I know!' said Monsieur. 'She noticed me!'

'Right,' said Max. Some courtship rituals were strange.

'We're going down here, this place has lots of lakes, both of them need a wash, there's a farm house over there for the humans and cats, the people will feed us. And bring our friends a sheep or two each. They're used to dragons here – they are tenants of Lord Rochester.'

'The Dragon Lord?'

'The very same: Geoffrey Wilmot 3rd Duke of Rochester. This is his land.'

Going down wasn't as amusing as going up, but both dragons landed gently. Her riders climbed creakily down and attendants came forward to remove the harnesses.

Andrew held out a hand to Max, and they shook hands. Max only realised that he was still holding Andrew's hand when Monsieur hissed in his ear, 'Go on, kiss him!'

Max blushed and let go. He put Monsieur on the grass. Andrew allowed Madame to climb down. Both cats looked at each other, then turned their backs.

'I don't know, confessed Andrew. 'She says he's impudent.'

'Probably encouraging,' said Max. 'Come inside? I'm hungry, what about you?'

'Starving,' agreed Andrew.

Over a pleasant meal of bread and cheese and fruits, washed down with a strong local cider, they began a conversation.

'I wouldn't like to be the directors of the Rendell Steel Works,' said Max. 'Have an apple?'

'Thanks,' said Andrew, then grabbed his wrist. 'Wait, the Rendell Steel Works? They had your dragon?'

'Yes,' Max did not try to release his arm.

'The Rendell Steel Works in Melonia had Powys?' repeated Andrew. His blue eyes were snapping with fury.

'Yes, I said so, why?'

'Gwynedd was bricked in under the Rendell Steel Works in Astonia,' said Andrew. 'The same company, and they were making weapons for a war–'

'Between Melonia and Astonia,' Max interjected. 'As was my Rendell Steel Works. Bastards! Wretches!'

'Indeed,' Andrew agreed. 'They would have made a fortune.'

'And killed thousands of innocent people,' said Max. 'Well, I think we put a stop to that. I don't feel like going back,' he said sadly.' I've nothing to go back to.'

'Neither have I,' said Andrew. 'I had once, but no longer.'

'But you do have me,' Max told him. 'My Monsieur has fallen in love with your–'

'Madame,' chuckled Andrew. 'It was clearly destiny.'

'Fate,' said Max, leaning closer, cupping the smooth jaw in his callused Engineer's hand. Andrew shivered pleasantly at the touch.

And this time when Monsieur prompted, 'Kiss him,' he did.

And Madame giggled when Andrew kissed him back.

THE CYMRU NEWS

In which is incorporated the Shropshire Intelligencer,
and the Monmouth Advertiser.

21TH OF OCTOBER IN THE YEAR OF OUR GRACIOUS LADY VICTORIA

QUEEN OF GREAT BRITAIN ETC., 1899

RETIREMENT OF FAMOUS ENGINEERS

Geoffrey Wilmot 3rd Duke of Rochester announces with regret that his premier engineers, Sir Andrew Herbert and Sir Maximilien Tolhurt, known for so long as The Twins, joint inventors of so many useful and beautiful things, (including the Nursery Project, which assures mother dragons that their eggs will always be kept in perfect conditions,) are retiring at the end of the month at age fifty-five.

It was the fearless actions of both of these admirable men which led to the release of Powys, *draig goch*, and Gwynedd, *draig glas*, who have since raised so many litters of strong and lovely dragons over the years.

The Twins are retiring to a house near the village. They built this cottage for themselves, and it has every invention to make their declining years comfortable. They have continued their tradition in every way, and will be settling down with a small number of cats, both the ebony and the tabby.

The Duke has caused an Illuminated Address to be made and presented to his engineers. We wish them the very best for the future.

THE ARTIFICER OF BEAUME

Gérard met the angel when he had retreated to his favourite hiding place and was preparing to put a blade into his heart.

It was a good blade. His father had given it to him, hoping that he would learn to fight. A vain hope. Gérard was lame, crippled, slow of foot, unlike his brave and beautiful brothers. He could ride, but lumpily; he could walk but with a graceless lurch. He could not dance. No marriage would be arranged for him, for what high born lady would consider a union with the third son of a king whose face was so ugly that his own mother had banned him from the women's quarters, lest a pregnant woman should catch sight of him and mar her unborn?

For in a land of dark eyes and raven hair and sweetly brown skin Gérard was bleached. His hair was flax, his skin as white as paper. His eyes were sea blue or sea grey, like the eyes of a blind person. He had always known how ugly he was.

He had some skills, but they were not valued. He could make clay figurines so animated one would think them alive. He could cast metal and make moulds for jewellery. He could mend anything mechanical. He could play a small pipe and call birds to his hand. Tricks, merely, said the court. Though he rode so badly, horses loved him. Cats brought him their kittens to lay in his lap. Dogs lolloped after his painful, halting gait.

The last straw was that he refused to use any of his animal charming abilities in furtherence of the hunt. His father and brothers loved hunting above all pursuits.

Gérard had made a present for his father, in an attempt to

please. He had felt the clay model of the angel grow under his hands like magic. He had made the wax for the casting. He had sat up all night, watching it cool, and polishing the silver figure when it emerged from the crumpled clay.

It was a creature of beauty and grace. An angel, standing on tip toe, wings slightly cupped to catch the wind, about to fly. It was the best thing that Gérard had ever made.

He had presented it to his father, who had barely glanced at it, flicked a hand at him, and looked away.

So Gérard was going to relieve the world of his unwanted presence. His masterwork was gone, to be left unregarded in some storehouse to gather dust. That had been his last try. Now he was leaving. That angel would also be the last thing that Gérard ever made.

His refuge was a niche in the castle keep. It had long ago been locked and forgotten. There he was safe but always had to come out and face the indifference of the court again, and this time he wasn't going to do that. He opened his shirt and felt down his left side, counting ribs and palpating them for the space between. His heart beat under his fingers. This would be over in one deep, final, swift stab. He folded both hands on the undecorated hilt.

Goodbye to the sun, to the light, to life. He closed his eyes and thrust.

And the knife did not move. Sheer surprise snapped his eyes open. His wrist was held in a firm grip. The hand was as pale as his own. He followed it up the bare arm to a shoulder and thence to a grave face and a pair of eyes as bright as stars. They flashed blue and silver.

'Who are you?' stammered Gérard.

'Astrophel,' said the stranger. 'Come with me.'

'Let me go,' Gérard struggled unavailingly against the clasp. The stranger did not even notice. Gérard tried to pry up the pale fingers, but they did not budge.

'I cannot,' said the stranger.

'Why not?' I am worthless. I want to die and relieve the earth of the burden of my loathsome presence.'

'I'm your angel,' said the stranger. 'You called me. I have to protect you.'

'I called you?' Gérard asked, finally allowing the knife to drop.

'You made my image in silver. I had not known I was beautiful before. Come with me,' repeated Astrophel. Gérard took his hand.

The angel led him to the top of the tower. It was a hundred feet high. To fall would be to be obliterated on the courtyard stones. Gérard heard horses neighing. His father and brothers were home from hunting. A deer carcass was slung across a pony's back. The hunters were all laughing, pleased with their day's pleasure.

Astrophel cupped Gérard's face in one long, cool, pale hand, forcing Gérard's eyes up to meet the angel's.

'We are going away,' the angel told him. 'You do not belong here.'

'Where are we going?' he asked, as the angel wrapped him in his feathery embrace. 'Forget I spoke. I do not care. Take me whence you will.'

'Put your arms around my neck, now, up! Lock your legs around my waist. Hold tight.'

Oh, beautiful, the unfolding wings, silver as a swan's, perfectly in order from flight feathers to tiny scapuli. They were white with a blue tinge; impossible, palpable. The angel's body was smooth, but soft down blanketed his back, under the pinions.

'Say farewell to the ungrateful ones,' Astrophel bade Gérard, then stood on tiptoe, flapped his wings once, twice, with a sound like thunder, and launched himself into the air.

He swooped low enough over the huntsmen to let them see whom he was carrying and force their horses to rear and plunge, then he was banking and climbing into the dazzling air. High above the earth, the angel asked

'Are you afraid?'

'No!' replied Gérard. 'Yes. This is wonderful. You are holding me so safely I do not fear falling. Am I not too heavy for you, graceless, leaden lump that I am?'

'I could carry four of you and feel no strain,' Astrophel replied.

He seemed to glide and soar, more like a falcon than a swan. All the world Gérard knew was fled away. He had never been over the hills which were his horizon.

The country beyond was green and fertile. Gérard saw barns and flocks and little houses, a watermill, a temple of Gaia. Astrophel set them down with barely a thump in the neglected garden of a small cottage.

'This is the home of the Artificer of Beaume,' Astrophel told Gérard. 'Go in, he is waiting for you. He is dying. He needs to speak to you.'

Astrophel gave Gérard an encouraging push in the small of the back and he limped to the open door, suddenly heavy again.

It was the usual design. Three rooms, a kitchen, a bedroom, a workroom. The kitchen was dusty, the pots unwashed, the floor littered with dirty cups and plates and garments. Gérard went to the door of the bedroom. He felt strangely unafraid.

'You've come,' whispered an immeasurably old voice. 'Come in, boy, I don't have much time.'

A very ancient man was lying in a disordered bed, propped up with pillows. He reached out a trembling hand and Gérard took it. Frail, shaking, hot. Gérard saw the old man's eyes were already glazing. He was dying indeed.

'Look after them all for me,' quavered the Artificer of Beaume. 'Make sure I am buried next to my Elizabeth. I can see her clearly now, she's waiting for me just over the river. Can't you hear the current running under the boat? The horse needs his hoof fomented for another two days. Give him a bran mash tonight. Take this...'

He reached under his pillow and gave Gérard a small bag which chinked.

'You'll need to clean and oil all the tools, buy more good coal for the forge from Fram. It's a good life, boy. I've been happy here. Kiss me farewell.'

Gérard kissed him on the forehead. He tasted sickness and death sweat.

The Artificer sighed, relaxed, and died as he watched.

'What should I do now?' he asked, but Astrophel was gone.

Stowing the gold, Gérard straightened out the corpse, closed the old man's eyes, and limped out to find the nearest house.

When he arrived there, the woman of the house said on receipt of his news, 'So he is gone then, poor old man. You took your time getting here, he's been sick for months. He wore himself out, waiting for you.

'Now I'll just take off this apron and send the boy for Mistress Aurore and we'll lay him out properly. While you go to the Temple of Gaia, just along there and to the right, down that lane, and tell the priest he'll need to have a grave dug. He'll want to be buried next to his Elizabeth, he missed her very badly.'

The lady gave Gérard a reproving look and bustled him on his way.

Bemused, Gérard did as he was bid. The priest of the Goddess was cheerful, plump and young. He sighed. He gave an order for the digging of the grave and asked Gérard to sit down and drink wine and perhaps take a little bread and cheese.

'You are the new Artificer of Beaume,' he told Gérard. 'For hundreds of years, a new one has happened along as soon as the old one starts dying. We've been watching the road for you for weeks. You must have slipped past us somehow.'

'But I'm no artificer!' protested Gérard.

'Can you play on a small pipe? Mend clocks and watches? Can you forge, make horse shoes, make moulds in wax and clay, smelt metal, mend broken things, befriend animals? '

'All of those things,' admitted Gérard.

'Good, then, that's settled,' said the priest, refilling his cup.

'By the way, how *did* you come here?'

Gérard decided that his new life should contain nothing but the truth.

'An angel brought me,' he said.

'Good,' said the priest. 'Now, I shall send you a couple of acolytes to help you clean the house. The old man got rather set in his ways and reclusive when his Elizabeth died. Everything in the house is yours. Drink up, Artificer, you have to meet your household.'

Gérard went quietly.

At the end of a very busy day, his house was scoured, his dishes and cups stacked, his clothes washed and drying on the hedges, his bed re-made, his one glass window polished, his cistern pumped full, his kettle boiling for his wash, his new linen scented with lavender and his vegetable soup cooking.

In the meantime, Gérard was making friends with his animals.

When the women had removed the corpse of the old man, his dog had been found, huddled beside him, whimpering. He crept to Gérard's feet and put his sorrowful head into his lap. He was an unsightly dog. A greyhound, perhaps, had been enchanted by the robust charms of a mastiff. A tag on his collar said 'Gelert'. A pair of calico cats with extra toes had accepted his offerings, but were uncertain as to whether he should be allowed into their inner communion. They were sitting either side of the skull on the mantelpiece, inspecting him for moral flaws.

His barn housed the lame horse, several indeterminate animals who might be sheep or goats, a cow, and many hedgehogs, rabbits and squirrels, who seemed to be making their home there.

His garden had many herbs, his barn was stacked with hay, and the old man's room was lined with books.

Gérard was happy for a long time.

Being Artificer of Beaume was interesting, difficult, and intriguing. He read the old man's books to find out the properties of herbs, the treatment of animal diseases, and methods for fixing carts and clocks. He tried harder than he ever had in his miserable previous life. For the first time, people liked him and trusted him as animals always had. Even the cats came round in a week and happily shared his bed as the winter came on.

But he was lonely. There were few young people in the village and they were all spoken for, boys and girls. In all the world there was no one to kiss deformed Gérard, Artificer of Beaume.

As he lay one night in his bed, flanked with cats, burning for a kind touch or any caress, he felt rather than heard wings and went into his kitchen to find Astrophel, seated at his table, his wings folded neatly behind him.

'The angel looked just the same. Unearthly, beautiful. The sculptured mouth was smiling.

'You called me,' he said to Gérard.

'Only with my longing. If I had known you would have come, I would have called when Mistress Radley was dying.'

'I could not have saved her, if you could not,' replied Astrophel.

'Then why have you come?' asked Gérard.

'I came to love you,' said the angel, surprised. 'Did you not want a lover?'

'Oh, yes,' said Gérard, as the angel's mouth closed on his, and the fine, long fingered hands slowly caressed his back, running down to his buttocks, squeezing, stroking.

Astrophel led him into his bedroom, stripped him naked and laid him down, kissing any stretch of skin revealed, while Gérard touched what he could, finding the angel's wings very sensitive, relishing in the texture of the down on the beautiful back.

As their bodies clasped, the angel wrapped his wings around Gérard, lifted him and pressed him close, thigh and breast. Inside that warm, weightless, feathery embrace Gérard tasted such joy as he had never felt before. Then he fell asleep in the angel's arms, wrapped in his wings.

When he woke in the morning the angel was gone. But on his pillow lay a long straight feather, which was not a swan's feather, in token of a promise.

Astrophel came when he called, mostly. The Artificer of Beaume was so contented that people forgot that he was crippled, if they had ever cared. There was always something amiss with the artificers, anyway.

Years passed. Gérard birthed calves, mended broken wings, staunched wounds, contrived watermills and kites, mended broken cart wheels and made toys. People came from several villages around for his Spring Tonic. And Astrophel came to wrap him in his wings and make love to him as though he was already in Heaven.

One day a very superior person came riding, leading a caparisoned horse. Gérard came out to the summons, courteously wiping his greasy hands on a rag. He had been changing an axle. The rider looked down on the grimy, limping figure.

'Are you Prince Gérard?' he demanded.

'Why do you ask?'

'The King is dead, his two sons with him. Hunting accidents. It was said that the heir to the throne was carried away many years ago by an angel. Do you know anything about it? The heir is eagerly sought. He would be warmly welcomed back to the castle.'

'No,' said Gérard instantly. 'No such person lives here.'

'Then who are you?' asked the rider.

'I am the Artificer of Beaume,' said Gérard. 'Farewell.'

THE NAUTILUS

It probably would have worked, if something very large with a lot of teeth had not surged past, white belly as wide as a keel, and severed, in one bite, the lines which attached the bathysphere *Nereid* to the mother ship *HMS Adventure*.

Professor Peter Aaronson remarked to his stalwart companion, Sir Hugh Repton, 'I believe that was a *carcereus*. It was too big, far too big, to be a simple *selachus,* or even a Great White. This is exciting, Repton. They are supposed to be extinct.'

'And soon,' Hugh pointed out with commendable patience, 'so will we. How deep is the bottom here, Aaronson?'

'Rather deep,' replied Aaronson. 'Too deep to survive, if we dive out. Pressure, you know.'

'I know,' acknowledged Repton. 'Well, it has been a good life. We climbed Kachenchunga; travelled the Nile; found that Inca village and learned their language. Neither of us have left wives or children to mourn.'

Aaronson turned his dark eyes on his friend. 'If you come closer, we can balance the sphere. If it tips over, we will be dead instantly.'

'I can do that, though I don't see that it makes a lot of difference to the little time we have left, unless–' Repton not only moved closer to the professor but took him in a close embrace. 'Unless I employ the last few moments of our lives by telling you how much I have always loved you.'

'Why not?' replied the professor. 'I have always loved you, too, my dear. My Hugh.'

'Tis a tragedy we left it so long to declare ourselves,' Repton said.

'Well, we may not be a youthful as Romeo and Juliet, we can at least die upon a kiss.'

'Peter,' breathed the explorer, and kissed his friend.

They did not have time to be embarrassed. The bathysphere plummeted. They clung together. Then it struck the bottom with the sound of a very large, very deep bell.

'Good Christ, it is the Inchape Rock,' Repton said, clearly dizzy with too much carbon dioxide.

'No, it's... we've landed on something hollow; something metal. Look down, see, there's some sort of hatch. Quick, Hugh, grab that knob, I'll take the bolt and latch. This must be another bathysphere or submarine mechanism, perhaps it has some air left.'

'Your wish is my command,' Repton murmured, moving from merely dizzy to actively hallucinating. For how they could've landed precisely on a hatch that wedded perfectly to their own could only be the wishful thinking of the soon-to-be-dead.

Nevertheless, the two of them, in their shared delusion, managed to open the hatch of their bathysphere, and the one below, wheron they fell into cool, clean air; tinged with a faint hint of engine-oil and onions. As they tumbled out onto a hard, cold surface, the lights came on. The hatch shut behind them.

'Don't let go of me,' the professor panted. 'I don't think I'm real, yet.'

'Nor me,' Repton replied, burying his face in his companion's shoulder and gasping for breath. 'Why are we still alive?'

'If we *are* still alive.' Aaronson said.

'Dead?' Repton thought about it, then bit the professor, quite hard, sucking a red mark into his neck.

Aaronson flinched and dragged Repton closer, kissing his mouth brutally, biting in return.

'Not dead,' Repton observed, feeling the nudge of an erection against his hip. 'And much as I would like to fling you down and ravish you – as I have wanted to do all these years, my dear chap – I would like to find a softer surface on which to proceed.'

'Quite,' agreed the professor. 'If you would help me to stand.'

Repton scrambled to his feet and drew Aaronson up to hold him close. The professor was shivering with cold and shock. His slender body pressed close to Repton's muscular warmth.

'I have always admired your aplomb,' Repton told him. 'Let us walk a little, warm us up. Which way, do you think?'

'Toss a coin, my dear, I can't see a single marking. Or a door. We seem to be inside a hull, of something far bigger than our bathysphere.'

'But it must be a wreck surely.'

'I don't think so,' said Aaronson, brushing his dishevelled hair out of his eyes. 'There's no sign of damage. And some of the engines must be operating, to maintain the light and air. Which raises the obvious, that there's no point in lighting it, or giving it atmosphere, unless people come here; which in turn argues that there must be a way out.'

Repton grinned. 'Good thinking, Peter. But I wonder who owns it and if they'll be cross when they find us on it. And whether we will discover anything to eat or drink in this tin shell.'

'The answer to both questions,' said a faintly-accented voice behind them, 'is that he is delighted to see you, and would like you to join him for dinner.'

Aaronson and Repton both flinched in surprise and turned to find a man with bright blue eyes and a strong, bony face, smiling at them. He was dressed in soft, loose trousers, cavalry boots, a plum-coloured tunic, and a heavy leather belt with a scabbard and sword. A black velvet hat partly covered his hair which was pale as flax. His hand was outstretched in greeting.

Repton shook the man's hand heartily. 'I am Sir Hugh Repton, explorer, and this is my companion, Professor Peter Aaronson. We are very pleased to meet you, for we thought we were surely dead.

Their host smiled. 'Welcome Sir Hugh; Professor Aaronson. You may call me Utis.'

'Captain Utis?' asked Aaronson, his mouth quirking as though he had heard a joke. Hugh did not understand. But the captain himself smiled and nodded, then indicated a previously unnoticed door. He conducted them through it and indicated a stairway.

'If you gentlemen will take the trouble of climbing this stair, you will find a cabin with the usual appointments. I am afraid that you will have to lodge together, my dear sirs, but I am sure that you will find your quarters comfortable.

'A wash and a change of garments, will make you feel more at home. And I will send someone to call you for dinner in about two hours. Refreshments will be delivered presently.'

And then he left them by another door, which hissed open and shut, seemingly of its own accord, after his trim, tall figure.

The professor, exhausted from the recent lack of oxygen, eyed the steep iron stairs wearily. 'We climb?'

'I climb,' Repton said, and hoisted his fellow onto his back, where he clung, laughing and protesting as the stairs weres ascended.

Repton set the Professor down at the top in a corridor, before the open door of a ridiculously spacious cabin. The two men stared in amazement. It was a proper bedchamber such as could be found in the best hotels. The walls were hung with red velvet and the four-poster bed was dressed in brocade curtains, worked with knights on horseback.

Repton clasped his friend's hand, walked boldly inside and pushed Aaronson back onto the great bed.

'Just lie there and catch your breath, Peter, and I shall scout,' he said. The professor stared up at a figured ceiling, then took his own pulse to see if he was fevered or possibly not alive any more. He closed his eyes.

'Now there, let's get these boots off,' was the next thing he heard. 'You shouldn't sleep in your clothes, my dear. I have drawn a nice bath of hot water, so let's get you all clean.

'Hugh?' The professor reached up, without opening his eyes, and gently pulled his friend's head down and kissed his mouth. That reassured him. 'Right. Alive. Not dreaming. Good,' he said. 'A wash would be divine. Then I have things to tell you about our captain.'

'I thought you might,' Repton noted. He stood and gazed at his professor. 'You know, I've never seen you naked, though I've often imagined what you must look like. Undress for me?'

'Of course,' said Aaronson. 'If you will match me, garment for garment.'

It seemed deliciously wicked to be removing jacket for jacket, shirt for shirt, sock for sock, and finally, breeches for trousers. And, as games went, Repton lost, for he did not wear the warm underclothing of his thinner colleague. He watched hungrily as Aaronson finally stripped off his underdrawers, and then tried to cover his body with his hands.

'I'm scrawny and ugly,' he apologised.

'Tosh, my Peter. You are delicate and elegant and beautiful. Now, into the bath. Shall I carry you again?'

'No, but come with me,' Aaronson said. 'I'm still not at all sure that this isn't some hallucination. Even if it is, I'd rather you were with me, Hugh, as it feels more real.'

'If it's not real, Peter, then we share a fabulous dream,' Repton said, and escorted his lover to the bath.

The water was hot and fresh, not salt, and the soap was scented with sandalwood. The bath was big enough for two, if they slid close together. They did so with alacrity, and the water washed all the evidence away.

The towels, of course, were fluffy, and the nightshirts they donned of fine lawn, embroidered with more knights in white thread. They sat down on the red plush sofa.

'Have some wine,' Repton poured a glass for his lover. For Peter was his lover now; not just friend, not compatriot, not colleague. Repton was glowing with satisfaction. 'There are also some little almond cakes. Have a few, my darling. You've had a shock.'

'So have you,' Aaronson sipped the red wine and ate a few of the little cakes.

'Yes, but shocks and surprises are part of my profession. So far no one has tried to sacrifice me to anything, which always improves your day. Our captain seems to be very civilised.'

'Ah, yes, refill my glass and I will tell you about him. He is wearing the dress of a Polish prince; sword and all. I'm sure you noticed his distinctive hat, that looks a little like a Tudor bonnet. And we are drinking Bull's Blood, a Hungarian wine.'

'Eastern European also fits with his accent.'

'And he told us to call him Utis.'

'So?' asked the explorer, baffled.

'You've heard of Odysseus, the Ancient Greek hero. He once called himself Utis, which means No Man. And what, dear Hugh, is No Man in Latin?'

'Nemo,' Hugh said. 'We used to say it at school: Who broke that window? Nemo, Magister.

'Oh, good Lord, Peter. You mean this is Captain Nemo? This is the *Nautilis*?'

'In all probability,' said the professor. 'Nothing more was heard of her after she sank that Russian ship and killed the tsar's son and chief executioner.'

'I never thought she was more than a legend,' Repton said. 'They say she went into the Moskenstraumen, the maelstrom. Nothing gets out of that.'

'Except, perhaps, a ship that also sails under the sea.' Aaronson ate another almond cake decisively.

'Except that, of course,' Repton agreed. 'But that means that we can never–'

'Leave,' said the professor.

They drank more wine, considering this.

They dressed in clean underclothes and their own suits just in time to greet the sailor who knocked on their door. Chief Watts, he said his name was, and he escorted them through more of the hissing doors to a large dining room and a grand table laid with dainties.

Captain Utis, wearing a new tunic made of dark green silk, greeted them and conducted them to chairs. Waiters began to ply them with all manner of fish: fried and pickled and grilled and raw, soaked in lime juice.

'You are a liberal host!' Repton observed. 'This is a wonderful dinner, sir. We thank you.'

'I hope that you will be happy here,' replied the captain. 'Because I'm afraid that once you join my crew, you cannot leave.'

'Tell me, captain, you travel the oceans? Study the deep flora and fauna? Things that no one else has ever seen?' asked Aaronson.

'I do,' the captain replied.

'And occasionally you do leave this ship, to hunt, perhaps, or otherwise see the sun?' Repton asked. Hugh Repton could not live without the sun on his skin.

'Yes, we have a base, the Island, where the crew's women and children live. There you may lie in the sun, Sir Hugh.

'Also, we are sometimes attacked by various creatures – the giant octopus, for example, seem to think that Nautilis is quite tasty – and then we need to swim out and fight.'

The captain beckoned someone who stood behind them. 'Chief Watts, will you show the gentleman your arm?'

Watts rolled back his soft sleeve to show regular round scars. It was as if he had been stamped by a tinsmith's gouge.

'Octopus, sir,' said the sailor. 'Woundy great big bugger. We got 'im, though.'

'Fascinating,' breathed the professor, peering at the scars.

'Now, now, my dear, give the nice man his arm back,' Repton told him. Then he looked the captain straight in the eye. 'We are lovers, this man and I. Have you any legal or religious objections to our relationship?'

The captain's lip curled. 'In this vessel, I am the law,' he said. 'And my Conseil would be very annoyed if I began to pass laws against my own heart.'

'Ah,' said Repton.

'Indeed,' agreed the captain.

'Then we are at one, sir,' said Professor Aaronson. 'We would be honoured to stay on board with you. I'm sure we can make ourselves useful. I have some scientific knowledge, and my... my lover is a great hunter and explorer.'

'To the crew of the *Nautilis*,' said the captain, raising his glass. They all drank.

Scientific Mystery: The Journal of Oceanography

Many papers have been received, over the years, from a certain Professor Smith. They have mostly been published as later explorers dived deeper into the sea and confirmed the findings.

The flow of papers appears to have dried up in about 1925. No trace of the professor has been found at any university in Europe or America, and the papers were posted from different ports.

Any reader who has any knowledge of this Professor Smith is invited to write in. He was a very skilled observer and natural historian. His papers were always dedicated to 'H.R. my dearest love'.

Information about him would be appreciated.

Editor

KHEPERREN AND PTAH-HOTEP

Sweating in the desert all day meant that when the night came with its deep cold, Pierre Duclos settled happily into his routine of a brief wash in water warmed by the sun, a final glass of cognac from his secret cache, and a luxurious roll into his blankets. The Valley of the Kings was a baking scree of rocks too hot to touch during the day. At night the geology gave back its heat, and his little tent was pleasantly warm.

His tent mate Sergeant Ciaran Paterson had not come in, doubtless carousing with the diggers. He would tumble in, late and intoxicated by kif, and Pierre would call him *crapaud*, a sot, and put him to bed. And Ciaran would demand a kiss, putting up his face like a child. And lately Pierre had kissed him. And enjoyed it far too much. It was no longer a jest between comrades, that goodnight kiss. Pierre had no idea what he was going to do about it, if anything, but his dreams, of late, had been heated and unclear, leaving him to awake sticky and puzzled.

Paterson was stocky, rather sunburned and rough, with a massive scar from some native battle on his chest. Nothing like the scented, epicene youths of the Egyptian brothels which Pierre had visited when he first arrived. Paterson was one of Howard's British soldiers, hired to secure the camp and the dig. He was upright and honest and would probably fell Pierre with the butt of that Lee Enfield if he made an approach to him. Yet he leaned into that one kiss, opening his mouth, offering himself to be explored.

And he was unaccountably desirable. Pierre shut his eyes resolutely and began to recite Arabic words in his head to disconnect his mind and sleep. But all the words he could remember were affectionate, Light of my eyes. My heart. My life. My friend.

Then he was abruptly asleep and dreaming. He rose on hawk's wings into the sky, over the Valley of Kings, and flew until he settled on a red sandstone ledge near the main gate. There were hieroglyphs there, ancient graffiti. He read a complaint about how much the labourers ate, especially in garlic and radishes. He read a home hint about repelling rats with a plaster plug of cat fur. He looked to the cliffs and saw a tomb opening, and a man at the door, embracing another man.

Then he was back in his own body. There was a weight on his chest. The voice of a goddess, a dark and powerful female voice said, 'Swear by all the Gods to find the tomb of Ptah-Hotep, and you shall have your heart's desire.'

'What?' he blurred, trying to stay in the dream, feeling his body awakening.

'Promise!' urged the voice, and he said, 'I promise,' and then awoke.

There was indeed a weight on his chest. It was a black cat, scrawny, underfed and dusty. She reposed on his pyjamas as though by right. He sat up and she slid down to his lap, opened her green eyes, and looked into his.

He had never seen such a self-aware glance from an animal. Goddess. Right. Heart's desire. Tomb. And this cat was her avatar, here to make sure that he did as he was bid.

He had better feed her, then. He called for bread and cheese, and a dish of the labourer's broth. Cooled, the cat found it acceptable. She also ate most of his cheese, drank her fill of the fresh water, and fell asleep on his bunk.

'Will you stay here, Oh Basht, Slaughterer of the Fiends of Evening, Lady of the Cunning Word, Keeper of the Door?' he asked. She licked a paw in assent. She had a regal presence.

Ciaran woke, groaned, and noticed her.

'Oh, no, cats as well as morning?' he groaned.

'*Si grognan ce matin,*' remarked Pierre. 'So grumpy in the morning! You would be happier in the morning if you didn't smoke so much kif at night, my dear sir.'

'Last night wasn't kif, it was some local drink, apparently distilled from cornplasters. Is that coffee?' asked Ciaran, weakly.

'It is, and you shall have it, because I love you,' said Pierre, which was not at all that he had been going to say. The cat pricked up her ears.

'If you love me so much you'll give me your only cup of coffee, you must love me indeed,' said Ciaran. 'So it's only fair that I should love you, too, Light of my Eyes.' He dragged himself into a slouching position. Pierre brought him the coffee and he gulped it, and the large cup of water which followed. Ciaran leaned on him quite unaffectedly. 'It's your fault I get so polluted, you know.'

'Mine?' asked Pierre, sounding very French. '*Explique-toi!* "

'I couldn't lie in here and watch you sleep any longer, without touching you, so I sent myself out bravely into the desert to find some way of knocking myself out,' explained Ciaran. 'You kissed me, when I asked, but you never touched me.'

'Mon cher,' said his tent mate. 'Had you mentioned that–'

'You might have denounced me,' said Ciaran. 'Blimey, my head hurts! Get me some aspirin, Ha'bi'bbi, and tell me about the cat.'

'I dreamed about the Valley of Kings, copain, and I dreamed the location of a new tomb,' said Pierre, fetching aspirin and refilling the water cup. He dosed Ciaran and sat down on the tent floor next to his feet.

'I read the graffiti on the cliff, I saw the tomb door open and two men in the adit. Then a voice said that I should promise to find the tomb of Ptah-Hotep, and I should have my heart's desire, so I promised. When I woke up this cat was here, sleeping on my chest. And do I have my heart's desire?' he asked, trying to steady his voice.

'If your heart's desire is me, yes, you do,' replied the soldier.

'Tonight, when I have recovered, I shall prove it to you, my Light. For the present, am I too disgusting to kiss?'

'You will never be too disgusting to kiss,' replied Pierre, and demonstrated this.

The cat went back to sleep, head on paws.

Supervisor Carter was pleased to allow his most promising French colleague leave to explore a little, even on the basis of a dream.

Howard Carter knew about the importance of dreams. A dream had informed him that there was still a royal tomb to find. This prevision sounded promising. He had been concerned that Pierre Duclos, a pale, thin scholar, might find the desert conditions and the heavy work too taxing.

'But you must not go alone, there are some rogue fellahin around, take a guard.'

Pierre knew just the guard for his expedition. He collected gear and food and water, for there was no water at all in the valley and the wells which the artisans had used had not been rediscovered. He also collected a donkey, a small one which had been recently beaten and needed some restful occupation, notified his soldier and picked up the cat.

'I can't leave you here, Majeste,' he told her. These people are cruel to cats. And you ought to supervise: you need to be able to tell your mistress that I have carried out her wishes to her satisfaction.'

The cat climbed onto the donkey saddle without comment and they set out. Sgt Paterson took the leading rein. Pierre noticed, as they paced evenly along the ravine floor, that he was carrying his military pack, as well as his rifle and ammunition belt.

'You could put your pack on the donkey,' he suggested. Ciaran laughed.

'It's no weight for me, I'm used to it – marched all over the world with this knapsack – and she's carrying enough. Bastards lambasted the poor little thing, she's bruised.'

'Should I carry my own things, Englishman? Your race cares more for animals than people, they say,' teased Pierre.

'Says a man who takes orders from a cat,' responded the sergeant. Pierre admired his easy, comfortable pace. He did indeed look as though he could march around the world.

'I nicked a sack of oats and hay for the little 'un, and we won't work her too hard, we ain't in a hurry,' Ciaran said. 'Couple of days rest and she'll be all right. I fair hate the way these wogs mistreat animals,' he added, as the donkey nosed him for another bit of ration biscuit.

'They have no souls, it is said.' Pierre took the sergeant's hand in his own, pulling to slow him down, and then forgetting to release it.

'Nonsense,' protested Ciaran. 'You've only got to look in her eyes and you can see she has a soul. Haven't you, my angel? And your cat. She's been watching me as if she was weighing up whether to give me a medal or put my name down for punishment duty.'

'Then she is mistaken,' said Pierre, relishing the feeling of the hard, calloused hand in his own, fingers holding just tight enough. 'If you are condemned, then I am condemned as well, and She of Silences needs me to find this tomb.'

'You Frenchies are so rational. We're out of sight of the camp, and of the sentries. You could kiss me again, you know.'

'Yes, but I will deny myself that pleasure until we have reached good cover, and have found a place to camp. If we are seen by the English, it's disgrace for both of us.'

'I know,' replied the soldier. 'Has it always been like that? For men like us?'

'Not in Ancient Egypt,' replied Pierre. He released the sergeant and reached for a water bottle. The sun was beginning to bite. 'There they had no moral objections at all.'

Just before the turn in the path, a shot rang from the cliffs, then another. Sergeant Paterson shoved Pierre and the donkey back against the rock wall and levelled his rifle, searching the heights for targets. The cat rose to her paws and hissed.

'One, south ten degrees,' said Pierre steadily. 'Another, fifteen, same cliff. More coming up.'

'I see them,' replied Paterson. 'You know this path – anywhere we can take shelter?'

'Nowhere – it was well chosen for an ambush. If this is goodbye, I regret nothing except that I have never made love to you.'

'I regret getting drunk last night,' said the soldier, never taking his eyes off his mark. 'I would have stayed with you forever.'

'I fear that this is as far as forever goes,' said Pierre.

As more shots scarred the red stone and the cat wailed a loud, impatient howl, a thunder cloud descended from a clear hot sky and covered the ravine in mist.

Pierre and Ciaran, astounded, did not move. They could see nothing. In the cloud were dreadful noises, a rising predator's snarl which broke out into a full throated roar, breaking over them like a wave, harsh as a slap in the face: powerful. Ravenous. Personal.

Then it was gone: cloud, attackers, roaring. Pierre passed a shaking hand over his face and found it faintly damp. The cat, satisfied, sat down on the saddle again with a smug expression and began to wash mist off her fur. Ciaran slung the rifle and grabbed Pierre by the shoulders and kissed him, hard. Pierre moulded his body into the soldier's embrace. They were both trembling. Finally Ciaran whispered against his lover's neck

'What was that?

'That, mon amour, was Sekmet Blood Drinker, Sekmet the Destroyer, Sekmet Slaughterer of Men. Goddess of War. She is the lioness aspect of the Goddess Basht. Evidently the Goddess means for us to be able to carry out our task. Shall we move? I'm feeling a little... shaky.'

'So is Angel and so am I,' replied Ciaran. 'The only person who isn't terrified is that cat. Come on, we'll find a bit of cover, have a brew-up, and it's bikkies all round. Except for Her Highness, there.'

'I have some dried fish which I think she will find palatable,' said Pierre, and they moved away from the manifestation.

As a British soldier, Ciaran could make a small fire and boil water in any conditions. They sheltered under a dry wall and drank tea improved with cognac, recovering their nerve.

Bashtet accepted a small dried fish from Pierre's hand. He stroked her as he awarded her the Goddess' titles: 'Nefert, Neferti, Bashtet Tashery.' She purred loudly, for the first time, rubbing her face against his hand.

'What does that mean?' asked Ciaran, finished his tea and stamping out the fire.

'Goddess, little avatar of the Goddess Basht,' replied Pierre.

'I think she agrees with you,' said Ciaran. 'Not much further, Angel,' he assured the donkey. 'Soon have you unloaded and rubbed down.'

Nightfall found them established. The tent was pitched, the donkey rubbed down and watered, tethered nearby with some hay in case of night starvation.

Ciaran felt unreal, but not unsafe. After that supernatural cloud, he was sure that they were all under divine protection, and he had always longed for a god who could take instant action and, preferably, had teeth. Basht had accepted more dried fish and had vanished into the desert.

At last, at *last*, Ciaran could shed his clothes and lie down in the accepting embrace of his most beautiful lover. Pierre was slender and elegant and pale, everything he was not: he wondered that so scholarly a man could find a rough soldier so delightful. But as the caresses grew more intimate and the bodies slid closer together, he was sure that Pierre wanted him as much as he wanted Pierre, and that was, after many other lovers, finally and forever.

In the darkness and cold of the desert, they were two bright lights, heart to heart, burning as steadily as Sirius, Sothis, the star of Horus, above. They wrapped themselves in their blankets and fell asleep, arms around each other.

In the morning, they rose and carried out the usual tasks. Basht returned for more fish and also nibbled the edge of a biscuit. She drank deeply, as though she had been adventuring during the night. She walked from one lap to the other, as the two men sat on a suitable rock, sniffing languidly at their mouths and then burrowing her nose first into one shirt and then the other. Then she gave a satisfied 'Prr't' and sat down for a wash. She was beginning to look much better. From a ragged dusty stray she was already filling out to be the sable beauty she would become.

'What was all that about? A kit inspection?' asked Ciaran.

'I think she wished to know if we were truly together,' replied Pierre, caressing her whiskers. The Goddess has some purpose in choosing us, you know.'

'Fair enough, I never argue with goddesses,' said Ciaran swiftly. 'Have some of this cake, it's the last I have. My mother sent it.'

'Very good fruitcake,' said Pierre. 'Have you thought what will become of us? Shall we live in your country, or in mine?'

'I hadn't thought,' confessed Ciaran. 'I'm a soldier. It doesn't do to take long views if you're in my trade. No, what's there for me in Devon? I'd never make a farmer, that's why I joined the army. You?'

'We might stay here,' Pierre had been thinking about this. 'Men loving men is not illegal here. I have a taste for my father's trade, which is antiquities. What say to setting up business in, say, Cairo? You shall be my bodyguard, the master of my house, and my escort when we are travelling. And lie with me every night? Perhaps?'

'That sounds...' Ciaran lost words, and kissed Pierre very gently, allowing his lips to linger on his lover's soft mouth.

'Yes?' asked Pierre.

'Yes,' said Ciaran.

They found the tomb in the afternoon. The seals were untouched.

'What's written all down the door?' asked Ciaran. Basht sat

impatiently at Pierre's feet, just like a house cat waiting for some dim human to recognise the signal and open the door.

'It's a curse, a very comprehensive curse, against opening the tomb,' replied Pierre.

'What shall we do?' asked the soldier, twining his lover's fingers in his own.

Pierre put their joined hands against the clay seal, and it crumbled to dust, taking the curse with it. The door swung open, groaning a little against the wind blown sand. Bashtet flicked inside, as though it was her own house, and sprang onto one of the two sarcophagi in the tomb.

The walls were festooned with vines. Fresh as the day they were painted. Globes of delicious grapes hung eternally within reach of two men, who were overseeing the picking, eating the fruit, supervising the pressing and maturing, tasting the wine. They sat at a table together, saluting one another, and the table was laden with a fine feast.

Pierre scanned the inscriptions. 'He is Ptah-Hotep, Great Royal Judge. Oh, this is not a royal tomb. M'sieur Carter will be disappointed.'

'This bloke, he's got reddish skin, he's bigger than the other, who's pale and thin. What does it say about them?' Ciaran urged his friend to translate faster.

Piere was still kneeling, his eyebrows rising in astonishment and he read. 'The stocky one is Kheperren, a soldier with General Horemheb. And the Royal Judge and scribe, Ptah-Hotep, was his– Yes, Ciaran, Ptah-Hotep was his lover; the man he lived with all his life.'

'A soldier and a scholar,' said Ciaran. 'And there they are, lying in the reeds, making love, just as we did. Face to face.'

'*Justement*,' replied Pierre Duclos.

'So it's all right,' said Ciaran, eyes alight. 'We've happened before, we'll happen again. It's all right, us.'

'Yes,' said Pierre Duclos. They embraced in the tomb, between the two monuments. 'We're all right, *mon coeur*, we're forever all right.'

THE BLUE GUIDE

– Advice to Travellers

If you wish to buy antiquities while in Cairo – and who does not want some fragment of Egypt to take home to Surbiton or Berlin? – then you should direct your steps to the emporium of Monsieur Pierre Duclos in Alexander Street.

The shop has only a small sign, but do not let that dissuade you. Monsieur Duclos has antiquities and copies to suit the smallest budget, and riches and treasures for the largest. His shop is an old house, in which visitors may sit in the former seraglio, drink mint tea in the cool shade of the vines and listen to a learned discourse from M. Duclos.

A noted antiquarian, M. Duclos specialises in objects from the 18th Dynasty. His partner, M. Paterson, is always an interesting speaker, especially when talking about his sanctuary for abused animals. A donation can be left with him.

Visitors may also see the latest generation of the famous Duclos Basht, a breed of night-black cat now famous in Egypt. M. Duclos discovered the orginal Bashet in the Valley of the Kings. She was, fortunately, in kitten at the time, as no wild sire has been found. The breed is elegant, svelte, and perfectly black, with a velvety coat and spring green eyes.

M. Duclos will allow some bargaining, but his prices are already fair, and he will not indulge in any sharp practices.

We at Blue Guide thoroughly recommend his establishment.

A NOTE TO MODERN READERS

The life and times of the Great Royal Judge, Ptah-Hotep, and the soldier, Kheperren – who lived during the tumultuous reign of Pharaoh Akhenaten and Queen Nefertiti – is told in the historical novel *Out of the Black Land* by the 21st Century author, Kerry Greenwood.

THE THEBAN BAND

'Cleon, do you remember?' asked the deep male voice, as a hard hand slid slowly down his side to his hip, leaving a trail of sparks. 'How I first saw you wrestling, naked and oiled, and fell in love? And you flung yourself into my arms, sweaty and tousled, and I kissed your mouth and tasted blood from your cut lip? You tasted of danger, Cleon, my golden one, of danger and battle.' Now he felt a body lie down and slide between his legs, the mouth descending to his neck, so that the voice was muffled. 'Oh, I wanted you then as much as I want you now. There have been so many battles,' said the voice, resigned and sad. 'And this will be the last one. And then when will we meet again, my love, my heart?'

Just before the bodies joined, Anastasios woke up with a start. Cursing, he found himself, again, whimpering with lust and wishing that he could stay asleep just a little longer. If he was going to have dreams about being this Cleon and having a man make love to him in such beautiful Greek, he should at least garner the climax. But he never did.

And a tent shared with three other men in the middle of a really very quiet desert was not the ideal place to try to take care of his arousal without attracting attention. In the dream, he had been conveniently without clothes. Waking, he was tangled up in his khaki underwear and t-shirt and blanket, all of which had somehow come loose and coiled around him with malicious intent, like Laoccon's snakes. Moving very carefully, he slid a hand down, found the affected part, and very quickly came, hard, biting his hand to muffle his sob of release.

He was Anastasios, he told himself firmly, unravelling and getting up to go outside and wash. Not someone from an ancient battle - Troy, perhaps? He did not recognise the name Cleon. He was a proud Greek fighting to liberate his country from the Germans, who had committed atrocities, who had murdered innocent Jewish Hellenes, who were squatting evilly on his motherland and shooting whole villages in Crete. He had seen the photographs, sent to British Intelligence. 'Here Stood Kandanos, which defied the might of the German State,' and no one had been left alive in Kandanos, not man or woman or child or dog.

Of course, that wouldn't work in Crete. There were Cretans here who had promised to cut out a Nazi's heart and eat it. And they would. Raw. And laugh. The Cretans had survived 300 years of Turkish occupation. The Nazis would not break them. And he himself was a proud son of Thebes, and the Thebans had always been fighters. Only defeated, in the end, by Phillip of Macedon. And he had been Alexander's father, and he had conquered the world.

He washed, drank some water, and sat down in the sand to watch the sun rise. It was always a spectacle. His Greek lover would have said, 'Hail Apollo!' and seen the chariot with horses mounting the horizon. And all that Anastasios, in late 1943, saw in the sky was a great ball of flaming gas. Not, he considered, an improvement.

David Stirling, a Philhellene and probably completely mad, had convinced the British that they should include a contingent of Greeks in his irregular army, causers of trouble, saboteurs, paratroopers, bomb-aimers, assassins behind enemy lines, which were presently called Special Air Services. For some reason he had limited the number of Greek soldiers to 300.

And here we are, thought Anastasios, all 300 of us, camped in a ragged group of tents in this God-forsaken North African wilderness, about to spread out and make life miserable for the enemy. And anyone who thinks we are unruly hasn't met the Australians yet. Stirling nearly court martialled the whole regiment when he heard what had happened about that train full of crates of beer and spirits.

And he hadn't heard it from any of us. They were andartes, bandits, those Aussies, and they had made a special trip to bring the Greeks all the ouzo in the shipment. Anastasios suspected that Stirling was not really angry with them. After all, he had accepted all that scotch they had saved for him, and they *had* blown up the train, as ordered, after it was unloaded. Our own Captain Tsigantes had drunk up and not said a word.

They wanted us, the bad boys, the bold ones, the ones that didn't fit in well with an ordinary army. He had said it himself. He wanted pirates who could follow orders. He wanted a force which could be sent anywhere to do anything, as long as it involved wrecking things, stealing things, breaking things, and blowing things up.

Anastasios liked blowing things up. The camp was just beginning to wake, the night guard was coming in to wash, eat and sleep. Something was itching at the back of his head. There was something significant about the number 300.

He thought about it as he went back into the cramped, evil smelling half darkness to dress and find his boots, shake out the scorpion, there was always one, and present himself at the mess tent for something which resembled food if you hadn't eaten for ten days, and greet his comrades.

There were 16 Thebans in the 300. He knew them as one knows people from one's own province. He drifted over to where some were sitting and put his tin plate on their table. Chrysander, Andonis, Georgi, Yanni, Cletus.

'Brother,' said Cletus, grinning, 'you're looking dreadful. You should cut down on the wanking, malakos.'

'And good morning to you too, Cletus,' he responded. 'What's happening today?'

'Kit up and out by nine,' replied Cletus.

Anastastios' hand strayed upward to the holy medal his mother had given him. The others were doing the same, touching a sacred icon or beloved object. Chrysander sat closer to Andonis. Everyone knew they were lovers. And Yanni was supposed to be pining after Georgi. Whereas he, Anastasios, had only an Ancient Greek as a lover. He remembered his question.

'Why 300?' he asked. 'Why are there 300 of us?'

'Really, what were you doing when you were supposed to be at school?' asked Yanni severely. 'Fucking goats again? The Theban Band, idiot, the Sacred Army.'

'Oh,' stammered Anastasios. The army of male lovers. Men who fought harder because their own darling was beside them. His schoolmaster's voice came back to him, quoting Plato.

'An army of lovers cannot fail,' he said aloud.

'That's us,' said Chrysander, nudging Andonis. He planted a big kiss on his friend's cheek. 'They have a lion statue at Cadmea, where they all died. A huge great memorial. I've seen it. I'll take you to see it, if you like, if we ever get home. They found 274 skeletons under it. The Theban Band.'

'And soon we will get back to Greece,' declared Georgi, allowing Yanni to move closer to him. 'And then those Nazis will be whimpering for their mothers.'

'What about the name Cleon?' asked Anastasios. The others were getting up.

'Don't you mean Creon? The King in *Electra*? Anyway, if that was breakfast, we've had it. How I miss real food! If someone gave me a kalamata olive at this moment, I'd suck his cock,' said Yanni.

'That would be nice, but I have no olives. We'll have to wait until the Aussies ambush another train,' laughed Georgi.

'Come along, my brave boys, it's time for a little fly.'

'It isn't the flying that worries me, but the falling,' muttered Anastasios.

'Falling is just like flying until the very end,' soothed Cletus, putting a hand on his shoulder. 'Wait a little, my Anastasios. Why did you ask about the name Cleon?'

'It's nothing,' Anastasios muttered and pulled away from under the hand. 'I just heard it somewhere.'

Cletus let him go without another word.

The mission went well. They scattered along a railway line. They removed rails, disrupted signals, broke down one bridge and burned another, before they began to return to their pick up point. No sign of any German troops, though this could not last.

Then the sand storm began.

The only cover were small caves, just covered over ditches, and they crowded into them. Anastasios found himself lying in a barely tank sized cave with Cletus.

The wind howled, the sand scarified everything in its path. They dragged in their equipment and wrapped themselves in both their blankets. Inside two layers of badly-woven wool, felted with use, there was air enough to breathe and even speak, if they put mouth to ear.

'This could last for days,' worried Anastasios.

'I've got some water, so have you, and it usually only lasts until sunset,' said Cletus, re-arranging them so that Anastasios lay with his head on Cletus' shoulder, filtering his breath through his companion's shirt. 'Try to sleep. I'll wake you, if it dies down. No one is going to find us here, brother.'

'And no one can rescue us, either,' complained Anastasios. He closed his eyes, comfortable against another body. He dozed, but he was not asleep.

'Cleon, my love, we fought well,' said the rich voice again. 'You looked so beautiful, so graceful, as your spears flew into the enemy ranks. Do you recall how we outfaced Aegesthilus? He roared up to our embankment, and we stood down, shield against knee, spears angled up to the sky, and started talking about which grapes were the best? He was so unsettled that he drew off his forces. We beat them later in the day. By then most of them had run away, remember? Ah, my Cleon, kiss me again. We haven't much time.'

And this time Anastasios as Cleon kissed someone, and they kissed back, and this time hands were on his body and he knew his companion's name.

'My Calliste, my most beautiful man, I remember you dancing in full armour, the firelight glinting off vambrace and greave, and I fell in love with you. Surely the Gods sent you to me,' Anastasios told Cletus, and Cleon told Calliste. They kissed with the fervour of a thousand years of waiting.

They did not speak again until they were wet and spent and panting kisses into each other's mouths.

'Where are we now, my golden one?' asked Cleon.

'In another body, my heart, and soon we must go,' said Calliste. 'The Gods let us touch again, kiss again, as humans, before they take us away to the isle of heroes. I drew the spear from your chest and drove it through the heart of your murderer, my only love,' he said. 'But they overran our position, and I died under the stones of the peltasts. I never moved from standing over your body, my Cleon, until I could stand no longer.'

Anastasios felt a sharp pain in his heart, and Cletus groaned as many hurts manifested all at once.

'Why these?' asked Cleon, embracing Calliste closer, nipping him on the earlobe.

'Ouch,' said Calliste. 'They love each other as we do. They fight to defend Thebes against a cruel invader. And they are the new Theban legion, Cleon, the sacred band reborn. In a thousand years they have not forgotten us.'

'And an army of lovers cannot fail,' murmured Cleon, and then both soldiers fell abruptly asleep in each other's arms, and when they awoke the sand storm had died down and their plane had arrived.

They dug themselves out, scrambled aboard, and were flown

home wrapped in the same blanket, each afraid to let the other out of touching distance.

'They honoured us,' murmured Cletus, embracing his lover.

'I am honoured and afraid,' responded Anastasios. 'But we will die together if we fail.'

'We will not fail,' said Calliste comfortably. 'We will liberate Greece and go home to Thebes and drink wine and grow old together, while my sister's children bring in the goats and at night we will lie together with the sound of the sea in our ears. Didn't you hear what they said, my golden one, my honey, my brother?'

Athanasios kissed him, hidden in their shared covering. His voice broke on a laugh as he replied.

'An army of lovers cannot fail'.

THE SECRET DIARY OF
DR JOHN WATSON M.D.

ASHMOLEAN NUMBER 991 –4027 –SH –CLOSED ARCHIVE

This document is a small brown leather-covered notebook, found in a strongbox beneath the floor of a cottage in Sussex where it is believed by some scholars that Sherlock Holmes and Doctor Watson spent their retirement. The box also contained various legal documents, including a will (list attached), several military medals, a pair of opal cufflinks, ten gold sovereigns, a phial containing a seven percent solution of cocaine and a syringe in a shagreen case.

Authorities believe that the box was buried and then later forgotten, as the later owners of the cottage cleared out all the possessions, especially written material, relating to the famous detective and donated it to this institution in 1938. Some of it was lost to enemy action. Some of the collection is now displayed in the Sherlock Holmes Museum in Baker Street, London.

The handwriting in this document has been authenticated by Dr J Somerville, the noted Holmes scholar as belonging to Dr John Watson. The contents are now the subject of heated scholarly debate. This is a closed archive. Special permission from the Director must be obtained to gain access to it, and it may not be copied, summarised, or photographed for any but the purposes of private study.

It begins without any date or even mention of a day. But it must, from internal evidence, date to March 21st 1895, when the impending trial of Oscar Wilde for Gross Indecency was reported in *The Times*.

In style and sentence construction it matches Dr Watson's usual work.

I came home from the club late, tired, a trifle bosky, and half disgusted by the attentions of the young man for whose time and skill I had paid.

Since Mary died I had no wish to try for another female companion. She had been a perfect specimen of her gender.

I preferred though, for relief and perhaps to ease my burning and unrequitable desire for my friend, to visit the discreet club I had attended as a captain. We were all military men, all of us with so much to lose that no guilt-ridden wretch was likely to peach on us.

I went there when I desired to be, for a little while, caressed and embraced and loved. For a fee, of course. But the club was respectable; we did not employ boys. All of our young men were clean, well fed, well paid, comely and discreet. They were charming and kind to me and my broken heart and my long held, long denied love for my companion.

I had moved back to 221B and it was as comfortable as before. Mrs Hudson, always a kind woman, was gratifyingly pleased to see me. I did examine her rickety knee and prescribed some massage and treatments which she said did her a lot of good. And I flattered myself that her pleasure at my return was not just for the security of the rent.

Sherlock, who had ample means, would often forget to pay. 'Take it from the brass bowl on the mantelpiece,' he would tell her, waving that long white hand.

And there might be cash in the bowl, or there might not. Mrs Hudson had no means of knowing.

Since I had returned, however, I was a tired man. Nothing amused me, particularly. I ate and slept and drank and visited the whores when I could stay away no longer, but something inside me seemed to be decelerating, like a watch with a defective mainspring. I was aging, slowing down, on the road to senescence and death. And I didn't really mind.

'Come, Watson, I have ordered us a tidy little supper,' exclaimed Holmes, leaping up from his couch.

'You have drunk, but you have not eaten. Although I do have some rather good wine to share.'

Thus spoke the man who knew everything. He was right. I had not eaten.

I hung up my coat, doffed my hat, and went into my bedroom to wash my hands, take off my collar and boots, and assume my slippers and dressing gown. It had been a cool night outside, and the flat seemed warm and cosy and comforting by contrast.

Holmes 'little supper' was a collection of excellent dishes from a very expensive Italian restaurant, perhaps Sardi's. The wine was a Chateaux Margaux. I wondered what we were celebrating. It all smelled very good and I was suddenly hungry.

Holmes helped me to some partridge and poured me a glass of the red wine. Then he held up his glass in a toast.

'To friendship,' he said.

I raised my own and drank to friendship. I picked at the pheasant with shallots and almonds. It was excellent. I tried the artichokes.

Holmes was up to something. He was fidgeting with those long fingers, as though he was longing to pick up his violin. He tasted the poulet royale, commented on its piquancy, and drank more wine.

Then he rose and locked first the outer door, so that no one could get in from the street, and then the door to our own apartment, so that not even Mrs Hudson could gain entry. I raised an eyebrow. What had he to say that must not be overheard by even our innocent landlady? The shutters were across the windows. No one could hear from the outside. It must be a case of the utmost secrecy.

He dropped the keys in his dressing gown pocket and I ate some more partridge, waiting for the exposition of the problem. But Holmes began talking about les Grands Vins, something he does sometimes to cover another train of thought. I always get lost around the varieties of Bordeaux, and in any case, I was tired. I was always tired these latter days.

'Watson!' he said sharply, and I jerked awake. In my defence, I had heard the lecture before. Several times.

'Holmes?' I asked.

'Did you so much as glance at the Times today?'

'I did,' I replied. 'To what item would you draw my attention?'

'Oscar Wilde is to stand trial for Gross Indecency,' he said.

'Always was a fool, lounging around at the Cafe Royale, flaunting his ... predilections for all to see.'

'Agreed,' said Holmes. He drank more wine. 'But these predilections are shared by many innocent people. This Criminal Law Amendment Act will give the police free reign, and make every blackmailer rub his vile hands with joy.'

'Yes,' I agreed. 'It will be terrible.'

'Your club,' he started. Then he stopped and gulped Margaux. He never drank this much. 'That club,' he went on. 'The one you attended tonight.'

'Yes?' I quavered. I had no idea he knew I was an invert. I had gone to such lengths to hide it from him. The idea of successfully hiding anything like that from Sherlock Holmes should have made me smile, but I was horrified. I dreaded his reaction to this discovery of my depravity.

'You must not go there again,' he instructed me, taking my hand in both of his own. 'It is watched. I deflected police attention from you by telling them that you were there gathering information for me. You have escaped the raid by the skin of your teeth. I have been waiting here, pacing, all evening, waiting for you – or for news of your arrest.'

'My God, Homes!' I cried.

'Promise me,' he said earnestly. 'Promise me you will not return.'

'I promise,' I said, my hand still clasped in his. Then I realised the implications. My last scrap of earthly comfort, closeness, satisfaction, was now gone. I put my head in my hands. I despaired, amongst the wine glasses and the remains of our feast.

He rose and rested his hand on my shoulder. 'I know what you are feeling, Where will you go for a human embrace, to ease your loneliness and grief? When will you next receive a loving kiss?'

'Yes,' I groaned, all pretence set aside.

'Now,' he said, and promptly kissed me. A sweet kiss. His lips were soft and wet with wine. 'Will I not do as an adequate substitute for the whores of the Military Club?'

'Holmes!' I whispered.

He looked away from me, candlelight on his sharp profile, his hand still on my shoulder.

'I am no longer young, but I am healthy and clean. I was never beautiful. We have been friends for a very long time. Might you accept me as a substitute? I would not have my best friend walk unarmed into a den of lions – or, rather, a pit of scorpions.'

'No,' I said gently, patting the hand. His kiss tingled on my lips.

'No?' he asked, with a return to his cold, remorseless manner.

'Not as a substitute,' I told him, taking the hand and kissing the palm. 'You are no whore. Only as a lover could I accept you. If this is what you want, my dearest Holmes.'

'It is,' he averred.

'Why did you not ask me before?' I was curious, aroused, and afraid. Would this new turn of events destroy our ancient friendship, which had lasted so long and borne so much?

'I didn't *know* you were an invert,' he said crossly, looking at me again. 'I suspected as much, I gravely suspected as much, I hoped as much, but then you married, Watson.

'Before I could make up my mind to declare myself to you. It is a huge risk, you know. You might have turned away from me in disgust.'

'Holmes, I would never–'

'You might have,' he snapped.

'I might,' I conceded. I kissed his hand again. 'Are you, like me then, an–'

'An invert? Of course, Watson. Consider the facts. I have never had even so much as a friendship with a woman except Mrs Hudson. All my close relationships are... well, with you.'

'You have had lovers?' I asked, dazed. He might have been dallying with a whole brigade of guardsmen, as far as I would have known. I have never seen him look at a man with lust, never seen him dishevelled or red-mouthed with kissing, never even scented sex on him.

He sat down next to me on the sofa. 'When I was young. There was Sebastian, at least, we kissed and toyed and fancied ourselves in love. Then I smashed his world and he went to America and I decided that I had done with love.'

'And you hadn't?' I smiled. He smiled, too, his rare and beautiful smile.

'Then a sturdy, strong, ex-army doctor limped into my life, and I found that I had not done with love after all.'

I nearly choked on my Margaux. 'You've been in love with me all this time?'

He patted me on the back. 'Let's have a glass of that Armagnac the Duc sent and consider the matter, since you have not run screaming from 221B in horror and loathing.'

'My dearest Holmes,' I whispered and leaned into the hand cupping my cheek. 'I am delighted, astonished, amazed. I have to tell you that I have loved you from the moment I saw you, I have always wanted you. I never knew you even thought of love.'

'You knew how much I relied on you, trusted you, confided in you, cared for you,' he said quietly.

'Yes,' I said. I accepted the small glass of cognac. I was what Mrs Hudson called 'in a state'. 'I knew. I saw it in your eyes.'

'And you knew I had no other friend but you?'

'I never saw you with any confidential friend, male or female,' I agreed.

'And you never will. Are you familiar with the myth that

the Gods made men two-natured, then found their creations to be too strong?'

'Split them in half, so they spent their lives looking for their other halves, and didn't try to challenge the Gods again?' I remembered the story.

'I have been aware from the first time I spoke to you that you are my other half,' he said.

'Oh,' I said, struck by a revelation. 'I am very dull. And of course you are mine.'

'Bravo,' he murmured, as he does when I make some halfway-decent piece of deduction.

Being in love would not change Holmes because, by his account, he had always – Heavens! – been in love with me. All that time, while I had been finding other lovers and despairing of ever engaging his regard.

That called for more Armagnac flavoured kisses. His lips were tentative. Whatever he had done with his friend Sebastian had been a long time ago. But I had – God save me – experience enough for 20. I would seduce him gently into making love, so that he would feel loved and cherished – and mine.

The thought was almost as intoxicating as the cognac.

He broke off the kiss, which was getting a little heated. I was aroused: he was, also.

'Rules,' he announced. 'This is a perilous enterprise, Watson, my dear Watson. Outside this flat we must be just what we have been. Agreed?'

'Of course,' I said.

'Inside we must lock all the doors, be sure that if inspected, raided, we have two adequately slept-in beds. That is what condemned Lucius Paul. And no signs otherwise that two men have had a criminal connection. To that end I have caused fine linen towels to be bought. We can burn them at a pinch.

'And no love letters, no public kisses, nothing before an audience, even Mrs Hudson. We are risking a great deal, my dear.'

'I know. I'll risk it if you will. We have enemies, Holmes, who would love to ruin us.'

'I have enemies, you mean,' he corrected me in his usual manner. Then he said wistfully, 'Is love so good, that it is worth such peril? That you would go to that place in search of it?'

'I went here to slake my lusts with paid companions, which is not the same thing. That is not love. It is a transaction. And, yes, love is worth it and so I shall convince you. I agree to all your conditions.'

'There is one more,' he said, staring straight into my eyes.

'And that is?'

'That I am the only lover. I will not share you, Watson. If you are mine, you are mine alone.'

'And you,' I responded, chuckling, 'Are mine. If I show you love and you acquire a taste for it, you may not then find a prettier man than a crippled doctor to share your bed.'

He looked almost ill as he promised, hand upraised, that I would be the only one. Forever.

'I never thought you crippled,' he told me. 'I have always thought you most attractive. You have shoulders that Phidias might have carved, an admirable torso. And beautiful eyes.'

'How long have you been preparing for this day?' I asked.

'I laid the towels in storage after the first month,' he confessed.

'It is so sad, Holmes that we never spoke, that I never spoke, and you have spent all this time alone.'

'I had you with me, and when you were gone, the memory of you,' he told me. 'It is late. Shall we retire?'

He held out his arm to me. I took it, and he led me to his bedroom. There, he paused. He had not taken Sebastian to bed, then. I shucked my slippers, took off my socks and trousers and underlinen, retaining my shirt and my dressing gown. Then I sat my lover down and unwrapped him as though he was a long desired gift, the very best of Christmas presents.

He did not flinch away from my touch, but I went slowly, allowing him time to object or draw back. I was effectively seducing a virgin, and I did not want to affront his modesty. He stripped pliably, moving so that I could remove various articles. I peeled his dressing gown away, and then his shirt. Finally I could kiss his shoulder, his skin. He was wiry and muscular, pale and smooth. I tongued a nipple and heard him make a sharp gasp, as he did when he had solved some arcane problem. I shed the remains of my own clothes, slowly. If he had indeed been waiting for this sight as long as I had, I wanted him to enjoy it.

I am not much to look at. I am flabby round the middle, stocky, scarred, especially my right thigh where they had dug as many fragments of that damnable jezail bullet out of me as they could find, leaving enough to lame me for life. His eagle eyes examined me with cool, deep intelligence. He reached out and touched my chest, sliding his hand down until he paused on a round scar on my hip.

'Bullet?' he asked.

'Yes, I had forgotten about it. Lie down with me, on your pristine linens,' I said.

'Such is courage,' he murmured, and lay down naked in my naked embrace, his head on my shoulder, our legs intertwined, and I know there were angels singing, because I heard them.

We had to do surprisingly little wriggling to lie easy. We fitted together, knee and hip and arm and chest, and we kissed luxuriously. We had the whole night. We had the rest of our lives.

We started to move together, soon enough. Heat grew between us. I found his sex and it leapt gratefully into my hand. He found mine, and I put both our hands and our cocks together, to slide together, thigh and chest, heat rising, mouths open and biting, kisses which grew wilder and wilder. I heard him panting, or was it me?

'Petit mort', they call it. Little death. If I had died then as my lover reached it with me, I would have died blessed.

I mopped us clean with his fine linen and folded him back into my arms.

'So strange,' he murmured into my ear. 'My dearest Watson, my... my love. It was not like that with...' he fell silent, perhaps not liking to name his previous lover while he was in bed in my company, though I did not mind.

'You were very young,' I told him. 'Making love is a skill like any other. Are you pleased, my dearest Holmes?'

'More than I thought possible,' he said. 'I see that you have much to teach me.'

'It will be my pleasure,' I assured him with perfect verity. No truer statement has ever been made.

He leaned up on one elbow and looked into my face, worried.

'Your pardon, dearest Watson, did my small effort please you? It felt so natural, so easy...'

'Two halves of the same whole, remember? Either knows what will please the other. I have never been so pleased, my love, my love.'

I kissed him again. He kissed me back. Then he broke the kiss. This was beginning to be a bad habit of his.

'Sussex,' he said flatly. 'I do not insist on the location, but it must have a good connection to a town line.'

'Holmes?' I asked, utterly confused.

'If we survive, when we retire,' he explained patiently 'I would like to go to a remote cottage in Sussex and keep bees. Will you come with me?'

I laughed. He had mapped out the rest of our lives, after only one encounter.

'Sussex, yes, I like Sussex, and I have no objection to bees as long as they are your bees. We shall have a small cottage and a woman to come in by the day, and honey for tea.'

'That's settled, then,' he said. He buried his long nose in my neck, tightened his arms around me, and fell asleep.

So did I. I slept deep. I rose in time to unlock the apartment doors, wallow like a hippopotamus in my own bed to convincingly unmake it, and return to Holmes. I locked his bedroom door then, before Mrs H came and brought breakfast,

I woke him with sleepy kisses and made use of his fine linen towels again.

I have never been so happy. I needed to write an account of it, to make it real to me, though no one will ever read it until we are long dead. And I hope that we have our Sussex cottage. I'm sure that Holmes will do very well with his hives, and I am very fond of honey.

Dr John Watson, M.D.

THE EVOLUTION OF THE VAMPYRE

I considered my thesis proved when a dark figure materialised from the deep shadows in the Research collection and pinned me by the throat against the 1884 Magnusson edition of the definitive *Old Norse Sagas*. In 12 volumes. I was now crushed against *Vol IV, Beowulf* – Bjarni Herjolfsson.

'So there is a vampire in the library,' I managed.

A larger than human hand was confining my speech to a croak like that of a heart-broken frog.

'What gave me away?' he asked.

I looked at him hazily. I was going to pass out soon if he didn't loosen his hold. 'Shall we sit down and discuss it?' I whispered.

Just in time, the hand was removed. He pulled out a chair and sat me down, holding me by the wrists, which was an improvement on the neck.

He stared into my eyes. 'Well?'

Just the hint of an accent. He had almost said, 'Vell?'

I looked him over. So this was our library vampire. He was a bit above average height, dark hair and eyes, pale skin. Not startlingly beautiful or magnetic. He looked quite human, apart from the pointed fingernails and the fangs which were almost piercing his bottom lip...

His full, red, luscious bottom lip–

I pulled myself together. He was still waiting for an explanation.

'The research staff,' I said. 'I use this library all the time, I know them all. Lately they have been slow, pale and stupid; as though they were short of something – like blood. At first I thought it might be a virus, but they didn't seem fevered or in pain, they didn't sneeze or cough. And every one of them, every one, had taken to wearing high collars, even in this weather. I'm a student of folklore, and I worked out that they all came here, where no one ever comes, except me; because everyone uses the internet now, and so–'

'You wanted to meet me,' he said, again with the faint 'v' sound. 'How courteous. Might I know the gentleman's name?'

'Evelyn Du Bois,' I said. As he had not released me, I could not get up and bow. 'And by whom do I have the pleasure of being held captive?'

He released one hand and smiled. 'Very pretty grammar. For a long time I have been the Graf Caspar of Mecklenberg-Strelitz-am-Rhine. That will do. You may call me Your Highness.'

'Your highness,' I agreed. 'May we converse?'

'If you wish. I am not hungry at present. And you will not remember meeting me, anyway. Why are you interested in my kind?'

'Popular legend has done many things with the idea of vampires,' I began.

He snorted, releasing my other hand to bang his fist on the table. I used both hands to rub my throat, which would surely be bruised in the morning; if I lived out the night.

'In the beginning,' he said in a dark-chocolate voice which one could just taste on the tongue, 'we were simple. The undead, returning to our families with a thirst for life, gradually sapping their strength until they died and became vampires in their turn. Treated easily by digging up the bodies, staking, removal of the head, and so on. Usually such deaths were caused by bad drainage or plague, but few actual corpses complained about their treatment, due to already being dead. When I was Marcus Flavius Drusus, that was what I was.'

'You were a Roman?'

He raised an eyebrow. 'Have I not said so? I was just such a rising corpse, stinking, ugly, terrifying. The enraged villagers caught most of my progeny, but not me, and I lay in my grave for many a year.

'And then I ranged Europe, looking for a nice quiet spot with a reasonable number of people. I wasn't greedy. It has been centuries since I have killed. I had a pleasant little castle in Mecklenberg-Strelitz-am-Rhine, a staff of obedientaries, and an uneventful afterlife.'

'Obedientaries?'

'Ones who are habituated to me drinking their blood. They do get slow and stupid after a while. I was always having to replace the staff. I shall have to move on from here soon. It's a pity; I like old books.'

'My lips are sealed,' I promised.

He gave me a sharp, intelligent look. 'Yes, they are,' he said. 'Or they will be. But then... doom.'

He seemed so downcast that I took his hand. It was warm, which I had not expected.

'Doom?' I asked sympathetically.

'Bram Stoker,' he whispered. 'A hundred thousand curses on his name.'

He went on cursing for some time in a variety of languages, including Latin, for I distinctly heard him pronounce anathema.

'He dined one night with one who knew us – the explorer Richard Burton; dangerously beautiful man. I recall him lying sprawled in a blue satin bed while–

'But that is not germane. He decided to fascinate Stoker, a literary young man who didn't get out much, with terrible tales of blood-sucking monsters and aristocratic vampires and glamour, which he stole from old stories about fairies. Don't get me started on that. And that wretched young creature penned his dire novel and created Count Dracula, a new sort of vampire.'

'What difference would a new book make to you?' I asked, stroking the warm hand.

His eyes flashed red, like a cat's at night.

'We are creatures of myth,' he told me. 'You yourself, sir

scholar, called us folklore. If the mythos changes, so do we. So we common peaceful blood suckers became aristocratic seducers of young women – how I dislike young women.

'When I was a Roman I didn't even have female slaves. Stoker based *his* Count on Burton, you see. Richard always did have a whimsical humour.'

'So, you were transformed by the novel,' I thought about it. 'And since then?'

He snarled. They were hollow teeth, I noticed, like a snake's, and through them I saw that he could suck up blood as in a straw. Though hopefully not mine. Not yet.

'Then there came Anne Rice, who made us intelligent.'

'And sexy,' I reminded him. I adore Anne Rice's books.

He nodded. 'That, too. We had not been either before. She made us suffer for our hunger. She made us sympathetic.'

'And so you became– sympathetic?' I ventured.

'It was horrible.'

He put his head in his hands. I patted his shoulder and then had a surprising armful of weeping vampire, crying tears of blood into my chest. He felt very good under my hands, very muscular, very male. His hair smelt of chestnut blossoms and pine resin. I held him close until he sat up, wiped his face on my sleeve, and went on

'We suddenly remembered. Everything. We became intelligent, scholarly, musical, debauched, interested in humans. I hadn't been any more interested in my humans – though I treated them well – than you are interested in the personalities of the sheep you slaughter for dinner. That all changed.

'Quite a few of us could not endure the guilt, and walked into the sun. I had not been a great hunter, so I contained myself. I had preyed mostly on the lone traveller, and when I came on bandits attacking a caravan, I usually killed the bandits, because they were better fed and had more nourishing blood. Not for any altruism, you understand.'

'I understand,' I soothed.

'Then after Rice came–' he shuddered.

'Buffy?' I asked.

He flinched. 'Do not mention that name. From the moment she existed, and enough people believed in her, then Slayers spontaneously arose. And then came Angel, the Good Vampire. With a Soul! Now we were not dark creatures of nightmare and blood, but angels of light. It was awful. The changes gave me such cramps that I lay in my coffin and cried with the pain for a week.'

'Poor Highness,' I soothed again. This interview was not going as I expected, at all, but I was fascinated none the less. Now he was wringing his hands.

'I thought the worst had passed until–'

'Twilight?' I hazarded.

My poor Graf cried aloud at the name.

'Sparkling vampires able to endure the sun! And werewolves!

He threw up his slendedr hands. 'Not to mention a girl so stupid she set feminism back a generation, and a vampire so inane Buffy would have staked him on sight. The world is a sad place now,' he whispered, laying his head on my shoulder.

'There are advantages,' I said. 'Now people aren't afraid of you. That must make them easier to enchant.'

'Pitiably easy,' he sighed against my neck. 'I used to be repelled by crucifixes and holy water would burn me. I used to know that if I walked into the sun, I would burn to ash. Now all I have to do is avoid *twinkling*. It is *so* humiliating.'

It struck me that having a vampire nuzzling my neck might not be a good career move, if I planned on living for the rest of the night.

'I bring good news,' I said, moving aside so that he was mouth to mouth with me, rather than mouth to carotid.

'You do?'

'Zombies,' I told him. 'Zombies have replaced vampires in popular imagination. Now only the really good writers are writing vampire novels. In which you do not twinkle.'

'Zombies?' he looked into my eyes. 'Pah! Zombies are Haitian and brain dead; creations of a sorcerer with a powder made of dead puffer fish.'

'They were. But like your evolution they have now become something else. Whether they were ever real enough to be affected, to actually appear, I don't know.

'But popular culture has moved on; which leaves you as you are, my dear Graf Caspar. Clever, beautiful, attractive, moral, scholarly, musical–'

'And you wish to talk to me about the past, don't you?'

'Yes. Were you there when Julius Caesar died?'

'It was messy. What a waste of good fresh blood.' He chuckled.

'Will you talk to me? Will you let me stay with you?' I urged.

'Oh, yes,' he said. 'If you wish. I am required to help you, ever since Rice; and especially since Buffy.'

'That would be wonderful,' I assured him.

'There's another thing that the new vampires are,' he whispered, his fangs retracted into his mouth, his lips on mine, soft and warm.

'What's that?' I asked, already succumbing to his erotic charm, which was like being hit below the waist with 240 volts of domestic current.

'We're sexy,' he said, his fingers slipping under my t shirt, 'and we like to make love to men.'

'Yes,' I said. 'Oh, yes, please.'

ALL ALONG THE WATCHTOWER

'Ave, Flavius,' said Quintus, climbing the plasti-wooden stairs. 'How goes your watch?'

'Ave, Quintus, glad you're here, you are a good relief, I'm freezing my bollocks off. Nothing happened until just now – there, see them? Two riders are approaching.'

'Wind's picking, too. Stay a moment, might need a runner. They're Equites. They don't usually hurry.'

'Might disarray their hair,' agreed Flavius, huddling in his red cloak. 'Or chip their fingernails. Oh, by all the Gods, this is bad. Focus the telescope. You see them?'

'Pantheres caeruleis, I've never seen one in the flesh, what brings the Pancae to us? With riders? They're not hunting them, they're running with them.'

'You know they can't eat earth protein,' Flavius reproved. 'Yes, they resemble huge blue leopards, but they worked that out early and since the Medicus cured that cub of the vitamin deficiency, they haven't laid a tooth on us. Sentient but aloof, that's the Pancae. They trade meat and skins, we trade salt and catmint. If they're coming with the Equites, something very nasty is about to happen.'

'And, it's going to happen to us,' sighed his friend. 'As usual.'

'You volunteered for this,' Flavius said. 'You could have stayed home in Colonia, eating honeycomb and communing with the cerapidae.'

'By Hercules' Balls!' swore Quintus. 'Beacon fire on Secundum! Sound the alarm!'

Flavius hauled on a cord and a klaxon blared, ear-shatteringly harsh. Shouts and stamping sounded below as the Optio turned out the guard. On the next hill Tertia, the third of the trimontium, Quintus saw the red fire flare. That beacon would alert Colonia, and they would alert the other watchtowers. Cerapids would wing out as soon as the Legion commander received reports from those two riders, their horses floundering, and the accompanying pancae, delivered the bad news.

Flavius heard the gate open and crash shut. He left Quintus on watch and ran down the steps. Horsemen were gently leading the trembling mounts away, to soothe and water them.

Horses were precious. Only two generations ago, when the Colonia had crashed on this planet, the machines had been working, and as the colonists were defrosted, the gene banks had engaged and produced those animals which could thrive on the grassy, rolling hills of Trimontium. Horses, goats, sheep but not cows: bees: dogs and cats, for company and other duties, donkeys for arid areas. A variety of birds, which throve.

One generation ago, as the machines died for lack of replacement parts, they had produced the next generation: an infant for every four people. These children were carefully selected across a wide variety of genes, so that the colony would not interbreed. They, too, were precious, since few women conceived on Trimontium. The Medicae had failed to locate the missing enzyme or vitamin. Then their machines, too, had failed.

But Trimonitium already had sentient races. The pancae, of course, leopard-shaped and blue as a summer sky in the Aegean; sarcastic, intelligent, and not particularly interested in humans. Until they had taken a whiff of the catmint which a certain Domina grew for her own feline companion. That established a base for trade.

Then the Medicus had cured the cub, and the pancae decided that they could tolerate the colonists. Only they could bring down the *bos*, eyeless, brainless, slow moving mountains of flesh which grazed across the plains, and when they did, they always had plenty of leftovers which could be swapped for catmint and various delicacies.

Trimontium did not have birds until chickens and ducks were produced by the ship, but it did have cerapids, flying creatures who adored honey to such an extent that they could be trained to take messages just by assuring them that honey would be offered at the other end. They were fast and had stings, and none of the other flying things bothered them.

Scientists had despaired of communicating with the Cloud Beasts, masses of opaque material who wafted around the sky, until the settlers completed their bathhouse and steam rose into the aether. A nebula, a small cloud, wandered over, and then rolled and bathed in the released warm steam. A shower of red things fell off it. Apparently, they were parasites. Boiled in steam, they were delicious. The other clouds drifted over to watch the young one wriggling in delight. Then the Nubulae had spoken, telepathically, 'If we have some skill you can use, may we, too, bathe in your {irritation removing, louse destroying, altogether delightful} hot wet air?'

The answer, of course, was yes, though no one had thought of a skill they had which anyone could use. But the sight of a grave, elderly cloud beast rubbing its length along the bathhouse roof, making a bare whisper of sound, and the shower of crustaciae rattling down to waiting plates, was one of Trimontium's pleasures.

'C..c...classis,' gasped the Eques, leaning on his friend. 'A warship is coming!'

'After all this time? Are you sure?'

'Nubulae are sure,' he gained some voice. 'They warned us. There's a hot spot at thirty degrees. Something is coming down.'

The cerapid sitting on the Legion commander's shoulder nodded, pecked at his check affectionately, then winged off towards Colonia. It would repeat the message and lick up its rightful honey. The settlement had grown up around the remains of the ship, most of which was still complete. Lately the Trimontium-born had decided to build their own houses. They seemed uncomfortable in the white corridors, painted with images of various gods.

'Muster!' shouted the Legion Commander, a child of the ship. 'Rangers!'

Flavius shucked his helmet and armour, put down his spear, grabbed his ration bag and his flask and donned his loose fitting woven garment, all shades of green and brown, made by his father, a notable weaver. He and four others walked out the wicket gate and slid away into the grass.

He had travelled too far! The classis had come down with a dreadful roaring crash, the grass about it all afire, and was now tipped over almost onto its side. It did not look like a healthy ship. The name was on its side: Classis Andromeda. The fire had died down. The legion from the colonia had come out and was ranged between the watchtower and the ship. A legion had exited the ship and was lined up before the colonists. It looked bad; the soldiers had modern weapons, the colonists had spears. Their leader was nose to nose with the colony leader, Consul Atticus. They were both shouting.

And Flavius could not get around the army and join his own people. He could not hear what anyone was saying, but it looked bad. He ground his teeth in frustration.

He was lying in a natural gully, made by water a long age ago, when he heard someone breathing, drew his knife, and then had a human body dropped on him by a large blue furred creature. The panca spat, and swiped at his muzzle with a clawed paw.

'He smells wrong, but he's yours. You eat him,' he said, and stalked off. Flavius unwrapped himself from the other human, and grabbed both his arms as he struggled.

'I am not going to hurt you,' he said, clearly. 'Can you understand me?'

'I can,' replied the soldier. 'I was just scouting, as always, and this blue leopard picked me up as though I was a kitten!'

'He says you smell wrong,' Flavius informed him. 'But they

don't eat people. I'm Flavius,' he said. 'You came from the warship?'

'I'd stand up and salute, friend, but I'm a bit unnerved. Blue leopards! What a place! Ave,' he said, recalling his manners. 'I am Sixtus Caesureus Athenacus of the Lost Legion.'

'The lost legion?' asked Flavius. 'Want a drink and a bite? I've only got bosmeat sausage and olives and bread, and some wine.'

Sixtus's pleasant face was transformed by greed. He was a handsome young man with dark hair and eyes and a Hellenic cast of countenance. Sixtus handed him the bag, and watched as the legionary ate precisely three of the twelve olives, two bites of the sausage, and a quarter of the bread. Then he took a gulp of wine and handed it all back to Flavius. And he smiled.

Flavius saw such pain and deprivation and loneliness in that smile that he enveloped his enemy in an embrace that was at least partly one of pure compassion. He saw a depth of suffering in Sixtus's eyes which defied belief. Those dark brown eyes had seen far too many horrors that no one should have to see.

'Oh, my honey,' said Flavius. 'It's all right. You're safe here. No one has troubled us for more than eighty years.'

The young man's body was meagre under his hands. Flavius could feel every rib, the hollow of the belly, the salt-cellar collarbones of malnutrition. This could be remedied. Ask the pancae for another bos, and they could feed everyone on roast beast.

'The empire has fallen,' whispered Sixtus into Flavius's neck. 'Commodus, the last emperor, ordered us away. Keep going, he said, never stop. So we obeyed. Mithras, we obeyed. And we fled and we died and we fought and now, here, we have come to an end of our journey. We can't get away this time. That ship will never rise again.'

'And you would be welcome here,' soothed Flavius. 'We need technicians and spare parts and your ship has them. Colonia is mostly intact, but we don't know how to use most of the machines. We can always do with more legionaries, or settlers, we can build a house and cultivate bees if you like, or grow olives, or hunt the bos with the pancae.'

Sixtus kissed him, suddenly and fiercely, tears striping his grimy cheek. 'Oh, yes,' he said. 'To stay in one place, to lie in the sun, though I observe that you have two, just to be a man again and not a soldier. But it won't happen. Our commander is a stubborn old beast, and by the look of him your consul is about the same.'

'Yes,' agreed Flavius. 'We'll have to do something about that before they start shooting each other.'

'The guns are for show,' said Sixtus. 'We haven't had any ammunition since... oh, I can't recall. That waterly planet with the dragons. What are you going to do?'

'We two are going to do it,' Flavius told him. 'Come with me? Trust me?'

'Yes, and yes,' agreed Sixtus. 'I'm so tired that if they kill me it will be something of a benefit. At least that way I get to lie down and rest.'

'No one is going to kill anyone,' said Flavius firmly, and rose out of the gully with Sixtus by the hand.

They walked unnoticed into the classis' line, and through it to where the commanders stood.

Still shouting, thought Flavius. You'd have thought that they would have run out of breath by now. Both sets of men looked anxious and were clutching weapons. This could turn extremely unpleasant really fast. Flavius hoped he knew what he was doing.

'Consul,' he said loudly. 'Legate,' he added. "There are things you both need to know. Will you let me speak?'

'Flavius, how do you dare?' demanded the Consul.

'Because I am a free-born Roman citizen, Consul, and you are an elected official. Listen. Two things. This is a peaceful colony planet and we have no evil intentions towards you.'

The Legate lifted a scarred eyebrow.

'Second, you are stranded, Legate. Your ship will not rise again. You need a home. This is it. It is called Trimontium.

We've been here 80 years, we know a lot about it, we can help you settle, and we will always need guards.'

'Sixtus, have you betrayed me?' demanded the Legate, raising his pistol.

'I, too, am a free-born Roman citizen, Legate,' responded Sixtus wearily. 'And anyone looking at the old *Andromeda* there can see she isn't lifting again. I like this place; this man gave me olives and wine when he thought I was an enemy. We have things to offer them, too, Sir. Their machines have died for lack of spare parts and knowledge. We have the knowledge. We can trade for what we need.'

'Cannabalise the ship?' the Legate sounded horrified.

On cue, a cloud beast settled on the nose of the classis, and it gave a groan and fell over, not too hard because it was mostly buried in sand already.

'You have technicians?' asked the Consul, eagerly.

They were in close conference instantly. Flavius drew Sixtus away.

'Come on,' he said. 'If we go now we can get to the bath house before all the equites. And if the cloud beasts have been basking, there will be crustaceae. With lemon juice, they are quite delicious.'

'This must be the Elysian Fields,' responded Sixtus.

'No, you're not dead yet,' Flavius told him, and proved it with a kiss.

Warm season came in wet and hot, so the cloud beasts writhed with pleasure in the sky. The pancae had taken to some of the legionaries, now that they smelt like Trimontium, and took them hunting. Flavius came back to the small house he shared with his dominus, Sixtus, just as he was taking a honeycake out of the solar oven.

'My grandmother's recipe,' he told his lord. 'Pour me some wine, my light, and let's sit outside under the vine. It's too hot in here.'

'A good idea, my jewel,' replied Flavius, sitting down under the grape vine and handing a cup to his lover. 'You know, I think this is working,' he observed.

'What, the honey cake? The wine? The cloud beasts cavorting over the bathhouse? The legionaries roasting chunks of bos over that fire? The new growth in the olive trees? Your sweet presence in our bed, your kisses, the endless delight of your love?' asked Sixtus.

Flavius sipped wine. 'All of those,' he said lazily. 'And that the Lost Legion is—'

'No longer lost.' Sixtus raised his cup in salute. 'The Lost Legion has found a Forever Home.'

It's So Very Lonely, When You're a Thousand Light Years from Home

I had one hour's air left. Fifty nine minutes. Fifty eight. Seven.

I wrenched my attention away from the counter. These escape pods were well made, comfortable for a given meaning of comfortable, and contained food and water and even entertainment.

For forty days. This was the thirty ninth day. I still had food and I still had water and I had been entertained with the second mate's whole collection of 20th Century noir films, while the automatic systems hunted across the galaxy for the nearest beacon or habitable planet, but now I was running out of air, without which all the rest were a little superfluous. And there was still nothing out there but the Big Black.

And asphyxiation is such a nasty way to die. I tried not to think about it. I tried to think about my last lover. A brief encounter at Marsport, a sweet mouth, a strong hand, all over in a moment. Never saw him again. I couldn't even remember his name. If I ever knew it.

And they had all been like that, I realised. Impossible to keep a planetside/traveller relationship alive, though some people always tried it. They were the ones who fornicated their way through the unattached members of the crew when they got that gram that said, sorry, I've met someone. I had been the delighted recipient of some of that attention. But people who form relationships will form new ones, and all my lovers had gone on to settle down with someone else, and make the lunchtime crew smile at how they doted on each other.

No one doted on me. I was an easy lay, a reliable comfort, to be applied to the ache as needed, discarded when replaced. If I died out here, as it was increasingly likely that I would, no one would weep for me.

So I began to weep for myself. I was actually sobbing, in a way I had not done since I was seven and my father died, when I heard a little voice that said, 'Lonely. Cold'.

'Escape Pod 459, Galaxy Class ship StarRover out of Syria Planum, Mars, requesting urgent assistance,' said the automatic message.

I held my breath, my face wet with tears. No answer. It must have been a ghost. There is a theory that everything said on any form of communicator is still bouncing around the universe. Bits and pieces of conversations, numbers, emerge out of the static between the planets. But I was in deep space, hence my present predicament, which would shortly become a plight. In, oh, I don't know, another fifty-three minutes?

'Speak again,' I asked. 'Is there anyone there?'

'Lonely,' said the voice.

'So you said. I'm lonely too. Where are you? Can you come and get me? Guide this pod? I'm running out of air,' I tried not to sound too desperate.

'Cold,' said the voice. It sounded like a man.

'Yes it certainly is,' I agreed. My surge of hope died. This was some last cruel trick of the gods. I hoped they were laughing themselves sick. But I had someone to talk to, even though it was just a spectre.

'Let me in,' pleaded the voice.

'Love to, but I can't open this pod in space,' I told it. 'Only in atmosphere. So you'll just have to talk to me.'

'Who?' asked the voice.

'I'm Sebastian Reynolds, first mate, StarRover, a good ship until she developed some explosive engine trouble and we all got thrown out here. I hope the others made it. I was the last to go. We shoved the families and the couples out first. But I had no one. Still haven't,' I concluded. 'You can call me Sabi. What's your name?'

'Spectre,' said the voice, after a pause for thought.

'Nice to meet you, though I would have liked to meet you when I didn't have, let's see, forty-three minutes left to live. I would have taken you to my favourite bar and bought you a drink. Mars ale, the finest that Syria Planum could provide. Tastes wonderful, once you get over it being blue.'

I was not really expecting a reply. These electronic ghost words almost never make so much as a sentence and they are not responsive. Unless you are sitting in an escape pod with twenty-eight minutes left to breathe. And hallucinating an Imaginary Friend to comfort your inevitable death.

'Let me come in,' breathed Spectre, sounding closer and louder.

'I can't,' I replied. 'I wish I could.'

Now was not the time to remember all those merry ghost stories about pods found with the occupant all wizened and drained of blood by space vampires who projected through the walls. But, I thought, so what, I was dying anyway. In twenty one minutes.

'Will you harm me?' I asked, a stupid thing to say.

'No,' sighed Spectre. 'I'll love you...'

Probably to death, but the odds were not in my favour for living more than eighteen more minutes, so I said, 'Come in, Spectre,' and opened my arms.

And he *flowed* through the hull, a lovely man-shape made of starlight, and wrapped himself around me and sank onto me, icy, beautiful, so cold that I thought he was just death in another form. But in atmosphere he warmed to human temperature and kissed me with lips that felt real, and coupled with me with a human body, so that I wondered if he was just a terminal hallucination my brain had given me to soften my dying.

Nice going, brain, I thought, as I stroked smooth buttocks, pulling them closer, and felt Spectre arch against me, gasping without breath into my mouth. I could only see him as a shimmering outline, but I could feel him as though blood pumped in his veins.

'Let me come in,' he pleaded, and I laid myself flat and open for him, and I have never felt so dissolved, so possessed. Something entered me. Something came to an orgasm as I did. Was his semen starlight, I wondered. His passion was scorching, his love was like a supernova. No one had ever loved me like that.

'Warm,' said Spectre, snuggling close to me, fingers searching my face as though he had never touched a human. 'So warm and sweet.'

That lovemaking must have taken up all my remaining time, so I kissed his hands, palm and back, and whispered

'Goodbye, Spectre, I'm so sorry I can't stay,' and he kissed tears from my eyes and...

I didn't die. Or, perhaps, I already had. The counter had run to zero minus thirty minutes. I was out of air and dead. Except that I wasn't.

'Are you keeping me alive?' I asked Spectre, who had both arms wreathed around my chest.

'Yes,' he said. His voice was firming. 'You are part of me, now. I am part of you. We are one. We can live in everything but water. We don't like water.'

'So you can live in hard vacuum?' I asked.

'We can,' he corrected, 'By myself I am just a wailing ghost, seeking human heat. We love humans. Humans taught us love. They taught us about the flesh. We never had flesh before.'

'Will contact with you kill me?' I asked. Not that I minded. I was already overdue.

'No,' said Spectre, and caressed my cheek. 'We don't die,' he told me. 'Humans tried to teach us about death, but we didn't like it.'

'So, we'll be together forever,' I said. 'And you'll be my lover?'

'Unless ... you, know, water,' he replied, resting his cheek against mine.

I stretched luxuriously. I was more alive, for a given sense of alive, than I had ever been. And since Spectre could not survive water – and I couldn't swim, either – we retained the ability to die, if we wanted to, if the centuries tired us out. Already his essence was saturating my cells. I was becoming my lover, and he was becoming me. For some reason I could smell apples, a hot orchard scent.

A quote from the mate's 20th century films came to mind.

'Spectre, this could be the beginning of a beautiful friendship'.

His laugh was like sunlight.

I NEVER GOT THE HANG OF THURSDAYS

I was, I admit, bemused. Also startled. One moment I had been tootling along in a standard orbit, scanning the fifth of an endless series of moonlets for useful minerals, listening to Monteverdi and eating dried grapes, and the next the whole pod had been swallowed at a gulp by a larger ship, my pod had been automatically docked, and I was removed from said pod by two large people in combat armour and helmets.

Even for a Thursday, this was unusual. The soldiers grabbed me by the arms, my feet dangling, and then allowed me to stand again as a tall, brightly coloured individual sauntered into the docking bay.

He had biolumes, chevrons of purple, gold and sable. He had long curly black hair, in ringlets like an eighteenth century wig. He had an android parrot on his shoulder – a long extinct bird called a macaw, scarlet and gold. It eyed me with disfavour. The frock coat in green brocade came straight out of a history vid. Probably a porn history vid, because he was startlingly beautiful, and if that wasn't a codpiece in those skin tight breeches, I almost didn't want to know what it was.

I did, though. A ridiculous reaction, because I knew who he was. His name was Dread, and he was dreaded for good reason.

'You are my prisoner,' he stated. Beautiful voice. Like chocolate sauce over raspberry sorbet.

'That does seem to be the case,' I admitted, firmly secured by a thug on each side.

'Your name?' he asked.

'Myrddin McLisse, and I have heard all of the jokes.'

'You now belong to me,' he said.

'No, I belong to me,' I responded. 'You have current custody of my body, though.'

'You will answer my questions,' he said, flickering a bit. I was gratified. He was going to kill me. Dread always killed prisoners. At least I could annoy him a little before he did. He approached and looked into my face. He smelt of rich fabrics and coffee.

'This is an ore detection pod. Where is your mother ship?'

'If they have any sense, half the universe away by now. They don't pay ransoms, but you know that. You don't ask for them.'

'Why do you work for the Company?'

I tried to shrug. 'I like eating and wearing clothes and sleeping in a bed. The Company has locked down my planet. You work for them, or you starve. I chose the more comfortable alternative that has chocolate in it. Why do you dislike the Company?'

'For those very same reasons,' he replied. I was disconcerting him. He remembered that this wasn't a conversation. 'I am asking you. What ship?'

'Ore Miner *Casseopeia*, out of Planetary Station Barnard's Star. Ten months out. On her way home, by now, as if her tail was on fire, missing one ore pod and useless pilot and heavy with a tummy full of rare earths. That's all I know; get on with it.'

'Get on with...' he trailed the enquiry, waving a long, elegant hand.

'Deleting me. I haven't any skills which might serve you, but I might be good to break down for spare parts.'

His eyes gleamed. 'No, no, I've decided to like you. Bring him to my cabin,' he ordered, and stalked away, his red lined cloak flourishing behind him. His macaw flapped blue green and red wings to keep its perch on his shoulder.

'Oh, dear,' murmured one of my guards. 'Sorry about that, son. Come along. Try not to annoy him, and he might just kill you quick.'

I thought about struggling, but it was clearly futile. I really don't like Thursdays.

The Captain's cabin was... lush, was the word which leapt to mind. Most of it was probably projections from a state of the art RealPlus I saw on the Chippendale table, but some of it was real. Real enough to sit on and be tied to, for example, this Rococo chair. The guards left, the door hissed shut, and I was alone with Dread. He allowed the parrot to fly off his shoulder and roost. He was pacing.

I took in the silk-hung walls, the Aubusson carpet under my bare feet, the bed with curtains of heliotrope gauze, the piles of pillows, the table laid with wine and dainties. Very 18th century, as was the man walking around me, close enough to touch if I wanted to touch – and I did. He was svelte and elegant and exhaled style.

But his eyes were chips of sapphire. He leaned close and breathed into my neck, kissed me briefly, put a forefinger to my bottom lip. I clenched my jaw. He took his hand away. I could not read the expression in his eyes.

'No,' I said.

'No?' he asked in that chocolately voice. 'Why not? Don't you think me beautiful?'

'Oh, yes,' I agreed. 'You are spectacular. I've never seen a human as beautiful as you are, Captain.'

'Then why an instant negative?' he asked, as if he actually wanted to know.

'Because I'm tied to a chair, at your mercy, and I don't get off on threats,' I said honestly. 'Your guards suggested that I ask you to kill me quickly, rather than torture me. That strikes me as foolish. If you like torture, and all the gossip I have heard suggests you do, then begging for mercy would merely make my torment last longer. So I'm not asking you for anything.'

'Why, then, tell me no?' he asked, still close, still not touching.

'Oh, that's for me,' I said. 'To make me feel better. So that I can't ever think that I played any part in my own ravishment. So that you know that this is not my idea.'

'I see,' he said, and moved to sit at the table, pouring himself a goblet of red wine. He sipped. His tongue slipped out and licked up a droplet of wine at the corner of his mouth. One of the most arch, self-consciously sexy things I had ever seen.

But I was still tied to a chair and I still didn't like threats and if he was going to kill me, I wished he'd get on with it.

'May I offer you a drink?' he asked.

'You may,' I replied. 'But while my hands are tied, I cannot accept.'

'And if I untie you?' he asked.

'I can't promise anything,' I said. I really would like a drink, he had real wine, by the look and smell of it.

'What if I untie you, offer you a drink, and tell you that my guards have a very basic sense of humour?' he asked, sipping again. His tongue was a sin and a crime.

'You could try it,' I suggested. 'Why did you decide to like me?' I asked.

'You're not afraid of me,' he answered.

'You're not very frightening,' I replied. 'And I haven't anything to lose. Lost my planet, lost my lover, lost my family. Only me left, and I don't matter.'

'How careless of you,' he murmured, rising and loosing the bonds by touching them with a ring on his finger. Atomic unbinding, perhaps? He extended a hand. I took it. He levered me to my feet and I stumbled to the table and sat down on another even more Rococo chair.

'How did you lose all of them?' he asked, gently. Well, why not, while he was talking he wasn't tearing out my fingernails for a necklace.

'The Company,' I replied. 'Nothing to do on our world but work for them, right? My parents were killed in a mining accident, a subsidence. My lover left me for a Company exec: he was sick of being poor, and my world only does two classes – poor and destitute.'

'Wine,' murmured Captain Dread. I drank. It was so good that I almost swooned. I sipped. It would have been criminal to gulp. Grapes and sunlight. Wonderful. I went on with my sorry history.

'So, I enlisted in the ore detail. High death rate, but I didn't care about that. More money if you survive. And I didn't survive, so I would like more wine, please, before we get on with my tragic demise.'

'I am not going to kill you,' he said.

'Not immediately, but eventually?' I guessed.

'Not at all,' he said. 'I shall ... chastise those guards. I am not the entity which tortures for fun. The Company does that. I have never hurt a prisoner. Usually I just dump them on a certain planet outside Company space.'

'But...' I really didn't want to believe him, but his hand was warm on mine, and I had been alone for so long. 'Captain Dread...'

'A convenient fiction,' he told me. 'The name produces great fear. Fear means that we fight very few battles. People surrender. It's so nice of them and saves a lot of trouble. And no one captured by SS Vengeance ever returns, so the legend remains.'

'Why don't they return?' I asked, feeling his fingers creep along my wrist, sliding up my arm, leaving sparkles behind.

'If you were out of Company space, would you yearn to come back?' he asked.

I had to admit that he had a point, there.

'And you, Captain, why do you want an ore-jockey as a lover? Do you seduce all your prisoners?' I asked. His hand cupped my cheek, stroking my scarred jaw.

'No, I have never done this before. You remind me...' he said, softly. 'You remind me of myself, you remind me that there is still courage in the world. And you smell divine.'

'I do?' I asked. He smelled of wealth and privilege, wine, musk and coffee. God knows what I smelt of, after a few days in an ore pod. I would have had me classified as Hazardous Waste and dropped out of a rubbish chute.

'You smell of engines and metallic ores and space,' he whispered, very close to my mouth. 'And wine and defiance. And sweat and yourself. If I kiss you, will you bite?'

'You will have to find out,' I said, leaning into him, 'by experment.'

He kissed. I did not bite. Until much later, and that was by request.

He lay sprawled in his big bed, pale against dark green sheets, all long limbs and alabaster skin, his biolumes flickering low, as they had blazed before, purple and old across his body. And I lay with him, my head on his chest, toying with a tress of that beautiful hair. I had never had a lover so generous, so fierce, so passionate. I gave silent thanks that my lover, Tailyn, had abandoned me and smashed my heart. Though that seemed to be healing with suspicious speed. Maybe it hadn't been all that broken after all. But this one – I could not even imagine being apart from him. I tugged at the ringlet.

'What is your name, Captain? What shall I call you, before you dump me at your planet outside Company space?'

He sat up abruptly, grabbing me by the shoulders. His mouth was red with kisses. I had quite debauched him, that elegant, self-possessed figure. But surely he couldn't want me! I was the absolute epitome of 'nothing special.' But he was shaking me, staring into my eyes, compelling my attention. His long fingers bruised my biceps.

'My name is Daniel, no one else in the universe knows that, and I am not dumping you anywhere! My Myrddin. Mine. You're coming with me, piracy is really quite diverting, you'll find.' He pulled me into a close, leg twining embrace, holding me hard against his heart. 'To get away from me, you will have to say, clearly, that you don't want to be with me. Say that, and I will let you go.'

'No,' I snuggled closer. 'I'm not going to say that. Not ever. Not until you are sick of me.'

'And since that is not going to happen, there is no need for it,' he decided. 'Will you come with me? I am the Thursday Captain Dread. We can do other things for the rest of the week. This, for example.'

'There are seven Captain Dreads?' I hazarded.

'Indeed,' he agreed. 'If one is killed, another takes his place. The Company has boasted that they killed Captain Dread several times, but a moment later, up pops another, all black curls and biolumes and Court Dress. It confuses them. Very amusing.'

'And I just happened to get the Captain Dread who would find me attractive?' I asked. He kissed me again.

'That is true,' he agreed. 'The others are all very ordinary.'

'I am going to have to entirely revise my views on Thursdays,' I said, and buried my face in his glorious, scented hair. His arms closed around me. I never wanted to leave this bed again. And very soon, it would be Friday.

Kerry Greenwood – historian, lawyer and writer – is the author of more than 60 books. Her fiction includes historical, fantasy, detective and crime novels – for adults and young adults.

She is the beloved author of 21 Phryne Fisher novels set in Melbourne in the late 1920s (and filmed for TV as *Miss Fisher's Murder Mysteries*); and six Corinna Chapman crime novels, set in the same city in this century.

Kerry holds both the Davitt and Ned Kelly Lifetime Achievement Awards for her crime fiction; and Davitt Awards for individual novels.

She lives in Melbourne with an accredited Wizard; and a few registered cats, who supervise her with loving paws.

In her spare time Kerry stares blankly out of the window and has no idea where she gets her ideas from.

Clan Destine Press is honoured to celebrate Kerry's love affair with the ancient world.

It began with our publication of her Egypt novel ***Out of the Black Land;*** then the extraordinary **Delphic Women** trilogy: ***Medea, Cassandra*** and ***Electra.***

CDP also publishes three eBooks in the ***Herotica*** and ***Mytherotica*** series which feature many more adventures in love and time and legend.

HEROTICA
ADVENTURES IN LOVE & TIME vol 1

Kerry Greenwood
Clan Destine ENCOUNTERS

HEROTICA
ADVENTURES IN LOVE & TIME vol 2

Kerry Greenwood
Clan Destine ENCOUNTERS

SALMANCIS

Kerry Greenwood
Clan Destine ENCOUNTERS

MYTHEROTICA
TALES OF LOVE & LEGEND

Kerry Greenwood
Clan Destine ENCOUNTERS